Chapter 1: Three Bodies, (

2015

I felt the blade pinch at the testy bits around my mouth and once again pondered the wisdom of buying generic disposable razors. Looking in the mirror I noticed I had shaved every area except that bastard piece just under my nose. It reminded me of my ex-girlfriend Kayla, who'd walked in on me in a similar position years ago and asked, "You're not gonna leave that are you?" To which I replied, "Yes. Yes, I am." And I goose-stepped past her, nearly forgetting to shave off the postage stamp 'stache before heading to work.Kayla...great legs...good kisser, and yet somehow, we drifted apart. Oh well, I was already running late.

"Do your taxes?" It was Housecoat Helen, my chatty, downstairs neighbor.

"Why, is it April 14th yet?" I cracked sarcastically, stepping into our shared vestibule.

She held up the early edition of *The Boston Globe* in answer.

"Crap," I replied louder than I wanted. Then I considered whether I should really do better hallway reconnaissance before venturing out in the morning.

I offered what I thought was a polite smile, which she obviously thought was not, then I pushed past and through the door. Maybe it was that third Natty Ice I downed for what passed as my breakfast, but I actually noticed the air smelled fresh and spring had arrived, dappling the leaves of the New England maples with subtle reds and browns. I briefly considered whether the presence of the word dappling, in my thoughts, may be indicating I had a burgeoning problem, you know, breakfast-wise. However, time was of the essence, and it seemed to be more a dosage issue than full blown dipsomania, so I put the matter to rest as I made my way across the parking lot.

I hopped into the Ford Falcon where I pulled the "Defroster Glove" from the hole in the dashboard, wiped the windshield, and prayed like Hell she turned over. That accomplished, I made my way downtown and took an angled spot on the Norman Rockwell-esque main drag in front of a narrow, two-story, brick office building with ARTFIELD HERALD printed across the bay window. As I approached the peeling paint of the front door, I noticed a piece of loose-leaf paper with a large magic marker "F," had been stuck to the window with a wad of gum, right in front of the "A" in ARTFIELD–the price of being located just down the street from the Calvin Coolidge Middle School.

I left it flapping in the light breeze and made my way inside. I waved to, but tried not to look at, the new 19-year-old receptionist with gravity defying breasts. The paper went to press today, and I didn't need any more distractions than the slight buzz I currently had. Copy Editor Gladys Nutwell was hunched over a laptop in the rear office area. She was 60 and very serious, in a New England-Puritan-at-a-witch-burning kind of way. She was decked out in her usual, seasons-be-damned, outfit: long solid colored skirt, frilly blouse pinched at the neck by a pearl pin, and shoes so sensible they probably had their own 401[k]. Her graying hair was pulled back with such severity it looked painful, and with the deadline approaching, she was a safe distance from a barrel of monkeys.

"How's it going?" I asked, turning toward the coffee machine in the alcove kitchen.

"How do you think it's going?" she spat—and we were off.

There was no milk in the mini fridge. Just some fancy-looking creamer and the only place I wanted to be, less than here, was at a tiny café table in Vienna. So, I left it black, but made it up to myself by leaning against a file cabinet, where I could engage Gladys, while still glimpsing the receptionist in my peripheral vision. Her brown hair bounced as she spun in her swivel chair to answer a call. I pictured diving into it nose-first and it smelling like opening a new can of tennis balls. Then, before I started creeping even myself out, I decided to get back to business.

"Did you see the middle school-ers 'F-bombed' us again?" I asked Gladys.

"Yes, I noticed that," she replied distractedly, while shuffling through papers with her left hand.

"It's not the crudeness I mind. It's having to scrape the gum off the window every time."

"Why not get Miss Magna Cum Perky of Secretarial School out there to do it?" Gladys sniffed, casting aspersions on a young lady who had done nothing but warm the cockles of my poor heart, or the poor heart of my warm cockles. I wasn't sure which.

I decided to take a different tack. "Is that the minutes of the Council meeting?"

She picked up the stapled pages, which I now noted were covered in more red ink than my Freshman Chemistry midterm. "No, it's Carol Hanselman's weekly editorial. She musta caught that *60 Minutes* piece on Campaign Finance reform and she turned in 1200 words in defense of the Citizens United decision and money in politics."

"No national stuff. We're a local paper. Bad enough, we agree to publish her rants about Freeholders and County Sheriffs every November. Isn't there a pothole on her street or unkempt lawn in her neighborhood she could go off about?"

"Consider it killed," replied Gladys with what qualified as a smile on go-to-press day. "I had already cut it down to nothing, removing all the crap about Charles Koch. I figured that would rub you the wrong way."

"Actually, my problem with Charles Koch is not political, so much. It's more that with a billion dollars he could be renting out The Louvre for a private viewing, riding dirt bikes up the Pyramids at Giza, playing a game of

A-S-S against the Great Wall of China. Hell, I'd be swinging from a chandelier in The Bellagio penthouse getting ready to do a Triple Lindy into an Olympic-sized pool filled with Dom Perignon and hookers. I mean the world is your oyster and you're worried about getting an anti-labor candidate elected in the third Iowa congressional district encompassing the greater part of Cedar Rapids? It's not the politics that bother me; it's the utter lack of imagination."

"What are we gonna use for filler?" Gladys asked, knocking me off my momentary soapbox.

"I'll come up with something," I replied, sipping the bitter coffee. "Lord knows they pay me enough."

Gladys shrugged, tossed the pages on top of her overflowing trash bin, and added, "While you're at it, Mrs. Kleinschmidt called saying she was sick all week and won't have a social column for us."

"Fabulous. Oh, the glamorous life of a small press editor."

"Hey, you coulda wrote for a city paper, remember. But you were no good at taking orders. So, you came back home. Now this is your job. You chose it."

"Maybe so," I responded, shaking my head. "But, trust me, starving came in a close second."

Gladys looked routinely unimpressed. "Just get me something for Hanselman," she intoned, rotating her swivel chair to attack the overstuffed IN basket on the other side of her desk. "I'll go through the notices folks sent in and fudge up what passes for a social column in this podunk 'burg."

I looked down at my still quarter-filled coffee cup, then tossed it in the kitchen area trash can, thinking I really need to get a flask for days like these. Meanwhile, Gladys went back to her keyboard, and I headed into my tiny, cluttered office to look over some last-minute advertising copy for this week. Next, I gave a once over to our meager finances, and fully depressed, decided to phone the Town Clerk.

Miriam answered in a voice so husky it should've been pulling a sled. I was momentarily titillated, until I remembered she was pushing 70 and built like an H-Back. I told her it was Luke Williams calling. "Is Wes in?"

"Not yet honey," she purred.

"Any revelations from the Council Meeting last night," I asked, hoping for a surprise that could fill Carol Hanselman's space.

"Nothing really. I have the notes. Should I read them to you?"

I flipped through the junk mail on my desk until I uncovered a Victoria's Secret catalog, which I noticed had gotten mixed in by mistake. Locating a particularly buxom, bustier-ed brunette, I bid her go on. Then I put the voice to the picture, until it seemed silly, she should be kneeling on a four-poster bed licking her finger, while discussing repairs to the town's septic system. So, I thanked Miriam and signed off.

Out in the office I saw Sandy Molesworth, a part-time reporter, enter. Her husband owned the biggest car dealership in the county, and she was dressed in a full-length fur in defiance of the rising temps. Despite the fact she thought she was the second coming of Ida Tarbell and Martha Gellhorn rolled into one, I tolerated her. If only for the fact she was happy to go up to Montpelier to cover the state legislature. Gladys claimed this was because she was sleeping with half the Assembly, but considering our sparse staffing I couldn't afford to look a gift whore in the mouth. When I noticed Gladys stop typing, I knew something important was up. So, I left the mystery of Victoria's ongoing secret unsolved, and walked out to see what was prompting Sandy's unscheduled visit.

As I sidled up behind Gladys' left shoulder, Sandy was just getting to the point. She seemed surprised at our ignorance, though I'm sure her already subterranean estimation of our abilities couldn't go any lower.

"So, you really didn't hear? Neither of you?" She placed her hands on her hips, but I fixed her with the sternest glower I could muster through the Natty Ice and caffeine. She caught her eyes mid-roll and continued. "Out on Logansport Road, a murder-suicide…"

"Holy shit on a shingle," Gladys exploded. Sandy stopped and we both stared dumbfounded. It was like catching your grandmother watching porn. Worse it was like catching your grandmother *doing* porn.

Murders just didn't happen here; let alone one with a suicide kicker. "Who was killed?" I asked.

"Ted Sheehan, he was Vice Principal at the high school."

I only heard of Ted Sheehan, but it was still sad and shocking. "I can't believe it. What happened?"

Sandy fixed me with a smug, more informed than thou look. "Apparently, he was dating an ex-student—of legal age and all—but 16 years his junior. She was 23, he was 39. The girl's father shot them both, then killed himself."

"A double murder!" It was Gladys again. "Son of an ass!!"

Though I was far from the touchy-feely type, I put a hand on her shoulder to steady her, while wondering if there was such a thing as shock-induced Tourette's. "Poor Ted," I managed. "I'd only ever heard good things about him."

"I got the news from Bob Carpenter," said Sandy, dropping the name of our district's State Assemblyman and one of her probable lusty liaisons. "He's a certified EMT. Picked it up on his scanner."

She fixed me with a contemptuous stare as if I was derelict in my duty. When in actuality the last thing I wanted, when I was trying to wind down with a Natty Ice and some Graham Greene, was background static keeping me posted on every old bastard's broken hip or police station donut run. "So, who was the girl?"

"He didn't get it. The signal wasn't great, and he missed some of the details. Isn't your brother-in-law on the police force?" I thought missing the names of the girl and her father sounded suspicious. But she re-upped on the disappointing looks when she reached the last part of the statement. I couldn't blame her. Having a brother-in-law on the force should've been a direct pipeline to big news like this. The problem was she didn't know my brother-in-law.

Patrolman Andrew O'Scanlon is a doughy, pasty, redheaded Irishman who could talk the balls off a brass monkey. To the extent I was never really sure whether he won my sister's heart through courtship or battering her into a conversational coma. And like most of the violently verbose, there wasn't a subject he couldn't or wouldn't discourse on with absolute certainty. I tolerated him for a while. First for her sake, then for the sake of inside info, but after she leaked that I referred to him as "the man Will Rogers never met," my pipeline to police secrets dried up in a hurry. Though, on the bright side, my ears finally recovered from their dog-toy-like consistency.

I checked Gladys again. She seemed to be coming back around. Her eyes no longer glazed over; her need to curse like a rapper in a strip club subsided. I then made my way back to my office and dialed the Artfield Police.

Sergeant Wally Reynolds was working the desk. I knew him well from years of playing softball and drinking beer together; the former really just an excuse to participate in the latter. "Hey Wally," I said, trying to sound official. "Give me Andrew will ya."

"Hi Luke, how's it going," he said too nonchalantly, and it was instantly obvious something was up. "Oh, uh, you mean your brother-in-law Andrew?"

"No, I mean Andrew Ridgeley, the other guy in WHAM! I figured he's not doing anything, maybe he can play my birthday party next month."

"Oh yeah, Andrew's not here, uh, wanna leave a message?" Sarcasm received and not returned was another red flag.

Big city departments may have layers of faceless, monotone underlings to steer the curious away from sensitive matters, but that wasn't going to fly here. "Listen Wally, I know about the double murder-suicide, no thanks to you guys. Now what's going on? I'm about to hold up the press here. Gimme something!"

I'd always been the laid-back type, but I saw an entire day of rewrites and rearranging coming my way and it gave my voice an unfamiliar edge. This obviously took Wally by surprise, and he switched to trying to level with me. "I'm sorry Luke, but we're under orders not to talk about that. Straight from the Chief."

The change in his voice indicated the aggressive approach was working, so I forged ahead. "Cut the crap Wally. This isn't the friggin' *Rockford Files*. It's 'Buttfuck,' Vermont. We went to elementary school together. That night we won the league championship; I saw you trip and pass out in your own vomit in front of Pete's Pub..."

"Yeah, and if I remember correctly," he cut in; "you didn't help me up, but stood over me yelling 'officer down, officer down'."

I suppressed a chuckle and kept working on him. "Yeah, and you once kept Pete's entertained with your impression of me crapping out on a headfirst slide and doing the Australian Crawl into third base. That's what I'm talking about. Give me something to work with. You know I won't throw you under the bus."

It was his turn to hold back a laugh and he softened a bit more. "OK. All I can say is try Glen Hubbard," he said, mentioning the name of the former Artfield correspondent for the nearest daily paper the *Burlington Bee*. "He's still in the loop. He might be able to point you to folks who can talk."

It wasn't much, but I couldn't play tough guy for long. "Thanks Wally, I'll give Hubbard a try. Next time I see ya at Pete's, remind me I owe you a beer."

"You owe me several, but one will do to start. Sorry I couldn't do more."

He hung up and I shot my drawers for Hubbard's home number. Found it under an old Molly Hatchet cassette. Noted it didn't feature "Flirtin' with Disaster," tossed it in the trash and dialed.

"Hello," Hubbard answered on the first ring. It was early, but I knew he'd be up. He was a family man after all. Three kids from a first marriage, all grown now, and twins, under the age of 5, from a second marriage. He even wanted more, but wife number two was not a player. He joked if she didn't come around, he'd dump her and start a third family. That's how much he enjoyed it. I told him once his obituary was going to look like the actor Tony Randall's: "He leaves behind two daughters, ages 54 and 3."

"Glen, it's Luke Williams. Did I wake you?"

"Are you kidding? I'm surprised you're up. Did Artfield repeal the 21st Amendment or is it a go-to-press day?"

"You know I only drink at home alone these days...like George Thorogood. I really called to see if you heard anything about the murder-suicide last night."

"In Artfield? Jee-sus," he was as shocked as the rest of us. "No. Not a thing. I can't recall a homicide ever happening up there."

"No one can and that's the problem. Seems like the cops don't know whether to shit or wind their wristwatches and so they've brought down the Cone of Silence. It's like a goddamn Benedictine monastery up here," I declared, stopping before I cross-referenced yet again. "Can you get me any info? Work a backchannel, call in a favor?"

"I'd be happy to, but I'm not on the beat anymore. Haven't been for a month," he said. "If you picked up the *Bee* occasionally and got your nose outta Evelyn Waugh, you'd know that. I'm big time now; on the Editorial Board."

"Who replaced you?"

"Some kid named Jeremy," he spat out the name with disgust. "Green as freakin' grass. Thinks he can do the job by text, email, Twitter and Google searches. Buncha BS if you ask me."

"Yeah, outside of gambling and porn, I don't really get the purpose of this Internet thing."

"OK, OK I'm a dinosaur. I get it. Listen, I'll reach out to the kid and see if he's got anything, but don't count on it."

"Thanks," I replied, hanging up. Another dead end.

I leaned back and pondered the options. I could try my brother-in-law's cell phone; hope he picks up and, via his congenital diarrhea of the mouth, spits something out for me. But just the way I phrased that in my head made the idea distasteful. I could go out to the scene of course, but that would take time. I'd have to push the press run back a day and the printer over in Farmingdale would no doubt charge us for the change of dates and rush job. Having just perused our meager monetary situation, this was not an option I was anxious to embrace.

By now Gladys and Sandy had taken up spots in my doorway. For lack of better options, I was in charge, and they were looking for me to make the big call on 3rd and long. Instead, I ran a draw and punted by calling my sister, Amy Williams O'Scanlon.

The phone ceased ringing, but there was no answer on the other end. "Hello. Amy. Hello," I tried.

"Gimme that you little shit," I heard, and remembered why her and Andrew were a couple. There was faraway laughter and then, "Yeah...hello?"

"Amy, it's Luke. Is Andrew there?"

"No. The phone rang in the middle of the night, and he took off. Stopped back this morning for a thermos of coffee and was gone again. Barely said two words."

"Lucky you," I replied, then wondered what those 'two words' might have been. "Where's your husband now?"

"Probably with anyone in the world *except* Will Rogers."

"Ouch." Things weren't going well.

There was a crash in the background and Amy held the phone away to yell something unintelligible. "Luke, I'm juggling three kids, two dogs and a cat that likes to piss in my shoes here. If you want somethin', tell me now so I can get back to livin' the dream."

Sarcasm apparently ran in the family. I got down to it. "I know about the murder of Ted Sheehan last night. I also know the cops aren't talking. What did Andy say this morning? Who's the girl?"

I shot the last question out as part plea and part opportunity to get me off her back. The sound of crying started up in the background and she gladly took the bait. "Monica Carson. She graduated in 2009 or 10. Her father had some weird name—Burly or Curly or something," she said, her voice fading in and out, the phone obviously cradled between shoulder and ear. "You good, now?"

"Hardly," I said, thinking about how I was going to sort this out on a deadline. "But thanks, and don't worry, I didn't hear it from you."

"Yeah." I think there was another "yeah" coming, but a dog barked, there was more crying, a thud and the line went dead. Suddenly I was looking more benignly at the prospects of chemical castration.

"Monica Carson," I said looking up into the expectant eyes of Gladys and Sandy. "Class of 2009, I think."

There was a stack of high school yearbooks on top of a filing cabinet in the corner. Before I could move, Gladys had maneuvered her sensible shoes through the detritus of my office like a halfback running the tires at an NFL training camp. She deftly plucked 2009 from the stack and flipped to Carson, Monica, by the time she laid it out on my desk.

We all looked down at a fresh-faced blonde with the kind of freckled nose that is cute in a young woman, melanoma in an older one. The caption was the usual jumble of recognition for sports, clubs, and awards over someday-to-be embarrassing shout-outs to good times with friends and the music of Miley Cyrus and Jason Mraz. Considering my own yearbook ramblings made Flock of Seagulls sound like the next Pink Floyd and included the ubiquitous "…it's a town full of losers and I'm pullin' outta here to win…" line, I was hardly one to cast aspersions.

Gladys was the first to make a connection between Monica and Ted Sheehan. "Flip to the 'Clubs' section," she said, leaning in closer. "There they are—the Random Acts of Kindness Club. I remember Sheehan sending in blurbs about their fundraising for Darfur that we printed. And there's Monica right next to him in the picture."

This was an excellent catch by Gladys. It wasn't so much my memory was shot. It was high schoolers were constantly collecting for one cause or another. I suspected it had more to do with how it looked on their college applications than a real concern with victims of some disaster in a place they would forget by the time they attended their first kegger. Plus, they seemed to always set up outside the automatic doors of the supermarket, where I didn't need any help feeling guilty while wheeling out with half a dozen boxes of Yodels in my bags. "Donate to the Native American Tribal Council," they'd beg. "I already gave at the casino," I'd reply.

"Interesting, but it doesn't really tell us much. It looks like half the student body was in the club," I mused.

We flipped through more pages not really knowing what we were looking for. Time was a wasting. A decision on the printer had to be made, when Charlie Grissom, our photographer, came in, his comb-over blown to crap, and went straight for the coffee.

Cup poured, he made his way over to the office and stood in the doorway next to Sandy. "Guess you know about the murder already. I picked it up on my scanner this morning and stopped over there on the way in."

Sandy looked at me, eyebrow cocked. "What is this 1977? Do I also need a CB radio with a 17-foot antenna for my car?" I lamented. "Anyway, what's going on out there, Charlie?"

"Hard to say, other than every cop in the force is there roaming the property."

"Sounds like a good time to knock over the liquor store," I joked to silence. "OK, what were you able to find out?"

"Not much. I got a few shots of the house and the commotion going on, but I couldn't get closer than the street. They had so much yellow police tape running from tree to tree I thought Tony Orlando and Dawn came to town."

If the comb-over that had now settled into a soft serve ice cream swirl on top of his head had only partially given away Charlie's advanced age, that reference clinched it. He was still an excellent bloodhound though. Twenty-something years at an Albany paper had honed his instincts. Even in retirement, he knew a good story and we were lucky to have him. I saw in his eyes a look that matched the feeling in my gut, so I pressed him for more. "Any State Police or even County cops out there?"

"Not a one," Charlie smiled, and I knew we were on the same page.

Outside of one minute to post at the Wonderland Dog Track, snap decisions were not my forte, but the time had come today as some forgotten 60s rockers once sang. "OK, here's the plan," I started. "Gladys, call the printer and cancel the run. Tell 'em we'll get back to them and when we do it'll be a rush job."

"That's gonna cost us," she replied, fully aware of our hemorrhaging finances.

"Don't care. Whatever the vig is, we'll pay it." Coming from a man who lived on Ellio's Frozen Pizza and drank gas station coffee that could rip the enamel off your teeth, this was attention grabbing. "Charlie and Sandy get over to the high school and see what's going on there. I'm heading out to Sheehan's place to see if I can crack this Blue Wall of Dumbness. Something's going on beneath the surface here. Let's see if we can pop this zit."

As that last line will attest, when it came to pep talks, I was more Rockhead than Rockne, but it had the desired effect. Thrilled to be chasing a story with potential, everyone bolted. I, on the other hand, sank back into my chair exhausted. As a man who once listed "napping" under hobbies on a dating profile, I was hardly a get-up-and-go(er), more like a lie-down-and-wait(er). Still, even I felt like I was in a rut, or maybe I was just sick and tired of waking up sick and tired. Whatever it was, I pushed myself out of the desk chair and set sights on the liquor store. Ted Sheehan's house could wait an extra fifteen minutes. It was gonna take at least another 30-pack of Natty Ice to get me through this ordeal.

Chapter 2: Smoke 'Em, If You Got 'Em

With a 30-pack and a Slim Jim secured, I started the drive northwest out of town to Logansport Road. Ted Sheehan lived in what used to be known as the Swinefield section. Pig farming area until it was bought by developers who were in the process of fitting it with some gentrified, Downton Abbey-ish moniker like Manchester Meadows, Havisham Heath or Stick-Up-Your-Bum Estates. Approval for a strip mall to house the ubiquitous Starbucks, Chipotle and Whole Foods was all that was holding up their plans of sub-divide and conquer, but that would certainly come soon. The only thing standing in the way being passage by the Town Council, a five-member board of Revolutionary descendent Yankees so old, dry, and crusty I could swear they farted dust. Sure, they were social reactionaries, but they also had the first two nickels they ever earned and at least one of them had a buffalo on it. So, it was just a matter of the price being right. Artfield's mayor and self-proclaimed "zoning expert" was Old Wes Willard, an octogenarian multi-millionaire so miserly he'd sooner "wet willie" a wolverine than touch his principal. He'd drive a hard bargain, but he would get his payoff in the end.

For a minute I considered whether Ted Sheehan's murder and the development of the Logansport Road/Swinefield section could be somehow connected. Were the developers after Sheehan's property, but he wouldn't sell? That's the kind of scenario that makes for a nice one-hour TV drama, but it was too trite here. It didn't explain Monica Carson and her father also coming up toe tagged. Or maybe the whole radio silence thing had to do with fear of bad publicity, in which case we were chasing after nothing. That was more likely until I considered the type of money-loving bastards that were going to be moving into the gated McMansions that were going up could care less. They ate working men like Curly Carson for lunch and the death of Ted Sheehan was simply a tax benefit in that it unburdened the public school's employee pension fund just that much more.

I continued to second guess myself as the Ford Falcon labored up the hill toward Swinefield. Since the road was literally visible through the rusting floorboards, I worried I might have to go "Flintstones" with my feet to get her up the last few yards. Kayla the Kisser had a litany of reasons beyond the mustache remark for breaking up with me, and the Falcon was at, or near, the top of that list. "It runs like a bear," I'd tell her. "You mean it barely runs," she'd reply, but I wasn't about to change. I loathed being burdened down with possessions, which should indicate a bohemian bent, yet I craved stability. I thought this quirk made me an enticingly enigmatic escort, but Kayla, and a host of other women, seemed to think otherwise.

Romantic reminiscing aside, I continued to worry about the motive here, but the one thing that kept me thinking I was onto something was the lack of State Police. When it came to brains Artfield Police Chief Harry Bowden wasn't going to Houston to build any rockets, but he did have enough common sense to know a double murder/suicide was out of his league. He was in his early sixties and could've retired long ago, but he was a fixture in the town for so long he couldn't give it up. In addition to law enforcement, he'd also served on the Town Council, the Board of Ed, and

County Highway Commission as well as doing a spell as Building Inspector. However, between suburban sprawl swelling the population and advancing age slowing him down, one by one he dropped the other hats to focus completely on the growing force.

Not that the Artfield Police Department was turning into the East German Stasi overnight, but it had come a long way from the days when the sound of a siren would be met by cries of "another cat up a tree" by laughing kids—even as a youth I could be brutal. These days, I realized, police work even in a small town wasn't so simple. The difference between the good folks and the bad had blurred. Thus, it took tact and professionalism to walk the line between friendly neighborhood officer and badass with a badge. For the most part the members of the APD, even my brother-in-law, did it well. Unfortunately, our relative remoteness from any high crime areas meant most calls were of a nature that they simply had make sure the so-called "victims" were fine. In other words, for all their good intentions, Harry Bowden knew his staff didn't have the chops for this situation, making his lack of a call for immediate help suspicious.

Though spring was in the air, there was still snow on the mountains. Locals often wound through Swinefield as a scenic shortcut to Sugarbush, the nearest resort and a pretty good stripper name if you ask me. The police had cordoned off Cliffside Drive, which led to the mountain and was the fastest route to Logansport Road and Ted Sheehan's place. Cars were backed up from there, some asking for an alternate route, others just rubbernecking.

The blockade looked hastily thrown up: a two-legged sawhorse, police tape and an old barrel straight out of a Depression-era cartoon. There was another entrance to Logansport Road on the opposite side of Burnet Hill. It was well out of the way and a much longer drive, so I decided to take a shot that the police hadn't gotten around to blocking it yet.

The problem was the giant Hummer in front of me. Seeing as the Falcon got approximately 3 gallons to the mile, and could still use leaded fuel, I had no cause for getting all environmentally righteous, but it was pissing me off I couldn't see around this friggin' monstrosity to make the left turn I needed to make. Unless you planned on cruising downtown Fallujah, it hardly seemed you needed a car of this proportion. Though hauling this generation of fat ass kids and gear to soccer games and dance classes did, admittedly, require some extra square footage.

Slowly I edged past the Hummer's back bumper, leaned forward from the beaded seat cushion, and seeing nothing coming immediately around the slight bend, gunned all 165 Vietnam-era horses and bumped noisily onto Evergreen Lane. Checking my rear-view mirror, I noticed a girl in a light green Volkswagen behind me trying the same maneuver. Maybe it was the bend, maybe it was the cloud of sooty exhaust fumes I released, but she failed to notice the garbage truck bearing down until it was too late. Already committed she had no choice but to mash down on the gas. Narrowly averting the trash mongers, but cleanly clipping the driver's side of my rear bumper before sliding off to a grassy patch on the far side of the road.

I eased the Falcon to the opposite side, got out and crossed over to check on the Volks. A girl was in the driver's seat. She had white-blond hair and a Scandinavian complexion that wasn't so much pale as translucent. I wondered if they even made an SPF high enough for her, or if at the beach, she had to slather herself in mayonnaise or Ranch dressing. As I got a better view of her makeup-free features, she definitely had the look that would make such a prospect enticing. In the presence of such a creature, I reverted to my usual coolness, leaned awkwardly forward, and mumbled, "Uh..You alright?"

Like so many women before her she proved immune to my suave patter and staring straight ahead answered with a nod.

She looked pissed, and her being young and pretty, and me being, well...me, I assumed instantly it was something I'd done. "It was nobody's fault," I stammered. "Between the Hummer and the bend in the road there was no way to see the garbage truck."

"That's nice of you, but I know it's my fault," she said. She looked up for the first time and while not as old as me she wasn't just out of school either. I guessed early 30s, or at least old enough to probably be thinking about things like her insurance rate spiking, which let me off the hook for her anger. "Is your car damaged?"

"My car?" I stammered, incredulous. We both looked at the battered Falcon and it seemed like her question was rhetorical. "I think I'm fine but looks like you banged up your front passenger side."

I walked around to the front of her car, but she stayed put. The headlight was busted and there were scratches along the side where she glanced off my bumper. I looked at the Falcon. The only noticeable damage was a tear in one of the previous owner's faded Boston Bruins bumper stickers that read JESUS SAVES...AND ESPOSITO SCORES ON THE REBOUND!

I walked back to the driver's side where she was searching for her insurance info, in what, even I could tell, was a rather expensive leather handbag–like the kind I've seen in the Coach Store at the Rutland Mall, when I walk in to get a lungful of new leather smell, then walk out.

"Don't worry about exchanging info. My car's good...uh, in a manner of speaking. You have a broken headlight and some scratches, but you might be wise to fix it out of pocket," I said, reassuringly. "You'll make it back in savings on your premiums."

This seemed to calm her a bit. She put down her bag, looked up and smiled, "Thanks."

"No problem," I muttered, noticing she had a young Gwyneth Paltrow thing going on–you know, before all the political proselytizing and peculiar parenting stuff. "I'm just glad you're OK."

Though we were probably only 10 years apart in age, I felt like she was giving me a "Thanks a lot, Gramps" look, that made me feel dirty. It was probably just my irrepressible insecurity, but I didn't have time to dwell on this before she started the Volks and sped off tossing a "You too" over her shoulder on the way out.

I went back to the Falcon, reached into the cavernous glove compartment, and found my emergency cigarettes. I'd given up smoking years ago but kept a pack around for just such an occasion, when the need to operate a vehicle and/or think coherently (I never found the two mutually inclusive) precluded a much-needed Natty Ice or six.

The smoke hitting my lungs felt good. Between the deaths, the decisions, the accident, and the girl, it had been an overly eventful morning already. Though I wasn't really sure why, the last one bothered me. After splitting with Kayla, a couple of years back, I decided to leave the hetero world, skip over the homo-, and bi-, and get an early start on the asexual. Neither gender, as far as I know, displayed any objection.

At first, I thought this would free up time to write my Magnum Opus, or at least some half-assed, snarky murder mystery, but instead all I did was write less, drink more, and watch every episode of the decidedly average *Mike & Molly* five times over.

I took another drag, coughed like a tuberculosis patient, and eased the Falcon back onto the road. My assumption was the police wouldn't bother to block this long and windy back route, and I was half correct. As I approached the turn for Logansport Road, I noticed something shiny and yellow crossing the road that turned out to be police tape tied to a sapling on the right and anchored down in the middle of the road by a pile of small boulders. The effect was like that of a mall cop car with a light on top. It looked official from a distance, but as you got closer you simply snorted thinking "whaddya gonna do, give me a ticket for doing 12 in the parking deck 5 MPH zone?"

I slid around the hapless obstruction and turned left. Ted Sheehan's place was the last on the right before the road ended at a brook and thicket of pine trees. The house was a small bungalow, which surprised me. Though not knowing the salary of a Vice Principal and having never lived in anything more than a one-bedroom apartment, I was hardly in a position to judge. Still, it seemed small and rundown, which suggested maybe there was a nasty divorce and a bad lawyer somewhere in Ted's past. I made a mental note, bunched up some phlegm, hocked it onto the gravel driveway and proceeded up to the house.

I immediately regretted my ear-catching expectoration, as I looked up to see, uh, I didn't get her name so thought of her as "Miss Iceland," and her Volks, up closer to the scene. Her blonde hair shimmered and seeing her out of the car and upright only increased her comeliness. She stood in profile as she talked to Woody Maynard, who'd obviously been assigned to protect the outer perimeter. He'd dropped his guard—and from his goofy look would like to drop something else—for her, but I couldn't say I blamed him. She had the kind of body that could make a Republican raise taxes and dressed to accentuate it. The clothes, like the handbag, reeked of cash.

I approached and smiled, as I noticed Woody struggling to suck in his considerable gut, and look authoritative, at the same time. "Hey Woody," I started, glancing over to catch the girl's reaction. She half-looked, then did a double take, recognizing me from the accident.

"Oh…uh…hi," she sputtered. "Is everything OK with your car?"

Obviously neither of us knew why the other was there. "Everything's fine. I'm here to check out what's going on," I said, taking a step toward the house.

"No chance," answered Woody. "It's an active crime scene, Chief's orders." Then out of vindictiveness or to change the subject, he pointed to the cigarette I forgot was still smoldering in my hand, and added, "I didn't know you smoked?"

"Uh, I don't. These are prescription cigarettes," I replied. "My doctor says I don't get enough *tar* in my diet." I quickly dropped the butt and ground it out under a stained Chuck Taylor. Feeling self-conscious for no reason other than Miss Iceland (the moniker fit so I was sticking with it) looked like the type who viewed smokers as worse than Hitler.

I needn't have worried. She couldn't care less about me, my crappy car, filthy footwear, and horrible habits. Instead, she stared down Woody and asked coldly, "So you're not gonna change your tune? About anything?"

"Sorry Miss," declared Woody, his gut inching out in direct proportion to how much he could see her estimation of him dropping. "No one allowed in, and no information released to the press."

"You're with the press?" I let slip out in a manner that would've caused Gloria Steinem to kick me in the balls.

She made a face, said, "Is there a problem with that?" then arched her back and ran her fingers through her long blonde hair. Her chest pressed against her tight white blouse, and if this had been a tennis match, you could hardly say she was "down a set." Considering Kayla was not so much flat-chested, as concave, I was certainly intrigued. I cocked an eyebrow at the suddenly aptly named Woody, and he averted his leer long enough to fill in some details.

"She's with the *Bee*," Woody offered, "Glenn Hubbard's replacement."

"I thought they hired some tech whiz kid for that spot?"

"They did," she interjected coldly, "but he quit two days ago. To work for a political blog or something. They hired me away from the *Concord Courier-Times*. I just started." I still didn't have her name, but based on her demeanor toward Woody and myself, Miss Iceland was still a go.

"New Hampshire, huh?" I said, nodding at the Volks' tags I was noticing for the first time. "Live Free or Die…great state motto, I mean, unless you're in prison and have to stamp it on license plates all day. Then it's kind of a cruel joke."

I thought this might lighten the mood. Woody chuckled, but she was all business, so I decided to act professional, though it wasn't really playing to my strengths. "Luke Williams. I run the local paper, *The Artfield Review*."

"Karina Leach," she returned, reluctantly, while eschewing my proffered hand.

Well, Miss Iceland it is, I thought, and turned to Woody to find out what the Hell was going on. "What the Hell is going on, Woody?" I started unimaginatively.

"Like I told Ms. Leach here I know nothing." I looked at his considerable girth, but a Sergeant Schultz comment seemed too on the nose, so I let him continue. "The bodies are gone. They're almost finished inside. Wait awhile and I'm sure the Chief will have a statement."

"He's nothing if not consistent," she sniffed. "But I've got a deadline and who knows when this so-called statement is gonna be released or if it's even gonna have anything I can use."

Woody shrugged. It seemed useless. We'd both have to run it as a general news piece, albeit a big one for these parts, and fill in the details later. This was easy for her working at a daily, but if I went to press and something juicy came out later, she'd have me scooped by a full week.

Just then I saw the curtains move out of the corner of my eye. I kept my head turned toward Woody but could see Chief Bowden give Miss Iceland an optical sponge bath. When I caught his eye, the curtain dropped, and he retreated no doubt to fill in those still at the scene about the latest talent.

I figured it would behoove me to play nice with her. Certainly, winsome and willowy had a better chance of extracting info than soused and sarcastic any day. Besides this looked like a mystery and didn't every Private Dick need a dazzling doll. Not to mention the fact since Kayla, my dick had been private as they come. A little quid quo "pro" action wouldn't hurt.

"You're right," I started, turning towards her. She hadn't softened, but being brand new on the job it looked like she wasn't averse to help from someone who knew the lay of the land. "Listen I've got a reporter and photographer at the high school getting notes on Ted Sheehan, the girl, and anything else that seems pertinent. I'll call 'em and tell them to put themselves at your disposal."

"Thanks," she replied. "I knew the male victim was a vice principal at the high school, but that's it. This will save me time."

She half-smiled, and I felt half-stupid for caring as much as I did, but such was my pathetic life. "I've got to get back to my office," I lied. A few of the Natty Ices were burning a hole in the cooler in my trunk and I figured I'd slip off the road and have one for lunch. "Give me your number and I'll call you when and if the Chief decides to release a statement."

She called up her contact info as I brought my phone out in a closed fist. She went to do one of those tap it from phone-to-phone things, like you see in the commercials. Unfortunately, my flip-phone didn't possess such capabilities, along with no camera, BlueTooth, WiFi, and a host of other things most 15-year-olds took for granted (I could text, but seldom did).

She read me her number, and I punched it in, while trying to keep my hand over the antenna that could be pulled out for better reception. She gave me a look of womanly disapproval that at this point in my life bounced off like bullets off Superman. She was obviously worried about who she trusted her professional life to, so I immediately addressed Woody to deflect her fears.

"Were Sheehan and this Monica seeing each other?" I demanded in my most reporter-ly tone. "Were they sleeping together? Was this some kinda relationship-gone-wrong thing?"

Woody looked shocked. Maybe it was because I'd stumbled on part of the key to the cover up. Maybe because he was conservative concerning their age difference. Maybe because the guy he once saw drunkenly karaoke "It's Raining Men," was going all Jimmy Breslin on his butt. Who knows, but he wasn't cracking.

"Listen Luke I got nothing for you. Why don't you go ask your brother-in-law. He was inside when I got here, but he went home about a half hour ago. He'd be your best bet."

"Your brother-in-law is on the force?!" Things suddenly took an ugly turn vis-à-vis Miss Iceland.

"Yes, but it's not that simple," I began, but she cut me off by turning hard and heading for the Volks.

"I'm heading over to the high school. Get in touch with your brother-in-law for chrissakes and call me if you find out anything–ANY-thing," she demanded, turning her pale, pretty face to me one last time before starting the car and driving off.

I turned to Woody who was standing mouth agape. "Pleasant sort," I shrugged and in a lot of ways I really meant it.

Chapter 3: A Real Ass Scratcher

It was no sense going immediately to my sister's house as Andrew would no doubt be catching up on sleep. Instead, I drove to the local convenience store and bought a pack of Yodels, one of those sugar-encrusted Hostess apple pies (because I have the cravings of a 10-year-old), and a coffee as big as my head. Keeping up with Miss Iceland, I suspected, was going to require arrhythmia inducing amounts of caffeine in someone as indolent as me.

Twenty pages of J.P. Donleavy and a bursting bladder later, I arrived at my sister's. She told me Andrew would be up soon. He'd only been given a four-hour reprieve before he was needed back for his regular shift. The kids, three boys ages eight to five, were all quiet—either napping or lulled into a Disney-Pixar contrived coma in the TV room. For banging out three kids in such a small window, my sister was still fit and reasonably attractive in a tomboy-ish sort of way. From the way she looked at me, however, it was obvious the feeling was not mutual.

"Looks like you've been doing crunches," she said, pointing at my recently expanding waistline. "Nestle's…"

"Well, I've never exactly had the body of a Chippendale Dancer anyway," I replied.

"Yeah, but now you look like you have the body of a Chips-Ahoy Dancer. There's plenty of room at your place. Why don't you get a treadmill or a stationary bike?"

"I already have plenty of places to hang my clothes. I don't need anymore. You know I'd never use those things."

Amy walked over to the counter, poured me a cup of coffee and I was reminded of my barking bladder. I made no move for the bathroom, however, as I accepted this penance as my payment for access to any information she might have gleaned from her husband.

"Then why don't you join a gym or take one of those classes they give at the Community Center. You could come with me to Zumba," she said, chuckling at the prospect.

"Sorry, I already have a workout program."

"Yeah. What's that?"

"I come home from work, smoke a cigar, and eat a plate of linguine while watching an episode of The Sopranos on Netflix. I call it Goombah. All in all, I'm feeling pretty good," I answered, only half joking.

"Better watch it or you'll be old before your time. You used to live in Boston, work on a big newspaper, and now look at you; locked up in your apartment eating mac and cheese, and reading books that went out of print 50 years ago." A child screamed in the next room, and without pausing for breath or diverting her eyes, Amy shot out, "Shut the Hell up in there!"

"Well, we all can't be like you, taking a big bite out of life and letting the juices run down our chins. By the way, I didn't know UGGs came out with a peep-toe these days."

"Very funny," she spat, hiding her stained, torn footwear beneath the chair. "I have kids, a house, a life here. You know, Mom calls me all the time asking when you're going to get married. What am I supposed to tell her?"

I never thought I'd welcome the company of my brother-in-law, but I found myself listening hopefully for his flat, splayed footsteps on the stairs. "You know what, tell Mom what I tell her. When she asks when I'm gonna get married, I ask when she's gonna break a hip–conversation over."

She gave me the patented family eye roll and went for more coffee. "Just think about it. I mean it's probably better you didn't marry that Kayla or any of the others. What you need is someone sweet, kind and not nuts."

"Hell, if I'm gonna limit myself like that I'll never meet anyone," I cracked just as Andrew rounded the corner rubbing sleep out of his eyes.

He wore a yellow-collared wife beater with matching briefs and his thinning hair was matted forward like William Henry Harrison coming off a two-day bender. He plopped down in a kitchen chair that creaked out for mercy, found a pack of cigarettes in what I originally thought was a fruit bowl (silly me), lit one and accepted the black coffee Amy handed over. "I know, not exactly the Breakfast of Champions," he wheezed while simultaneously clearing his nose with a low rumbling that seemed as if he was producing, not bodily fluid so much, as molten lava.

"Actually, sex is the real Breakfast of Champions," I joked as he opened the napkin and examined its contents. "But not much chance of that I suspect."

After my lame chuckle died out, a silence came over the room. The comedian Steven Wright once opined, "There's a fine line between fishing and standing on the bank looking like an idiot." I knew exactly what he meant as I sat there, full bladdered, waiting for Andrew to start blabbering about the murders.

"What a mess," he said after what seemed like an eternity, but was probably no more than fifteen seconds. "You couldn't have stomached it."

"Have you ever seen my apartment?" I quipped reflexively, then shut my mouth.

"This was no joke Luke," he said flatly, without the more-officious-than-thou attitude he usually took when talking to me about police business. "Blood everywhere—Ted in the bed with a hole blown through his chest. The girl slumped in the corner, her white dress soaked red. And Merwin in the bedroom doorway with a bullet in his temple. It was ugly, man."

Amy reached over and put a hand on his arm as I took mental notes. "Wait a second, who's Merwin?"

"Curly Carson, the father. It was a family name. He never liked it."

Suddenly the name struck a chord in my mind. Years ago, when we were having trouble getting players for one of our softball teams, Wally Reynolds, the desk sergeant I'd spoken to earlier, offered to "...get this guy Merwin, he played Double-A ball." When we jumped at the chance to get someone who was a September call-up away from the Major Leagues,

Wally corrected himself, "Not Minor League Double-A ball, I mean he played Sunday mornings in the Alcoholics Anonymous League." That meant either alcohol didn't play a part in this case, or something had caused Curly to slip off the wagon and possibly propelled the fatal spree.

I made a note to check out the local AA chapter and tried to gently push Andrew for more information. "Any clue as to the motive?"

"I shouldn't say anymore," he said and drew on the cigarette. I wasn't exactly The Mentalist, but I knew that meant he would say more, and I went back to standing on the bank again looking like an idiot.

It didn't take long. "It was the age difference. She was only twenty-three, and hell, she looked like she was going on twelve. Very pretty, but naïve. The Chief is pretty sure that's what drove the father mad, and I agree with him. It's a matter of interviewing folks, searching his house, and checking everyone's phones and emails. I'm sure we'll find something to indicate that."

I, however, wasn't convinced. Monica Carson may have looked young, but Ted Sheehan wasn't exactly Abe Vigoda. In the yearbook pictures, he was fit, handsome, and had a thick, full head of hair. Men don't fall apart, present company including myself excluded, that quickly. Besides the *Cosmo* I flipped through last time I was at the doctor's office told me 40 was the new 30, 30 the new 20, 10 the new embryo.

Well, I'm guessing on that last one, but still it was only sixteen years, not Anna Nicole Smith and J. Howard Marshall for chrissakes.

At this point, a generic rock song part Led Zeppelin, part *Hocus Pocus* by Focus, came blaring out of my pocket; the default ringtone I had no idea, or inclination to learn, how to switch. It was Charlie Grissom telling me no one at the high school was talking, but he did get pictures and a lot of good background on Sheehan's career. "Did a blonde show up–from the *Burlington Bee*?" I asked.

"Yeah. Quite a looker. A lot better than old Glenn Hubbard, huh?"

"Not bad. I'd throw her a chop," I said, trying to evoke a nonchalant "screw her, I did," attitude while really not knowing what in the Hell that was. "Um...er...well, just give her any help you can. She seems like a good kid."

The phone flipped closed with a loud pop, causing Andrew and Amy to look up from their coffee cups. "Sorry," I said sheepishly. "I really gotta upgrade. Nobody has these things anymore."

"Actually, Curly Carson did. I bagged all the items on his person for evidence," Andrew continued, "Someone said it looked like a disposable. Probably lost his phone and was using that while hoping the real one turned up."

From what I knew of him, Curly seemed like an old school kind of guy. His daughter probably made him get a phone, and he chose one of those cheap Consumer Cellular ones. And being resistant to change–as opposed to me who was just lazy–he never upgraded. It didn't merit a mental note.

He looked haggard from the all-nighter, so I figured I should push for a few more details before it was too late. "Did she have a key to Sheehan's place?"

"I don't think so. Her chain had only two keys on it. One car key, one apartment key. She was renting one of those townhomes in Dorset. We'll eventually check it out."

"*We* will? Three people died. Why aren't the State Police being brought in?"

He made a face as if he'd just sucked on a lemon and stabbed out his cigarette in the remains of his coffee. I'd finally gotten under his skin, but, of course, that was inevitable.

"Why do we need the State Police? This is an Artfield matter involving good Artfield people," said Andrew, rising from his chair. I could tell he was simply mouthing Chief Bowden's words, but these were likely the last I'd get from him, so I let him go on. "Sure, old man Carson got crazy over the whole affair, but what's the point of dragging the State Police into it. They'll only turn it into some kinda CSI circus. We can handle things just fine."

And with this he turned and walked out, a hand reaching back under the boxers to scratch a cream cheese white butt cheek, not exactly instilling me with confidence.

Chapter 4: God May Forgive You But I Don't

I had two choices. One was to return to the office, write up my notes into a background piece, and begin the myriad machinations that would send this issue to press and keep our sinking ship afloat. Frankly, though, that didn't sound like me. The other option was to retire to my couch with a beer, a book, and the afternoon Red Sox game muted on the TV. But while that seemed to be playing to my strength, I decided to split the difference, and phoned in the story to Gladys before heading over to the Episcopal Church.

I'm not a religious guy so I don't know much about the Episcopalians other than they believe Joe Piscopo is The Messiah, but don't quote me on that. I'm more what the "now you're showing your age," comedian Flip Wilson described as a Jehovah's Bystander. That is, I believe in a higher power. I'd just rather not get involved, thanks. What I did know, however, is the local chapter of Alcoholics Anonymous met there for coffee and sadness—I'm assuming the latter, which may indicate I have a problem come to think of it—three nights a week.

The church itself was a Department of Corrections, halfway-house-style, clapboard box on Washington Street, between the last surviving Ben Franklin Five-and-Dime store, and a new breakfast/lunch place aspiring for hipness, called Johnny Java's. The latter was popular with the pass-through ski crowd, but still hadn't lured the locals away from The Short Stack Pancake House two blocks over.

I figured if there was something bothering Curly Carson, he may have shared it or shown it at the meetings. I wasn't sure what the etiquette or legality was regarding sharing what went on in these things, but Hell, three people were dead in a town that was an Aunt Bee-pie cooling on a windowsill away from Mayberry, so I was hoping everyone was on board in trying to understand what happened. That said, I really had no idea what went on behind closed doors in these groups. The closest I'd come was through Derf, my former roommate in Boston, a man with a taste for gambling so intense my monthly request for rent money would invariably be met by "let's see how the Celtics (or Bruins/Red Sox/Patriots) do tonight and I'll get back to you." In reality, though, I never learned much from Derf, since he only attended GA meetings sporadically, and generally with a deck of cards in hand, because "When am I ever gonna find myself in a room with a bigger bunch of losers than this? There's money to be made!" Well, I couldn't argue with his logic.

First, however, I had to pee like a racehorse. An idiom Derf assured me did not translate into a profitable wagering theory (as in bet on the horse that relieves himself during the Post Parade—he'll be lighter), though Lord knows he tried. Thus, I ducked into Johnny Java's, only to find the lascivious lusciousness of Miss Iceland at the counter ordering a mocha-venti-latte-grande-macchiato thing at $6.50 a pop. If I had any notions, and I was still fooling myself I did, of getting more than friendly with her, this trendy side of her pretty much blew a John Holmes-sized glory hole in it. As I looked down trying to determine which cost more, her coffee or my entire ensemble, I heard her voice call out to me.

"Hey. If I didn't know better, I'd think you were stalking me," she said with just enough of a smile to hold my guilty paranoia at bay.

"Well, I'd love to stalk you, but to tell the truth it seems like a lot of work on my part," I cracked. "Plus, what with binoculars, ladders, infrared glasses, it can get really expensive. And not to mention the time, I could never be that focused. Seriously, back in the 90s Courtney Thorne-Smith doesn't know the bullet she dodged."

She seemed to soften for the first time. Maybe she appreciated the help I'd arranged at the high school or maybe she was finally getting me. That last idea had even me chuckling when she offered, "Can I buy you a coffee?"

"Thanks, but I'm about an espresso shot away from a heart flutter. Let me just use the restroom and we'll compare notes."

The bathrooms were in the back, past two rows of empty bistro tables and walls lined with reproductions of impressionist paintings by guys who never felt the need to enunciate the last consonant in their name— Monet? Renoir? Degas? It took a while to relieve myself of the Big Gulp worth of coffee I'd consumed and then figure out the pretentious planet-friendly hand dryer. So, when I got out, Miss Iceland had already spread her laptop out on a table (unfortunately not a euphemism) and was talking to Wally Reynolds still in uniform and looking completely out of place.

"What're you doing here?" I questioned Wally, who was wearing a Miss Iceland induced shit-eating grin that would no doubt disappear the moment we broached the subject of the murders.

"On a coffee run for the Chief and the guys," he replied nonchalantly. Behind him I could see the young barista and her lumberjack bearded manager stacking various drinks in those cardboard holders. I wasn't sure what I found more disconcerting, that looking like a Civil War general had suddenly become hip, or the thought of Andrew, Chief Bowden and the boys walking around with steamed milk mustaches and licking the whipped cream off their White Chocolate Frappuccinos.

"You were in there for quite a bit," Miss Iceland smiled up at me, "and Officer Reynolds and I were just wondering number 1 or number 2?"

They chuckled. I rolled my eyes. "First, let me say if this really was what you were discussing, I weep for the future of conversational discourse in this country. Second, if you're going back there, you may wanna light a match."

Miss Iceland laughed a little too hard, but it occurred to me she just might be getting the hang of things around here. As an outsider and newbie, she wasn't just going to roll into town like Kolchak the Nightstalker and start uncovering secrets. She had to soften up the troops and Wally, at least, was eating it up.

Just then Paul Bunyan called out that Wally's order was ready. He said goodbye to Miss Iceland with a touch of his PBA baseball cap, as if he'd just been introduced at the All-Star Game and waddled off. I kept an eye on him, wondering if the reason the police switched over from the diner was because they were getting some kind of discount. No money changed hands–though it could have when the order was placed–but Wally did sign some kind of receipt before walking out with a wink that certainly wasn't directed at me.

"So, how'd it go down at the high school?" I asked, figuring she'd want to get down to business.

"Your people were nice. They got me up to speed and introduced me to the administrators," she said while tapping away at her laptop. "I got some good background on Ted Sheehan, but they couldn't give me anything on the girl, due to student record confidentiality. Still, the second I asked about anything relating to the murders or motive, they clammed up like Marcel Marceau."

"Nice," I replied. "I woulda went with Shields and Yarnell, but Marceau works." She smiled at me, and if it hadn't quite melted the police enough to get information, I had to admit my PIN numbers were hers for the asking. Not to mention Mr. Peabody, as I called it, was up and inquisitive.

"So, if you're not getting coffee, or stalking me, why are you here?"

"Well besides the fact this bathroom is silverfish-free unlike my one at home, I was about to drop by the church next door."

"No offense, but you don't exactly come off as a man of God..."

"Hard to slip anything past you," I responded sarcastically. "But actually, Curly Carson was a recovering alcoholic. AA meetings take place at the Episcopal Church. I figured I'd check in with the priest–uh, minister–pastor guy or whoever runs the program. See if he can shed light on his recent mental state. Care to join me?"

"Yeah sure," she agreed, and packed up her laptop, picked up her coffee. A slight tug on my jeans to adjust Mr. Peabody accordingly, and we headed out.

A door to the left of the main entrance read "OFFICE." A light was on in the window, so I tried the knob, but no luck. I knocked lightly at first, then louder, and after what seemed a long time, a face peered through the square of the window and began to unlock the heavy door.

I recognized the face, as Logan Brooks, the reverend or what have you. He was just the man we were looking for, but that was to be expected. He ran the church, and all its various projects, almost single-handedly. From food drives at Thanksgiving, to Toys for Tots at Christmas, to clothing collection year-round. Though in his early 60s, he possessed an energy level I couldn't match on a 3-pack of Red Bull and a fistful of Adderall.

My erstwhile Artfield Review-er Gladys was a parishioner and friend and handled all his work at the paper. Therefore, I only knew him through his occasional visits to the office, and Town Council meetings, where he was often to be found promoting a cause, or recruiting assistance, with varying degrees of success, for said cause. He generally dressed casually; a black jacket over a white polo shirt or cardigan, depending on the season. But he was most recognizable by a shock of dense gray, black hair, which shot up and back off a shockingly low forehead, and I suddenly noticed it was coming at me at an astonishing speed.

I never thought I'd put myself in these shoes, but I felt like a slave trader accidentally trying to solicit the abolitionist, John Brown. All I saw was a forest of hair, fiery eyes and a craggy face demanding, "What do you want? Why are you here?"

I took half a step back, bumped into Miss Iceland, and she dropped her quarter filled coffee cup on the pavement. It made a small, harmless mark on the sidewalk, but this only seemed to enrage him more.

"And get that crap out of here," he rasped pointing at the cup Miss Iceland was dutifully retrieving. A blue-green vein throbbed on his temple, and for a second, I wondered if I could even spell the word "aneurysm" close enough, so spell check would at least know what I was going for, when I wrote up his death for this week's edition.

I could sense he was about to slam shut the door, so I made a quick appeal to his better nature. "We just wanted to talk about poor Curly Carson and what might've driven him mad."

"You drove him mad. This town drove him mad. And now his blood, his daughter's blood and Sheehan's blood is on all your hands. And now the diocese is closing the parish down and forcing me to retire. Not enough parishioners to justify this size building, they say. I'm finished with you people. May you all burn in Hell!"

With that the door slammed, the lock turned, the lights went out inside and Miss Iceland turned to me dumbfounded.

"You've been a pleasure," I said, facetiously, to the shut door. And though now I knew for sure we were on to something; I didn't have a freakin' clue what in the world that was.

Chapter 5: Somebody Hates My Car

By next morning the paper was on its way to press, Miss Iceland was back in Burlington, and I was where I was at my best—on the couch with a coffee, a stack of dollar store Oreos and a volume of Alan Sillitoe short stories. As I dove into the tale of how a 1950s British working-class hero was *not* something to be, despite what John Lennon sang, I pondered putting my own life into novella form. *The Loneliness of the Long-Distance Drunkard* leapt to mind as a possible working title when my phone rang.

This was, for me, a record-breaking third out-of-office phone call in less than 24 hours, and as I angrily jammed the torn piece of newspaper I used as a bookmark into place, I pondered how I was supposed to get anything done with all these interruptions. I checked the flip phone display before answering. It was my sister. "What's up?" I asked, while realizing Caller ID had rendered the art of exchanging pleasantries practically moot.

"Hey. Andrew wanted me to call you."

"Really?" I replied, thinking this sounded very CIA back channel-ish, like I was about to be asked to broker an arms deal with the Mujahideen.

"He said to tell you the State Police detectives came out this morning, reviewed the evidence, and signed off on the department's theory of the murders. As soon as the mandatory toxicology reports come back from Montpelier, Chief Bowden will issue a statement," she said very matter-of-factly. Then added, "Oh and you and your little floozy should stay out of Johnny Java's and the Episcopal Church."

"Floozy?" I answered, cocking an eyebrow then uncocking it since I was on the phone. "Well, you know the plan was to meet Scott and Zelda for some bathtub gin, but the speakeasy was closed. And why shouldn't I go to the coffee place or the church for that matter." The first part of her message came straight from the Chief. It was this latter part of the message that I found most curious.

"Listen, you don't like those pretentious drinks anyway and you wouldn't know a scone from a hole in your ass so just stay away," she said. "Plus, I heard you and your friend scared old Pastor Brooks right out of town. Stop trying to impress Blondie and do like I've been telling you. Go on the internet and don't be too choosy—Rubenesque is not a deal breaker."

"OK, we're done here," I started, but by the time I was finished there was a scream, a cry, and then a dial tone on the other end.

Well, tbedroom andy morning, so I downed the last cookie, took the coffee to the bedroom and got dressed. Clean-wise I was down to a Nehru jacket and a pair of my dad's old Bermuda shorts, so I pulled a Kris Kristofferson, found my cleanest dirty shirt, pulled on yesterday's jeans—that at this point were more like last week's jeans—and headed for the Falcon.

An internet search the night before had yielded the info Ted Sheehan was indeed divorced. The filing date was six years ago and, as far as I could tell from subsequent searches, there were no children involved. The reason for parting was not part of the public record, but the fact

Monica Carson was a nubile senior the year it went down, had me intrigued.

The plan was to hit Artfield High first and dig amongst some of my contacts on the staff for anything they might know about this supposed Ted Sheehan-Monica Carson relationship. I'd parked around back to avoid Helen, and pretty much any neighbors. A chatter, I am not. Then, just as I was about to put the key in the car door—because on the Falcon you still had to do things like that—I saw and smelled it. On the hood, amidst the rust and chipping paint, a large, fragrant turd.

It was clear someone had placed or shat (I believe that's correct; however, I did not anticipate having to conjugate the past participle of the verb "to shit" at this point in my life, so bear with me) it there on purpose. This is because it occupied point (0,0) had the hood been one of those X, Y charts students are forced to work with in Freshman Algebra. In fact, if the perpetrator had gotten up there to do it in, say, muddy shoes, I could've calculated the slope-intercept of such an effort using the formula $y=Mx + b$—or in this instance maybe $y=Mx + bm$ would be more appropriate.

I had no idea who would do such a thing. What I did know was, it was intentional, it was human, and they were apparently going for a bow before running out of steam. None of my exes would've wasted this kind of effort on me, and I hadn't given Miss Iceland any reason, though it was still early in our acquaintance. Besides I couldn't imagine anything coming out of that apple of an ass but rainbow sherbet.

Between the difficulty in trying to wrap my head around such an act and the smell, I decided it was time to act. I went to the nearby recycling bin, grabbed a piece of cardboard, and flicked the offending pile into the bushes. I'd ponder the whys and what-fors later, and since the Falcon couldn't look any worse, I eschewed trying to find a hose, fired her up, and headed out.

On my way to the high school, the smell began seeping in through the holes in the dashboard where things like a radio and glove compartment door used to be. I was thus forced to open both front windows, which required a pair of pliers and the flexibility of a gymnast, while trying to give at least a minimal nod to the rules of the road.

I reached Artfield High a little after 9:30 a.m. and chose a spot in the rear of the student lot, in range of a security camera, hoping to catch The Midnight Pooper in the act. Though I realized this wasn't likely given normal digestion time. Plus, based on the size and firmness noted earlier, he/she appeared to be reasonably healthy of colon, so I'd probably have to wait them out.

The high school itself was large, relative to the town population, since it was a regional school drawing also from more rural communities to the north and east. However, despite its stately lawns and blasé brick exterior, inside it resembled nothing so much as the bar of a Bangkok brothel. Now I assume there is a dress code designed to guide the fashion choices of the 14- to 18-year-old girls in attendance, but apparently enforcement was, to be kind, lax. Bare midriffs, Daisy Dukes, yoga pants, mini-skirts, tiny tank tops, it was like Pat Robertson's version of a Hieronymus Bosch painting. Of course, I could never feel sympathy for those creepy male teachers who slept with female students but considering what passed as "school appropriate" clothing, I was stunned one of their lawyers had never tried entrapment as a defense.

I showed my ID, signed in at the office, and got a visitor's badge. I realize 9/11 and Sandy Hook were the reasons for these precautions, but I also felt it was an equally good idea to keep track of any indiscriminate men walking around these halls. I could only imagine the leering of middle-aged outside contractors. The corridors had cleared by now with the ringing of the late bell and I quickly made my way to the gym to see what info I could shake out of Lip.

Max Lipper was the fittest, tannest 60-year-old Jew this side of Boca Raton. He spent his days playing basketball, volleyball and what have you with students, and his evenings participating in practically every adult sports recreation league Artfield and the surrounding areas had to offer. When he wasn't pitching in a softball league or posting someone thirty years his junior low in the paint, he could be found on a stool at Pete's Pub sipping Absolut and cranberry and hitting on anything that moved.

"I can't believe you're still teaching," I said, sneaking up from behind, as he set up plastic cones for that period's activities.

"My 33rd glorious year," he replied, turning around and grinning ear-to-ear. He then bypassed my outstretched hand in favor of a giant bear hug.

"So, I guess you were grandfathered in on Megan's Law?" I joked.

"I miss you, bud. When are you coming back to play with us?"

"With my knees, forget it. You have a better chance of seeing me here teaching than on a softball field."

"You don't want that," he said, laughing and shaking his head. "Those that can do and those that *can't* teach."

"Yeah, and those that can't teach, teach gym."

We could've busted balls and told war stories all day, but the first kids were trickling out of the locker rooms, so I figured I better get to the point.

"Bud, can you help me out? What did you know about Ted Sheehan?"

"Not much. As Vice-Principals go, I liked him because he left us alone."

"Are you saying he wasn't doing his job?" I questioned. If so, maybe he *was* screwing around with Monica Carson; texting and SnapChat-ing his way through a midlife crisis.

"No, I just mean he was good. Didn't sweat the little stuff. No drama."

I'd heard the high school could be a crazy place. In elementary schools, they went on Lockdown every time a kid cried. At the high school, on the other hand, any day they didn't have to bring the cops in was considered a win. "So, what was he like personally?"

"Don't know. Nice guy, always said hello, unlike most of the administration around here. But outside of school stuff, he kept pretty much to himself. Even when he was teaching, he never did Happy Hour or the Holiday or year-end parties."

The gym class was completely in and, while the clothes were actually more sedate—baggy shorts, long t-shirts—there was enough Spandex to make me wonder if turning Lip loose in here wasn't akin to inviting Roman Polanski to a Sweet 16 party.

Lip dropped the last cone in place, blew his whistle and the milling students dropped into their squad spots, just like we used to in our Supertramp *Breakfast in America* concert shirts and shorts over sweatpants —why the latter, I'm still not sure.

I was about to cut out when Lip had one last thought. "You know who you might want to see is Mr. Barton, 10th grade English teacher. I heard he was friends with Ted. They always did lunch duty together. We've got sophomores here now. Check the lounge or Room 130 or 131, he should be free this period."

Lip gave me another huge hug and I shoved off to find Barton. I knew the school fairly well from covering various functions here for the paper. The Faculty Lounge came up first, with nothing between it and the gym, except the Special Ed. rooms—tiny boxes where a teacher and classroom aide are crammed in with 6-8 ADHD and Oppositional Defiant students in what looks like a Texas Tornado Steel Cage match. It's a noble job, for as the humorist David Sedaris once commented, "I'm sure there are plenty of kids with legitimate learning disabilities, but aren't a lot of them just assholes?"

Pondering this, I peeked into the lounge, which was just a converted classroom with a dining table, second-hand furniture, a bank of computers and a giant, overworked copy machine that probably chewed up a rainforest of paper a day. Still, it was large and brightly lit, unlike the dank caverns of yesteryear, so filled with cigarette smoke that it wasn't clear whether exiting teachers were leaving the Faculty Room or the back of Cheech and Chong's van. Through the window, I spied three female teachers: two at the table grading papers, the third feeding stacks of papers into the copier as part of what I once heard referred to as the "give 'em worksheets till their hands bleed" theory of education.

I continued on, made a left, then a right, before winding up in the boiler room, where a custodian with a key chain so heavy it could've been used for the Olympic hammer throw, directed me to Mr. Barton in Room 131. Walking in, I was confronted by a man that was everything I could've been if I'd done the things I should have done. Approximately my age, neat, fit, well-dressed, and groomed to within an inch of his life. I was exhausted just looking at him. I used to joke with Gladys at the office that I was always late because it took me two hours to get ready in the morning. Then I'd run a hand up and down my slovenly self and crack, "Do you think this just happens?" Ron Barton could say the same thing, only without sarcasm.

"Hi, I'm Luke Williams from *The Artfield Review*. Do you have a minute to talk about Ted Sheehan? This won't take long."

"Sure," he said, extending a hand and giving mine a firm, confident shake. "There were some reporters here the other day, but I was doing grief counseling in the Guidance Office and must've missed them. Ted was a great guy. It's been tough."

He finished writing that night's homework on the polyurethane whiteboard that had replaced blackboards in all the rooms, I'm guessing, because chalk dust was afflicting too many teachers with "white lung disease." Capping the marker, he took a seat on a stool, and motioned me to a one-piece desk/chair in the front row. Dropping down and squeezing in, I was reminded just how bad my knees, and how big my waistline, had become.

"So, I hear you were fairly close with Ted," I began.

"Close as anyone I guess."

"He kept pretty much to himself, huh?"

"Personally yes, professionally though, he gave everything he had to the students."

"I noticed. Going through the yearbooks, it looked like he was involved in every fundraiser there was. What was the name of the club he ran?"

Barton had gotten off his stool and moved over by his desk. "The Random Acts of Kindness Club. It was one of the most popular in the school because of him."

"Right. They didn't have that when I was here. Though me and a couple of guys made up the 'Vicious Acts of Vengeance Club,' but I don't believe that was ever sanctioned by the administration."

He laughed politely and opened the big file drawer on the near side of his desk. "Ted loved fundraisers because they were all-inclusive. Jocks, nerds, cool kids, artsy types could all participate. And they were into everything," he said, as he began pulling novelty giveaway items from the drawer. "Here's a 'Donate To Darfur' button, a 'Hurricane Katrina Aid' magnet, 'Autism Awareness' drink cozy, 'Red Nose Day' noses."

He held out one of the latter as if to give it to me. "No thanks. I prefer to get my red nose the old-fashioned way–alcohol." As he shoveled the giveaways back into the drawer, I looked around thinking perhaps I missed my calling. Maybe I should've been an English teacher, surrounded by books and saying things like "There are no stupid questions, only stupid students," or "I don't know *can* you go to the bathroom?" not so much because I thought it funny, but because I felt contractually obligated.

"Have the police released any information about the crime?" he asked, waking me from my reverie. "I can't understand why anyone would want to kill Ted."

I figured this was the perfect time to leak the police theory and gauge the reaction of someone who actually knew Sheehan. "The word I'm hearing is Ted and the girl were involved and the father didn't approve."

"*Involved* in what?"

This was not the reaction I was expecting. I thought "involved" could only mean one thing in this scenario, but Barton was clearly confused. "You know–romantically," I clarified.

He shook his head. "Not possible."

This was the standard line on shows like *Dateline* and *48 Hours*. It was never possible that the brother, cousin, son, or neighbor could've chopped up his family with a Ginsu knife and buried them in the backyard, but of course in the end he did. So, I pressed him. "Why not? Ted was single, on his own. And Monica Carson was a looker."

"Doesn't matter," he said, and fixed me with a look of absolute certainty. "Ted Sheehan was gay!"

Chapter 6: Holden Caulfield At The Bat

It's been said, if you can't pick out the sucker at the poker table in the first two minutes, then it's you. In other words, if you've only got the info your competitors want to give, you're sunk. Now, however, thanks to Barton, I had inside information and for some reason I wanted to run out of the room and text it to Miss Iceland with a Happy Face emoji immediately. Fortunately, I was able to refrain from such high school hijinks long enough to hear Barton out.

Of course, my first question was how did he know this, but he instantly fixed me with a "Have you no gay-dar at all?" stare and it suddenly became clear. Next there was the whole marriage/divorce thing.

"Ted never really talked about that. He wasn't bisexual, as far as I know, so it's kind of a mystery even to me."

"He was very ambitious from what I heard. Education was his life," I offered, trying to get a fix on the man.

"Absolutely, it was all he ever wanted to do. He had two Master's Degrees, his Doctorate, was highly qualified in both Science and Math, published in multiple education journals," Barton rattled off. "He could have been an administrator years ago, but he wanted to stay in Artfield and right the things he felt were wrong here."

I recalled a story told by former Dallas Cowboys coach Jimmy Johnson of how he married young, not for love, but because as a no-name assistant, he needed to show stability, and have someone to bring to dinner parties and events. Once he got his first college head coaching job, he dumped his wife because at that point wins and losses were all that mattered. He no longer had to put on a show. Vermont may be a Blue State politically, but there's still a strong strain of Yankee conservatism socially, particularly in the more rural areas. I considered whether Ted Sheehan's marriage was just a convenient façade.

"What did he feel was wrong?" I asked, trying not to get ahead of myself.

"Same as everyone, money, funding. Less emphasis on meetings and paperwork, more on the students," he answered.

We sat and talked about the myriad ways money is wasted on everything but students and learning. From teacher workshops that taught how to "lead with love," ("I tried that once," Barton cracked, "they called Family Services.") to proms that made the Court at Versailles look like a Chuck E. Cheese, it sounded like a shit show of considerable proportions. I knew well old Wes Willard, Riley Chase, and the rest of the curmudgeons on the town council and school board were stingy with the buck. Balancing increasing technological needs, parent expectations, and payroll pressures against an ever-tightening budget, was a constant tight rope walk. Had Ted Sheehan lost his footing?

Eventually, he looked up at the digital clock mounted under the regular school-issue clock and told me he had to get ready for the incoming class. "Kids can't read analog clocks anymore," he said when he noticed my gaze lingering on the wall. "If I didn't tack the digital up there, they'd be looking at their phones every other minute, and once that starts you've lost 'em."

Things had certainly changed since I roamed these halls, though I did notice from the stack on Barton's desk they were still teaching *A Catcher in the Rye* to sophomores. "Still spoon feeding 'em J.D. Salinger huh," I observed.

"You've read it?"

"Yup, sophomore year."

"What'd you think?" he queried.

"Well, after I got about 50 pages in and realized it wasn't about baseball I kind of lost interest. And don't get me started on the Somerset Maugham they made me read in college. *Of Human Bondage*, what a tease."

Barton wasn't sure if I was joking or stupid, but before he could confirm that it was a little of both, I unwedged myself from the desk, thanked him for his time, and was off. Outside it was the kind of gorgeous spring weather that took me back to my college days, when we'd grab a Frisbee and a cooler full of beer, pop the Grateful Dead's *American Beauty* in the cassette deck, and drive up to the mountains debating how it was possible we were failing Western Civ.

With those memories in mind, the scoop on Sheehan in my notes, and my car delightfully feces-free, I pulled out the flip phone to call Miss Iceland in a state of euphoria, delightfully free of gin and/or Xanax.

"Hello," she said a little too formally, as if she didn't recognize the number.

I leaned up against a rare rust-free spot on the Falcon and dropped my bombshell. "Ted Sheehan was gay!" I exclaimed.

It was not exactly Hiroshima August '45. "Who is this?"

Mr. Peabody was just waking up, but this put him down for the count. "It's Luke, Luke Williams, from *The Artfield Review*, the double murder suicide," I was running out of details and octaves in my panicking voice when she finally cut in.

"Oh yeah, hey Mr. Williams, what's up?" Mister Williams? I quickly looked around for my father and just as quickly felt my heart shatter, like when you dropped the piece of gum that came with baseball cards on the floor.

She did sound distracted, so I still hoped to bring her back around. "Ted Sheehan, the VP at Artfield High, who was shot, was gay. He couldn't have been fooling around with the young girl. That shoots a hole in the whole police theory. We were right, something more is going on here."

There was a fair to middling pause before things started to register. "Gay? Son of a bitch you were right." I was happy we were back on the same page, but her shock at my actually being correct was a little off-putting. Also, she didn't seem excited, or suggest she'd be right down so we could have a romantic tete-a-tete, as I was hoping.

If my dating life proved anything, however, I was not one to take "never in a million years" for an answer, so I forged on. "This opens up a ton of possibilities. Why don't you come out here, and we can work on it together," I tried.

"I'd like to, but the paper's sent me to cover an event at the planetarium in St. Johnsbury."

"Planetarium? What's going on there—*Laser Zeppelin*?"

"What...uh...no, some kind of new educational program for grade schoolers," she said, sounding dejected.

"That shouldn't take long. Come to my office afterwards." Then, still feeling good, I added, "I'll take you out for dinner."

"I can't. I'm off the story."

"What? Why?"

"I pitched our angle to my editor and thought he was on board. Then out of nowhere he called me up at home last night to say I wasn't ready for it yet," she went on sadly, which perversely made me feel good, until it made me feel like a bad person, and things came full circle back to miserableness, as they usually do in life. "They're having the kid that was here before me work it freelance."

My brain was too sober to wrap my head around these myriad machinations. I was thinking I needed to get back to the well-stocked mini fridge at the office, and discuss everything with Gladys, when she cut in again. "Gotta go. I'm pulling up to the place now," she alerted me, as I began to pace, while brushing paint chips from the Falcon off my ass. "Good God! There must be a hundred snot-nosed bastards waiting to get in. This is gonna be a nightmare!" And with that, she clicked off and I thought, for the first time in a longtime, I might be in love.

Driving back to the office I felt strange. When I moved back to Artfield, the plan was to hopefully live another 30 years, drink beer, play ball and read everything I could get my hands on. Ambition, investigative journalism, and especially women, be damned. The latter three had brought me nothing but frustration, yet here I found myself, as P.G. Wodehouse used to say of Bertie Wooster, "back in the soup again," only with no Jeeves in sight.

It was Miss Iceland, however, that was bothering me the most. My history of getting jazzed up as regards a woman, only to be crushed, was legendary. Folks had been predicting my impending nuptials to every woman that passed through my proverbial transom, because I talked each one up like the greatest thing since self-adhesive stamps (seriously, what took so long). The closest I'd ever come, though, was one drunken proposal to Kayla, using the chorus from Eric Clapton's "Wonderful Tonight," as she drove me home from Pete's Pub; to which she replied "Wonderful *tonight*? What was I yesterday, or the day before that?" Hey, at least it wasn't "You

Are So Beautiful...To Me" or even worse "I've Grown Accustomed to Your Face," I thought.

Miss Iceland's fingers told me she wasn't engaged, and she'd mentioned she lived alone, but for all I knew she could be a dominatrix lesbian with a fetish for feet porn—which by the way, produces the message "Did you mean Sweet Corn?" when you try to Google it, uh, you know, for a story.

By this time, I had reached the office, there were three people dead and what appeared to be a coverup taking place, so I decided it was time to "put childish things aside," as Nick Nolte was told ad nauseam in *North Dallas Forty* and get back to business. As I looked up and down a main drag quaintly devoid of chain stores and fast-food restaurants, I realized Ted Sheehan was onto something. I too needed to stick around and see this matter through. I'd grown up here, and it was my refuge in adulthood when times got tough. Following up seemed like the least I could do, and frankly, "the least I could do" was generally my M.O. Of course, it wasn't going to be easy, so I entered the *Review* offices in search of cheap liquid refreshment and the counsel of Gladys Nutwell.

What's-her-name, the 19-year-old receptionist, sat at the front desk popping a chocolate in her mouth with her signature bored-but-beautiful look. "Not sure four out of five dentists recommend a 100 Grand bar for breakfast, but I guess when you're young ...," I said, wisecracking.

"Want one?" she said, looking up but leaving me unsure she was registering who I was.

"No thanks. I just look at one of those, or a Goldenberg's Peanut Chew, and the fillings start leaping out of my mouth. Besides, I'm trying to watch my girlish figure."

"Oh, don't worry it's Fun Size, see," she offered, holding up the tiny wrapper.

"Yeah, that's what I told my last girlfriend, 'It's not small, honey, it's Fun Size.' That didn't work out well either." She tilted her head like a well-endowed Labrador Retriever, and I looked into the back office which was unkempt and empty.

"Where's Gladys?"

"Oh, she had to run out to the bank. She didn't say when she'd be back."

The reception desk was shockingly uncluttered, but for her personal phone and a single "While You Were Out" slip. I gave her a second, even tried to lead her with my eyes, like some kind of Clever Hans trick, to the message, until silence gave way to awkwardness and all my memories of high school and pretty girls started to breach the dam of repression. "Is that for me?" I asked, pointing decisively, as it was clear she was more a visual/kinesthetic than auditory learner.

"Right, uh, some guy named Derf called," she said, finally handing over the pink square.

"Thanks," I said, taking the paper that read only "Dirph," with a smiley face dotting the "i". "You're doing a heckuva job." She shrugged as she bent over the desk for another candy, and regret over my tone was instantly assuaged, by the knowledge my sarcasm had no effect on cleavage such as that.

Back in my office, I popped a Natty Ice, and rummaged around the desk drawers for a snack. Finding an ancient jar of peanut butter, and a fistful of cracker packets left over from a long-ago aborted soup diet, I settled in. Gladys running an errand to the bank, concerned me. She ran the place and rarely left her post. If she did, it was at lunch. Not to mention leaving—I wanna say Naomi—the receptionist in charge, was not her ultra-efficient style. We weren't exactly heading up NORAD here, but still, having Ms. Breasty McRacksome at the helm, was akin to putting a 10-year-old in charge of the Space Shuttle.

I tried smearing peanut butter on a stale cracker with a letter opener, gave up and used my finger. I put a second cracker on top, popped the sandwich in my mouth, and took a long pull, letting the beer swirl around my mouth, washing the sticky snack from between my teeth. As I did, I gave up for the moment on worrying about Gladys and the errand, Miss Iceland's aloofness, and where exactly this investigation was leading me, and why I even cared so much. Then I picked up the phone and dialed Derf.

Derf generally called for only two reasons. First, to set up our yearly weekend at the races in Saratoga, and second, to settle a bet. Many nights I'd been awoken to hear:

"Is Brown in the Ivy League?" "Yes." "Crap." Click.

"Who kidnapped Patty Hearst?" "The Symbionese Liberation Army. "Son of a ..." Dial tone.

"What was the name of Tennessee Tuxedo's sidekick?" "Chumley." "Mother ..." Silence.

"Luke!" Derf answered, surprisingly upbeat.

I paused for the inevitable inane trivia question, but when it failed to materialize, I waded in. "Hey Derf. What's up?"

"I need to ask a favor." My wallet immediately shriveled up like testicles at a Polar Bear Plunge. "My brother-in-law hooked me up with a job as a food merchandiser ..."

Never one to let a little thing like work get in the way of gambling, he paused to let the "job" part of the statement sink in. "What the hell's a food merchandiser?" I asked, jumping in.

"I hand out samples in supermarkets for a new product, Amalfi's Gourmet Sausage," he said, unenthusiastically. "I'm like the Abe Froman of Northern New England. They have me in six stores in three days up near you, and I need a place to crash Thursday and Friday night. Can you put me up?"

If I had any style this would've cramped it, but lacking the same, I had no ready excuse, so I stalled. "Doesn't a big intestine stuffing concern like this give you travel expenses?"

"Yeah, but it came last week in the form of a per diem check and let's just say me and Javier Velasquez didn't remember the stretch at Suffolk Downs being quite that long."

"Sure, no problem," I buckled.

"Thanks, and I'll hook you up with all the sausage you can handle."

"As long as that's not a euphemism," I added, drolly, "I'm onboard."

I was calculating what this was going to cost me in dinners, reading time, and other sundry matters, when he suddenly changed the subject. "Hey, what happened up there? I heard there was a triple murder or something?"

The Boston papers must've picked up the story from Burlington or Montpelier. Three dead in the sticks is hardly worth the newsprint in major cities these days, so Derf probably didn't know the details, and I wasn't about to fill him in, as my Natty Ice warmed. "I'll tell you about it when you get up here."

"How come it's not on your website?" he questioned, as the sound of a banging keyboard came faintly over the line.

"Because we don't have one. Try the Burlington Bee site," I responded, looking for an exit.

He typed away and I figured I'd stick around long enough to get his opinion of Miss Iceland, whose photo was in the byline. But before I could ask, he was strangely distracted by another picture altogether. "Hey who's this guy about halfway down the page...beneath the ad for Canadian Viagra?"

Since no photos were allowed at the crime scene, I recalled they ran a shot of Harry Bowden decked out in his dress blues. "That's our police chief here. He's been hush-hush on the whole investigation. Why do you ask?"

"Cause, I know that dude," he said, incredulously. "He owes me money!"

Chapter 7: Of Ed McMahon and Air Supply

"He owes *you* money. Are you sure you got the right guy?"

"I think I can remember who *owes me* money," Derf answered, assuredly.

He had a point. He'd always been the owe-er, seldom, if ever, the owe-ee. Like a list of 80s heavy metal, hair bands that aged gracefully, the list of folks in arrears to him was short. On the contrary, Derf was into everybody for something. A walking advertisement for the reinstitution of Debtor's Prison, I could swear when we lived together, he once received a letter from Publisher's Clearing House saying he owed Ed McMahon $10,000,000. I pressed for more information.

"So how did this happen?"

"Well, I'd just cashed for six bills on a show wheel off a bridge jumper at Sam Houston," he began, cryptically. "Meanwhile he just went bust when the top of his tri-key got blind-switched at The Red Mile. So, he hit me up for a C-note and then disappeared."

"Oh well, that clears it all up," I said mid-eye roll, and then tried a more specific tack. "When did this happen?"

"About 5-6 weeks ago I'd guess."

"And how'd you meet?" I questioned, while scrambling to take notes on a beer can-ringed Post-It.

"What can I say? He was there at the dog track three nights in a row," Derf explained. "Losers of a feather, eventually, flock together."

I'd seen this particular phenomenon in action. Anytime Derf entered a Boston area racetrack or OTB, he was greeted like Norm walking into Cheers, complete with a witty rejoinder. Slouching his 6-foot 5-inch frame through the crowd bestowing his benevolent betting benediction on all and sundry—May the *horse* be with you—like some sort of Pope of Degenerate Village.

This was all too freakish. It had to be connected to Sheehan and Carson, but how? I drained the remnants of the Natty Ice and tossed the empty. I overshot the blue recycling basket, but it landed in the regular trash, which was just as good, since I knew from working late that the 4'9"

Spanish cleaning lady just dumped both baskets into a larger can and tossed the whole contents indiscriminately into the dumpster out back. "What time will you be here Thursday?" I asked, not wanting to waste any more time on the phone when there was drinking, and brooding, in that order, to do.

"Do they still have that dog track in Pownal?"

"Yes, but no live racing. Simulcast only."

"That works," he announced, agreeably. "I'm doing a demo near there at one. How 'bout I meet you at the track, say 3:30?"

"You'll be done by then?" I questioned but felt stupid before the words even left my mouth.

"Usually, I put in three good hours a day. I mean what are they expecting, I'm not a machine."

"Indeed, they probably don't know how lucky they are," I replied. "OK, see you there, and if you can recall anything about your exchanges with Bowden let me know. We might have a whole thing going on up here."

Derf signed off and I grabbed another Natty Ice. From the front, I could hear the door open and Naomi—screw it, that's what I'm calling her—speaking, "He's in the back, check his office." Her nonchalant tone made me assume it was Gladys back from her errand, so I didn't bother to hide the beer. She'd long ago accepted drinking on the job was part of my muse, as if I were Charles Bukowski with (slightly) better hygiene. However, just as

I popped the top, through the door from reception came a complete stranger.

It was a woman who could best be described as bland; to the female form she was what Air Supply was to classic rock. She was a veritable plain rice cake of a woman. Of middle height and slender build, she wore a formless denim dress beneath a faded black raincoat. Her middle-parted, coal black hair fell limply on each side, with the top of an alabaster white ear poking out left and right. She looked undernourished, underfed and anemic, and wore an expression that led me to believe the Oxford English Dictionary might want to consider adding "miserablesucks" to their upcoming edition—she looked like Shelly Duvall on Day 3 of a juice fast.

"Hi, are you Luke Williams?" she began, as I groped for a flat surface to ditch the cocktail. Finding none, I switched hands for no good reason, and she went on. "A police officer named Andrew said I should talk to you. I'm Debra Townes—Monica Carson's mom."

"Oh crap!" was my first thought, then considering the situation, I offered Gladys' desk chair, which was the only one not piled high with paper, books, or boxes. She accepted and sat at the very edge of the seat, like Kayla used to do on my sofa, but for different reasons.

Now if the philosopher/mathematician Pascal was correct and all men's problems did stem from an inability to sit in a room quietly alone, then I'd be the happiest S.O.B. around. Solitude was my jam, so to speak, but it was becoming obvious if I wanted to continue this investigation, I'd be jammin' out less in the coming days. Barton's revelation and Derf's

Bowden connection were about all I could handle at that point, but it was obvious more was coming.

See Debra Townes had a story to tell. It was going to be sad, and I was going to sit and listen sympathetically. As a reporter I should've been excited, but as a functioning alcoholic with a more than mild case of agoraphobia, I was chagrined. Still, I'm not a monster. She had just lost her daughter. I have a conscience, and since conscience is inversely proportional to ego, I also had a problem moving forward. But that was a dysfunction to deal with later.

Now, if I had more ego and less conscience I'd listen to her tale, file it away with the others, then nod and look sad. Then I'd strip it all down to what it was worth to me, and the headline grabbing story I'd write, and be on my semi-merry way. Not being of this ilk is why I had crapped out at the *Boston Globe* several years before, though several women, my sister and mother included, would add lazy, passionless, and indolent to the list. Thus, I sat on a milk crate full of back issues, tucked my beer on the floor behind me, and waited for her to begin.

"Thank you for seeing me," she started, soft but steady. "They said they couldn't give me any information at the police station. That there will be a press conference tomorrow or the next day with details. Then the Andrew fellow pulled me aside and said you might know some details."

It sounded like they were pushing the revelatory press conference back already. Suspicious, but why? It was a theme, like most in life, that was becoming less and less interesting the more I encountered it. "Not sure how much I can help you," I replied, keeping my cards close, mostly because I was as confused as anyone. "It was a fairly gruesome scene I'm told."

"I know. They wouldn't let me see the bodies, due to procedures. But I was probably better off, they said."

"You may want to take their advice on that. Particularly in Curly's case. Head wounds are never clean like in the movies."

She shifted in the chair, crossing her right leg over her left knee, the raincoat falling back and the dress riding up, till I was reminded I needed chicken. "Oh, not Curly. I was done with him long ago. It's Monica and Ted I wanted to get a last look at."

"You knew Ted Sheehan?" Once again, I was aroused, momentarily, till the usual tide of lethargy rolled back over me. It's a feeling that could also pass as the story of my sex life, but I digress.

"Yes. I guess I should give you some background," she began, as the alcohol and shifting stack of papers made my perch ever more precarious. "Curly and I married right out of high school. It was a beautiful ceremony, shotgun, and all, if you get my drift. By 25, we were divorced. I stayed close and we shared custody of Monica until she was 15 and entering Artfield High."

This sounded like it was going to be long, so I reached behind me and groped for the beer. I took a pull without shame, because she'd already seen it, I wasn't going to stop and, least proudly, because I had no intention of wanting to sleep with her.

"That's when I got a job over in Mount Olive, New York," she continued, while I bit my tongue on the old joke—last time I went to Mount Olive, Popeye kicked the crap out of me. "Monica wanted to stay here with her friends, and though it broke my heart, I left her with Curly. Ted Sheehan was the Orientation Coordinator. I met with him to make sure she'd be OK and had someone to turn to at AHS. I guess we hit it off and started seeing each other…"

"Whoa, whoa..," I said a little too excitedly and slid off the papers.

"Oh! Are you okay?"

No problem," I responded, getting to one knee, beer can held overhead like the Olympic torch. "Not a drop spilled. But what do you mean you were 'seeing' Ted Sheehan."

"Just getting together, sharing a bottle of wine, talking, that type of thing." Obviously, my poker face (and balance) needed work because she quickly added, "Not dating. It was nothing like that. He was just a sympathetic ear."

"Did Curly know? Could he have been jealous?"

"That was long ago, but no, we met at Ted's place. It was very discreet."

"I guess it would be," I said, thinking of Sheehan's place at the end of that desolate road. "He was out where the corn don't grow."

"Oh no, not the house where the murders happened," she interrupted. "He was still a struggling teacher then. We met at his apartment in that building next to the Episcopal Church. I'd use the back stairs. I'm sure no one saw me."

I recalled the good Reverend getting up in my face and pressed the issue. "Wasn't Curly attending AA meetings next door?"

"Not at that time, Curly was still a practicing, as opposed to a recovering, alcoholic then. It was one of the reasons I wanted to make sure Ted was looking out for Monica."

"What about this Random Acts of Kindness Club?" I began, hoping to see how deep the Monica/Sheehan relationship went, when suddenly Gladys swept into the room, bun wildly askew, which except for "one in the oven" was the most frightening "bun situation" I could imagine. The look on my face easily cut Debra Townes short. It was obvious...

We had a PROBLEM!

Chapter 8: So, This Is The End My Friends?

As Vince Lombardi's accountant said (I'm assuming), "Money isn't everything. It's the only thing." Heck, every time I go to wipe my ass it costs me fifty dollars until it makes a man want to install a bidet.

"We're cut off!" Gladys lamented.

"Cut off?"

"Yes! Cut. Off!"

I didn't think it was possible, but these words stung, as much outside as they did inside a barroom. Perhaps even more so. I could always stumble home and find more alcohol; money was a much more precious commodity.

When Gladys had ambled in, disheveled and white-faced, I was worried. When she went straight to my office, opened the fridge, cracked a Natty Ice and collapsed in a leaky bean bag chair, I was shattered–like seeing Superman searching for "roaches" under seats at the end of a Phish concert.

I quickly wrapped things up with Debra Townes, promising to meet again before, or right after, the police press conference. I then retreated to my office, where it took both hands and all my strength to unearth Gladys from the beanbag chair. I helped her navigate through the now near ankle deep hail of beans that had blown out and now covered the floor. Next, I deposited her in my desk chair from whence she began her tale.

"Cut off!" she reiterated, and took a decent-sized pull on the Natty Ice. Her blouse had come out of her skirt during the beanbag fiasco, but she paid no mind. "They're calling in our line of credit. We'll have to close down—immediately."

"They," meaning the Green Mountain Savings and Loan, and that "line of credit," being the only thing keeping us upright these past two and a half years. "Why? Why now?" I asked, confused.

"Who the Hell knows," Gladys said, with surprising candor, as she pulled the ubiquitous bun loose from the back of her head. The gun metal gray and silver strands fell Medusa-like. Snakes alighting on her shoulders.

"Did you talk to Henry?" I asked, referring to Henry Chase, the rotund, happy-go-lucky bank manager, who handled our account. I'd gone to school with Henry and talked him out of trouble junior year in high school, when his "City College of Business" fake ID nearly got him arrested in a Rutland package goods store. Remembering that, these days he was happy to extend our line of credit to get us through the rough patches.

"No, they brought the Old Man outta moth balls to deliver the news. Hank just stood behind him with his finger up his ass, which is no mean feat for that fat bastard," she spat. I wasn't sure how I felt about this new, foul-mouthed Gladys, but when she downed the rest of the beer, crushed the can, and motioned for another, like a biker's booze-bag, I figured now wasn't the time to question it.

The Old Man was Riley Chase, Henry's grandfather, Bank President, and a Founding Father of our humble little town. According to the older crowd, he was once a strapping young buck that drove the ladies wild. Now he was 88 going on 120, weighed 87 pounds in a nightshirt with a candle, and had the bone density of a sparrow with spina bifida. At Town Council meetings, Mayor Wes Willard decreed his standard somnambulant state to be a vote in agreement with his, and no objection was put forth in deference to saving time. "You met with Riley Chase," I blurted out, stunned.

"Yup, the Crypt Keeper himself."

"He hasn't been down to the branch since the Johnson Administration."

"Yeah," snorted Gladys, "Andrew Johnson!"

"And what did he say?"

Gladys cracked the can and sucked the foam off the top like a pro, then continued. "He said our deal stipulated if we exceeded our line it kicked in a clause that allowed them to call the loan at any time. We needed to re-apply for a new line every time we wanted an increase to avoid that. Hank Chase was helping us out, but in the end, it screwed us."

"Sonuva bitch!" I exclaimed.

"Exactly," Gladys said, taking a long pull. "We got anything stronger around here?" She rose from my chair and started searching the shelves and file cabinets for a bottle, I'm sure, she always assumed I was hiding.

I rarely drank the hard stuff. Max Lipper had brought over whiskey one late November night, when he was feeling blue about his kid from his first marriage snubbing him for the holidays. We drank "Thanksgiving Specials"–Wild Turkey with a splash of cranberry juice–but I was pretty sure he had taken the bottle with him. Nonetheless, I let Gladys search because I needed a minute to let the news settle in.

So, that apparently was how it ended. On the one hand I sensed relief. Derf, a quitter of many jobs, once said there were few feelings better than giving notice, and I realized he had a point. I felt lighter, like after a post-Chinese food bowel movement. On the other hand, I was angry, the end was premature–a feeling, sadly, I was all too familiar with–and not a by-product of my own inevitable apathy. At his age, Riley Chase hardly gave a damn about our two-bit newspaper. He spent most of his time up at the 9-hole Artfield Country Club dozing, drinking Old Fashions, and trying not to sit on his sack. Someone wanted us done in, and knowing Hank Chase was too soft, they brought the Old Man out of dyspeptic dementia long enough to do the deed.

As Gladys continued her quixotic search for the bottle of Applejack, she thought I'd hidden, I returned to my desk chair to mull things over. So far, I'd learned Curly Carson was an alcoholic, the police investigation was hiding something, the chief may have a gambling problem and, between the Episcopal minister, the dump on my car, and someone using the bank to shut us down, perhaps I wasn't as beloved in this town as I always believed I was around last call at Pete's Pub.

I reached across the desk for my own beer and accidentally bumped the mouse. When the screen came back to life, I noticed the email icon flashing against the generic beach background screensaver Windows chose, for a man who views the beach like Michael Jackson did a Cub Scout meeting—it's hot, sticky and, frankly, no one wants to see me there. I opened the email to find the police press conference was scheduled for the next morning—Friday 10:30 a.m. In government, politicians generally schedule release of bad or controversial news late on a Friday, then hope something more newsworthy deflects attention over the weekend—call it the Gary Condit-9/11 Effect. Chief Bowden had a weekend place up at Lake Champlain. With the weather turning warmer, I figured he'd give a short statement that wrapped up the police theory nicely, fend off a few questions with non-answers, then hightail it out of town until Monday. Considering we were belly-up; it was a plan that just might work. Glen Hubbard told me the kid who'd come back to replace Miss Iceland wasn't exactly the second coming of Mike Royko, and the stringers sent out from Boston, Montpelier, and Concord, would swallow whatever Bowden told them, in hopes of getting out of a place I'd heard a guy from the *Boston Herald* call, "not the end of the Earth, but you can see it from there."

I was sitting there with a hopeless, Native American after the Battle of Wounded Knee, hundred-mile stare, when Gladys gave up the ghost on the Old Grandad, straightened up and addressed me, "What the fuck are we gonna do?"

"First, I think we should try to dial it back to PG," I started. "I'm glad you've loosened up, but I find your cursing disorienting, and well, that's what the beer's for. Both at the same time tend to cancel out, and I can't face this situation sober."

"Sorry," she said, brushing smooth the front of her blouse. She placed her beer down on the corner of my desk and tried again. "So, what are we going to do now?"

I sat there pondering, which to the untrained eye probably looked like someone trying to pass a stone. I could overthink anything into inactivity, so I wanted to keep it brief. I'd gotten into this first for the story, then for Miss Iceland, and finally to honor the memory of Ted Sheehan, the Carsons and this town. Of course, now the romantic angle was gone, from what I could tell, and, as for those other reasons, I'd have almost certainly grown weary of them and qualified my giving up in due time. It's what I do, unfortunately. But now it was personal. They'd poked the bear, or at least the lethargic hairy guy, who'd spent most of the winter sleeping.

Now, however, it was spring, and between the shot of Vitamin D from the sun and just enough alcohol, I had the energy and inhibition to make a snap decision. "Are we paid up on this place? Rent, heat, electric, telephone?"

"Yes."

"OK then—usually I'm not that picky, but this time I wanna know who's screwin' me. Let's try to round up the troops, such as they are, and find out what's going on," I declared, trying to rouse myself, as much as Gladys. Then I stopped and remembered one expense I would have to do away with. "Guess I gotta fire the receptionist, huh."

"Oh no," said Gladys, faking sadness. "Not your 'unusually long shower' girl." Giving "unusually long shower" air quotes to indicate some old witticism of mine she'd been saving up to bite me in the ass, which, come to think of it, was part of that shower scenario, if I remember correctly.

"It's war now, we all have to make sacrifices," I said facetiously. "Plus, those were the only showers I came out of feeling dirtier." Although I didn't mention it, the receptionist wasn't one of my fantasy girls. My age having reduced me to using office supply catalog models, and the women on FOR SALE real estate signs, as more believable substitutes. "By the way what's her name anyway?"

"Winifred," Gladys answered in, what it took me several seconds to realize was, all seriousness.

"Uh—OK—well, that takes a little of the sting out of it."

"If it helps," she added, "I caught her and her boyfriend making out by the dumpster the other day, while the phone was ringing off the hook in here."

"Thanks," I responded. "That does help. I mean if I'm involved in the PDA it's a beautiful expression of love, when it's other people, it's just disgusting."

I let Winnie down easy, not that it mattered. She simply shrugged, emptied the candy dish into her purse and walked out with a smile. I wasn't the firing type, but I figured she'd be fine. In fact, with a body like that, I considered, if she screwed up her life that was on her.

Back in this office area, Gladys was at her desk and already working the phones. Charlie Grissom, our comb-over photographer, was already in, and Gladys indicated she'd take care to notify the rest of the staff in due time. That left me to bring in the outsiders. I returned to my office, grabbed another beer, and made a mental note that if Gladys was to continue her newfound imbibing, we were going to need more stock, and perhaps a bigger fridge.

Sitting down, I realized this wasn't going to be easy. The problem was cellphones. To a young person their phone is a device that brings the world to them or helps them escape it. To a middle-aged person with a wife, kids and a job, the same phone is just a watch that yells at you. Thus, while time had swelled my list of friends and acquaintances, things like longer working hours, helicopter-parenting and a lack of anywhere to hide, had shrunk their usefulness in a crisis.

I took a desultory pull on my Natty Ice and began to have second thoughts. It was, to say the least, deflating. Anyone connected to the police was out, for obvious reasons. Derf would be in, for a sack of White Castles and a trip to simulcast, but if his work record was any indication, the help he could provide would be minimal. I phoned some softball buddies, a couple of Pete's Pub regulars, and my reporter friend Glen Hubbard, but like a Larry King wedding vow, their commitment was tepid and imminently changeable.

In the main office, I could see Gladys working the phones, but couldn't imagine she was having much more success. After all, in this Internet age, the saving of a small-town press with mostly part-time employees was a hard sell. Gladys and I had agreed to meet here tomorrow morning at 9 a.m. Unfortunately, I was starting to think that our matching hangovers, and the expected sparse turnout, would then make shutting things down the only logical conclusion. I nodded to Gladys, drained my beer, and started for home, where a Tree Tavern frozen pizza (yes, they still make those), and some Muriel Spark awaited. I flung the can at an empty plastic garbage can, caught the edge, and tipped it over into a tower of back issues that collapsed with a mocking flourish. "Well, that's just about right," I thought and was gone.

Next morning, I woke up late and dressed slowly. Shave? Why bother? I'd parked the Falcon out front under a light because I really couldn't take another visit from the Mad Shitter at this point. Like its owner, it wheezed and coughed its way into action, and I headed for town. As I drove, I mused that like Billy Joel's "Brenda and Eddie," I'd gone from the "high to the low to the end of the show." Or, more correctly, from the middle to the bottom, to a state of limbo, from which everyone, no doubt, would assume I'd recover. Perhaps Neil Young was right, I thought, maybe it was better to burn out than fade away. However, considering he was now 70 and clinging to an ill-advised "Godfather of Grunge" gimmick I decided to seek counsel elsewhere.

It was already 9:20, when I eschewed the main drag, and decided to park around back to avoid being seen in my death throes. Additionally, I figured it would be easier to load my personal belongings into the Falcon, by pulling right up to the backdoor that accessed the office area. The dumpster against our back wall was already filled with crap, indicating Gladys, Charlie and anyone who might have stumbled in, probably by accident, was already in the process of burying the corpse.

I tossed my coffee cup into the dumpster and, managing to stay upright on a mix of caffeine and Zoloft, I pushed through the door.

"Where have you been? You're late," intoned Gladys testily. I thought this rather harsh, until my eyes adjusted to a whole new world. Gone were the paper stuffed milk crates, the overflowing garbage cans, along with the crumbling furniture and lopsided bookcases. The walls too, had been cleared of the plethora of push pins holding up long useless notes and outdated calendars. Though I was happy to see my velvet "Dogs Playing Poker" print had held its place of prominence. The desks were arranged in a loose circle, creating a War Room type atmosphere. There was even a couch with pillows for late nights. I felt like one of those women on HGTV, who see their room makeover and scream "Oh my God, oh my God, oh my

God!" (of which Derf once commented it seemed easier these days to give your wife an orgasm by redecorating the bedroom than screwing her in it).

"Welcome to your new home," said Gladys. "We've got a month to find the bastards who killed Sheehan and screwed us. We're ready if you are."

A small roar of approval went up, and for the first time, I registered that 15-20 friends were clustered along the wall prepared to offer their support. "And there's another 8 to 10 folks who couldn't be here this morning, but wanna help," Gladys added, as she saw me scan those assembled.

"Check it out, bud," it was Max Lipper, calling out to me from next to a full-size fridge standing next to my office, where once a rusting overstuffed file cabinet held sway. "All your favorites," he crooned, as he pulled open the doors to display frozen pizza, boxes of Stouffer's mac-n-cheese, salsa, dips, and, of course, a 30-pack of Natty Ice. "Don't know how you drink that swill, but God bless," he added, closing the doors, and pointing to a shelf next to it. "Plus, we picked up these for you at some dead lady's estate sale."

"V.S. Pritchett, Pat Barker, Kingsley Amis, Nadine Gordimer," I rattled off the names from spines of well-worn paperbacks. "Too bad the old bag's dead. She sounds like the woman of my dreams."

Just then Gladys leaned in, grabbed my arm, and said, "You may wanna hold out for something a little younger," and turned me toward the backdoor. There, Miss Iceland snuck in and was taking a place among the gathered.

When I turned back Gladys was wearing what I always thought was an oxymoronic, shit-eating grin. "So, how'd I do?" she queried.

"What can I say, I guess I'm all in," I replied, and her grin just got shittier.

Chapter 9: I'm Touched, But Not In The Good Way

I delivered a heartfelt thank you to all; barely remaining dry-eyed by remembering grown men were only allowed to cry at the end of *Brian's Song* (and maybe *Bang the Drum Slowly*; for Robert DeNiro's cancer, not his cringe-worthy batting swing). Then everyone got down to mingling amongst the Boxes O' Joe and doughnuts Gladys had laid out. Max Lipper threw an arm around my neck and pulled me close. His teeth were so large and white next to leathery brown skin, I felt like I was staring into a row of urinals at Fenway Park.

"You see, bud, folks love you," he said, gesturing in an arc around the room.

"Who'd of thought," I began, "or, as my father said when I graduated college, 'sometimes even a blind squirrel finds an acorn.' He was tough, but fair."

"We're gonna help you figure out what went on with this murder," Max continued. "Then I figure we'll have a fundraiser down at Pete's and collect money to get the paper back on its feet. How's that sound, bud?"

It sounded pretty good, but as for how it looked, well, that was another story. I knew going in we weren't exactly going to amass the faculty of Harvard at this get-together, but as I surveyed the room, it seemed we might have trouble rustling up even a community college adjunct among the assembled.

To my immediate right, I watched as Derf handled an emergency sausage call, before going back to looking up offshore point spreads on his phone, all the while muttering, "How can I get anything done with all these interruptions?" Further along the wall stood our intrepid reporting team. Sandy Molesworth had her iPhone on speaker so she could talk and manicure her nails simultaneously. While next to her, photographer Charlie Grissom was performing origami on his comb-over, as our octogenarian social columnist, Mrs. Kleinschmidt, nodded off on his shoulder, over a once-bitten cruller.

Amidst a gaggle of children, I spotted my sister Amy chatting with my reporter friend Glen Hubbard, Miss Iceland's predecessor on the Artfield beat. There were a couple of softball buddies, Bean and Tombs, that weren't going to crack any cases, but maybe a few heads if that type of thing became necessary.

Just then Max Lipper elbowed me in the side and, pointing past Bean and Tombs, asked excitedly, "Do you think they're real?"

I followed his finger to Naomi—er, I mean Winnie, the receptionist, who was either planning on pitching in or had forgotten I let her go. Had Derf known her, he would most likely have been laying 3 to 5 on the latter.

"Do you think they're real?" Max repeated, wide-eyed.

"She's only eighteen."

"So what? There are seniors, and even a couple juniors, at the high school I would swear had 'em done."

"Sounds like you're not exactly re-making *Stand and Deliver* over there," I stated. "Besides, why should I care if they're real? Implants are like professional wrestling—I know everything I'm seeing isn't what it seems, but that doesn't mean I can't just sit back and enjoy it."

Max became transfixed, like a deer in her headlights, so I continued to peruse the room. Then I grabbed him before he could dive headlong at Winnie, and pointed to a huddle in the back corner, featuring the English teacher, Barton, and two bespectacled sweater-clad men. "Who's that with Mr. Barton?"

"Two guys he recruited from the English Department to help out," Lipper tossed over his shoulder, trying to keep one eye on my ex-receptionist.

"Kind of a 'Legion of Whom'," I deadpanned. "Is it wise for all of you to be out at the same time? Won't someone at the high school ask questions?"

"Naw, they can't, even if they wanted to. It's called tenure—and it's a wonderful thing. Short of showing up drunk, they can't get rid of us. Now, where did Miss Knockers go?"

"Sounds like you might be pushing the envelope on that whole tenure thing," I surmised. "But I think she's over talking with my staff—uh, my former staff."

Lipper bolted toward Charlie Grissom and the gang, only to be "knocker-blocked," by the mellifluous mu-mu of Miriam, the smoky-voiced town clerk who was staring down despondently at an empty donut box. Then, eyeing the dozing Mrs. Kleinschmidt's uneaten cruller, she made a beeline to my crew with Max drafting behind her.

    All things considered, though, I had to hand it to Gladys, not simply for the quantity of the attendees, but the eclectic quality as well. Mrs. Kleinschmidt notwithstanding, she had culled the best of the *Review* staff. Charlie Grissom was a professional journalist, Sandy Molesworth merely competent but with connections in high places, and Winnie, the receptionist, possessed attributes that, Lord knows I, or in lieu of me, Max Lipper, would find something to do with. My sister gave us a link to the police through my brother-in-law and Miriam, if adequately supplied with grazing, would be our eyes and ears at Town Hall. Of course, the teachers gave us a strong presence at Artfield High, not to mention Barton also knowing Ted Sheehan in the–um–biblical sense (Queen James Version, I assume). And thankfully we had Glen Hubbard, a real investigative reporter, who just might be able to pull this whole shit show together.

    Oh, and there was also Miss Iceland. Surprisingly, I'd almost forgotten her. Now I spied her standing in the back corner near a small closet that had become home to our fax machine, non-digital cameras, answering machine, and a small mountain of folding maps. Gladys referred to it as "where technology goes to die." The girl was looking so washed-out and willowy, I could practically hear Procol Harum's "Whiter Shade of Pale" playing in my ear. And I was about to "trip the light fandango" over there as soon as I figured out what that meant.

Gladys sidled up beside and caught me eyeing Miss Iceland up. "So, I never knew you were into blondes. I thought you went more for the dusky Latino type."

"Why? Cause you caught me in here watching *Sabado Gigante* one night?"

"It wasn't the 'watching' part that made me think that."

"You'll never let that die, will you? But if you must know, I lean in the other direction. Sex with an albino? Now that would be something."

"You're disgusting," she stated, rhetorically.

"Tell me something I don't know. But if you must inquire, I think my taste developed the same way it did for most guys of my generation," I philosophized. "While watching reruns of *Petticoat Junction*."

Gladys raised a quizzical eyebrow, so I clarified. "They had a blonde, a brunette, and a redhead of reasonably equal attractiveness. I always picked Billie Jo—big Meredith MacRae crush—there and on *My Three Sons* as well."

"Fascinating," she spat, obviously unimpressed with more of my oddball ontology. "But are you gonna stand here talking about mediocre sitcoms, or go talk to the girl? I tracked her down for a reason you know."

She gave me a shove in the general direction, but it wasn't that easy. For starters, I wanted to make sure I let Miss Iceland know I was interested, but I have no game, no opening line. Back in the day, my routine move was to scour the ATM garbage before hitting a bar or party, find a receipt with an abnormally large balance, then write my number on the back and surreptitiously slip it to a single girl who caught my fancy, in hopes she would be intrigued enough by the "mysterious rich guy," to call. Obviously, that wasn't going to fly now. And, come to think of it, it didn't fly too well then either.

The other problem was ordinary men, like me, looking to step out of their league, need one of two things: money or a willingness to commit. I have neither. With the former, an average looking guy could dazzle his way into a hot girl's pants. With the latter, he could grind her into submission. Either way, it sounded like a lot of work on my part.

"Just go over and be yourself," Gladys insisted, noticing my hesitation.

"Yeah, that's never worked," I lamented, but lacking any other option, I sallied forth to my humiliation.

I kept my eye on her, as I tried to circumnavigate Miriam, and fend off well-wishes from Bean and Tombs. Not knowing anyone, she hadn't ventured far into the room. Her back was to the rear window with the blind, that was perpetually higher on the right side than the left, no matter how I manipulated the drawstring. She wore a blue hooded sweatshirt that read "Rice Owls"; great academic school, but all I could think of was the old University of Texas cheer:

UT Cheerleaders: What comes out of a Chinaman's ass?

UT Fans: Rice!

I decided I wouldn't open with that.

The jeans and sweatshirt were putting me at ease, and then, just before I addressed her, I remembered her real name was Karina, which allowed me to ditch the catastrophic "Hey, girlfriend" opener I was entertaining, I did feel things were looking up.

"Hey Karina," I nonchalantly started, getting the name out of the way early. "Did you go to Rice?"

"No, it's my ex-boyfriend's," she said, just as Miriam stepped on the foot of one of my sister's kids who let out a blood-curdling yell.

"I'm sure she said ex. Yeah ex. Ex-boyfriend," is all I could think as the commotion died down.

"He moved back to Texas and left me this, and his collection of Kinky Friedman and the Texas Jewboys cassettes," she added, dropping my heart rate back into the normal range.

"If he's got "They Don't Make Jews Like Jesus Anymore" in there, I'll take it off your hands." She rolled her eyes, and I realized our musical tastes may not exactly mesh and tried a different tack. "So where do they have you working?"

"They have me on the School Culture beat," she said, and I winced visibly, knowing that on any decent-sized paper this was the lowest a reporter could go. "They've got me lined up for more middle school Spring concerts than should be legally allowed. I attended one last night, and I gotta say I had no idea how many Oriental kids attended the Admiral Dewey Junior High in Rutland, till I saw their string ensemble."

I needed to towel off the sarcasm. It was so dripping, and for a second, I thought I might be falling in love. "I didn't know Dewey was a Vermonter," I began, wondering if 'Vermonter' was even correct. 'Vermontan?' 'Vermontite?' Then I returned to my senses and asked the burning question, "So what brings you here anyway?"

"Your co-worker Gladys tracked me down, told me what was going on, and I figured I'd get to work with the great Glen Hubbard, so I dropped everything and rushed right over."

That seemed like quite the kick in the ass, but as I turned toward Hubbard, my hopes reeling, I felt her slap me in the back of the head. "Hey Dumbo, I didn't come here to work with Hubbard, I came here to work with you. Something's up, and you're not the only one getting jerked around by it, so let's figure it out together." I flushed, feeling stupid, but in the end, chalked it up as physical contact and a pet name. Or based on my usual interactions with women, impressive progress.

As I was regaining my composure, and half straightening my hair, half feeling if I had a bald spot working yet, Gladys approached in her usual efficient mode. "Press conference, town hall, ten minutes," she said, verbs be damned.

"Crap," I blurted out, and not just because I'd forgotten the presser in the morning's activities. I'd also neglected to contact Curly Carson's ex, for whom I had several more questions. Her relation to the other two victims would round out the team Gladys assembled nicely. At this point I didn't even know where to find her number, but figured she knew where Town Hall was and would want to hear the Artfield PD's theory, so we would catch up to her there. "Let's go," I said to Miss Iceland, in a 70s TV detective series style. Then I fumbled for my keys, feeling like Jim Rockford, but probably looking more like Cannon or Barnaby Jones, in her eyes.

"Uh, that's OK," she said, reaching into the pouch pocket of her sweatshirt and producing her own keys. "I've seen your car. I got this one."

She made for the backdoor, but I lingered next to Gladys momentarily to watch her walk away. "Nice girl," "Great ass," we muttered, though for the life of me, I'm still not sure which one of us said which.

Miss Iceland artfully negotiated the local streets at limit-busting speed, but as we pulled into a spot near the center of town, I noticed we needn't have worried about ticketing. Two police cars were parked in front, as well as the Chief's Chevy Suburban which, I noticed, was loaded with fishing gear. Since the town only owned two cruisers, I momentarily debated knocking over the Krauszer's Convenience Store while things were left unattended, but in the end realized I wouldn't get far on the meager scratch-off lottery and take-out coffee receipts in the register. So, I groaned my way out of the Volks, and we jogged across the street and up a wide flight of concrete stairs.

The Artfield Municipal Building is a square, white-washed, brick building that appears like a giant snowdrift, winter, or summer. Entering through one of the huge double doors, one is met by a bland lobby with paneling that looks like it was taken off my dad's old station wagon. From there, one is presented with three options, as if one were a contestant on the world's worst episode of *Let's Make A Deal*. To the right, were the huge oak doors of the Municipal Court, where Mayor Wes Willard's buddy and investment partner Clem Nielsen self-importantly presides once a fortnight over matters stupid and small. Straight ahead behind a simple, plasterboard door, was the domain of Miriam, the town clerk, who made sure nary a dog went unlicensed, or a shed went up unpermitted. To the left was our destination, the Council Meeting Room, where the press conference was being held.

The Council Meeting Room was the site of the twice monthly meetings that decided property taxes, building approvals, school budgets, and civil service salaries, along with more picayune concerns. It was the preponderance of the latter that made attending and reporting on these sessions such a chore. When the housing development, near where Ted Sheehan lived, was proposed, and the outside developers came in to make their pitch, I stopped sending Charlie Grissom or Gladys to cover these, and began attending myself. Like most folks I enjoy a good ball-busting, long as it's not my nuts being roasted on an open fire, but when things went surprisingly smoothly, I gave up the ghost, and turned to reading through the minutes that Miriam supplied.

Miss Iceland and I pushed through one of the large double doors, and found ourselves in what I assumed for a second was a Yoko Ono poetry reading. Chief Bowden stood at a podium flanked by the two on-duty officers, but he hardly needed the protection. There was one tiny tripod camera, manned by what looked like a couple of bored students from UVM, a handful of only slightly older "stringers" from the *Boston Globe,* and the more local papers, and Wes Willard sitting, arms folded, in a chair next to the podium, looking like he was pissed at being there, or just sucked on a lemon, or quite possibly both.

Looking to the left, I noticed Bowden had set up a genius display of distraction along the wall. A long table filled with coffee, juice, bagels, bacon, pastries, and assorted other breakfast fare stood beckoning, and from the heaped plates in the reporter's hands, it had been liberally visited. Having once been an underpaid novice in the industry, I knew finding free food during working hours was a never-ending quest. I could still recall working the overnight sports desk at the *Globe,* and fanning out with my counterpart in obituaries, to find leftovers from meetings earlier in the day. Once found, we'd page each other in code over the PA: "The eagle has landed in Sector E," equaling turkey sandwiches in the Editorial Department. If pride comes before a fall, they'll probably have to bury me standing up.

It was obvious in this atmosphere, the Chief would get off easy, so it was lucky Miss Iceland and I had arrived just in time. We took two of the dozen or so chairs set up in two rows in front of the podium, just as Bowden stepped forward, and began to read a prepared statement. Old habits die hard, so I kept peeking to the left to see if they had lox to go with the free bagels, as Bowden sped through a statement so bland it could've been shredded and sprinkled on the meals served to ulcer patients.

"...and having examined phone records, ballistics, and the coroner's report, this office has determined Mr. Carson shot both Mr. Sheehan and Ms. Carson, in a fit of alcoholic infused rage, before turning the gun on himself. Therefore, this matter has been deemed a murder-suicide, case closed. Are there any questions from the press?"

I raised my hand from the second row, but Bowden pretended not to see. The college kids were already trying to negotiate their camera back into its plastic case, as the young reporters, happy to get out of town with most of the day ahead of them, dumped their plates in the garbage, and went to grab one last cup of coffee and Danish for the road.

I stumbled through the chairs, pushed past the kids at the buffet (there were no lox I sadly noticed. Hey, I can multitask when need be) and confronted Bowden and Willard as they made their way to a side exit. The two officers, younger guys who I didn't know, stopped short. They obviously had mistaken me for someone important and had inadvertently blocked Bowden and Willard's path.

"I have a question, Chief," I said as authoritatively as someone of my meager self-esteem could muster. In fact, I had several questions and no idea which to lead with, but Bowden saved my already overloaded brain from having to parse and pick.

"This conference was for press only," he stated, condescendingly.

"I'm press," I replied, unconvincingly, my voice cracking like Peter singing on *The Brady Bunch*.

"Not as of yesterday according to Riley Chase and Green Mountain Bank." It was Wes Willard chiming in; his face breaking into a smile that seemed painful.

This was obviously splitting hairs, but I was too sober to argue. Thinking fast I turned and pointed at Miss Iceland. "She's with the press. Karina, uh, um, (here I coughed out something that sounded like 'Schmedberg' then continued) of the *Burlington Bee*."

Chief Bowden chuckled mirthlessly, then indicated with his head over his shoulder. "We've already spoken to the reporter for the *Bee* and as far as I can tell, he has no questions."

I followed his gesture to the right front corner of the room, where for the first time, I noticed Curly Carson's ex talking to a hair-gelled, horn-rimmed, bespectacled, bowtie wearing, hipster nerd, who appeared to be making love to an iPhone with his thumbs.

When I turned back, mouth agape, I saw Wes Willard's bony ass slipping through the exit and heard a faint "dumbass" waft in with the slamming door. Man, I thought, and not for the first time, "nothing's ever freakin' easy."

Chapter 10: Of OCD And OMGs

"Yeah, that's the little pissant," exclaimed Glenn Hubbard, when Miss Iceland and I described the hipster geek we saw talking to Curly Carson's ex at the press conference. I wasn't sure if "pissant" was a colloquial New England term, but now that I turned 40, it sounded like the perfect way to describe anyone under 30. I made a mental note.

"I'll make some calls to the *Bee,* see if anyone knows why they called the kid back for this story," said the veteran reporter, closing his laptop. He'd nested at one of the desks—he could write his opinion pieces anywhere—which gave my confidence an always needed boost. Meanwhile, Miss Iceland was retrieving her keys indicating she had to go.

She had the dedication of a new gymnasium wing to attend just across the border in Winchester, New Hampshire, then 4 hours to kill before reporting on the scintillating doings of the Rutland Board of Education meeting. I extended my most heartfelt condolences.

She made for the door. I followed at a respectable distance, but noticing her sweatshirt came down over her hips, I decided to pick up the pace. She turned to me at the exit, and looking into her pale blue eyes, I wondered if I was in this thing to save the paper and find the killers, or just to get in her jeans. I figured a little from Columns A and B, a lot from Column C. But, as a person who will only give blood after confirming they're giving out a big cookie at the end, my standards in such internal moral debates are not high, so I'd get by.

"If anything comes up, call me," she tossed over her shoulder, her blonde hair bouncing seductively. At the door, she turned three-quarters and looked at me. It seemed something on my part was called for, but damned if I knew what. We hadn't even been out on a formal date yet, but my mind ranged from a peck on the cheek to a pat on that hidden, apple-shaped ass. Considering she hadn't just converted a third-and-long from deep in our own territory, I eschewed the latter and went for the former. It felt awkward, but I perceived a "lean-in" and felt satisfied.

"Enjoy the Board meeting," I said smarmily because I just can't leave well enough alone. She stuck out her tongue and departed, leaving me a visual that would tide me over till lunch.

Glen Hubbard was on his cell, feet up on the desk, talking to folks at the *Bee* I assumed. Meanwhile, Gladys was center stage, off the sauce, and running the show, as it should be. With a phone cradled on her shoulder, she tapped at the keyboard, and I knew she was in the process of squaring up accounts with our advertisers. Unfortunately, due to the benevolence, and possibly pity, of the good business folks of Artfield, most accounts were paid for in advance, so this process most likely involved considerably more refunds than collections. We were in the death throes at the paper, but having come to grips with my unambitious, slothful ways sometime prior, I'd begun socking away a decent, but hardly substantial, sum of money preparing for the inevitable. I now began to calculate mentally how much of a hit this bankroll was about to take.

With the phone on her left shoulder, Gladys motioned with her right hand at the piece of paper I was to take. It listed the institutions that would need to be notified that we were no longer publishing their event schedules as usual: Library, Little League, Senior Center, Schools, Religious Institutions, and so on. Never one brimming with self-importance, I simply assumed they'd all just turn to posting on the internet without a second thought. It was faster, free and the future. Still there was something sad about losing the print touch. After all, if technology was always better, the only place one saw a Segway wouldn't be when TBS runs *Paul Blart: Mall Cop*.

I was saved from this drudgery by the entrance of Derf, in his usual manner, hunched forward over his phone looking for the next wager. "Did you know there are only two Major League games scheduled tonight?" he lamented.

"Yeah, it's an early season travel day," I informed him. "Besides, haven't you, as you so eloquently put it, been 'getting my ass handed to me' in baseball so far."

"But I'm due," he started.

"Yeah, for 14 years now," I interjected.

"Still, if I get hot, I can't dig outta the hole I'm in with just two games."

"NHL playoffs start tonight—8 games."

Derf twisted up his face as he heaved his bulk into a precarious desk chair. "Hockey? What the Hell do I know about hockey?"

We seemed to have reached a merciful impasse. I turned for the office, list in hand, when Derf's voice, brightening now, called me back. "I did get my $100 back," he smiled, brandishing the single bill between middle and index finger.

"You tracked down Bowden," I said, incredulously. Not so much for his getting the money, as for his putting in any effort at all to get the money. Derf was a rare one, even lazier than I.

"No, we just kinda ran into each other. I went to get a bagel and tea at McCarthy's Bakery," For the first time I registered the bag and cup Derf had carried in and deposited on the empty desk. "By the way, what kinda town has a bagel place named McCarthy's?"

"Listen, you grew up in Northern New Jersey, where there were seven bagel shops in every town, and they were turning 'em back at the door. We're behind the times here," I said, getting agitated. "Now what happened with Chief Bowden?"

"OK, OK," Derf began, putting aside the Irish-American-Jewish breakfast treat for the time being. "I was coming out of the bakery, when I saw him pull up in front of the sporting goods store."

"Larry's Outdoor? He musta went there straight from the press conference."

"Anyway, I knew it was him, so I waited, and when he came out with an armload of fishing crap, I confronted him." Derf took a tentative bite from the bagel, pulled back the top half, and peered inside.

"And he just reached in his wallet and gave you a hundred?"

"No. First I had to remind him about Boston and the dog track," Derf continued. "He was acting nervous, like he was in a hurry to get away, get rid of me."

That was understandable, since it's not every day a semi-rural New England Police Chief gets shaken down for cash by a 6-foot-6, compulsive gambling, Jewish sausage salesman. I needed more though. "So, he gave you the money, so you'd go away? Did he say anything?" I prodded, thinking I was uncovering something important, but not knowing what.

"Well, first, he dumped the fishing stuff in his car. Then, he took me around the corner to this fruity coffee place." That was Johnny Java's, the new coffee place, where I met Miss Iceland the other morning. It was located strategically on the main drag to draw business away from McCarthy's, particularly among commuters and the ski/resort crowd.

"What did he do there?"

Derf took a healthy draw from his tea and smiled. "He just went behind the counter, opened the register, took out the Benjamin and handed it to me with a look that said, 'Now get lost.' You know, like every girl I've ever dated."

Like a tampon on a stick, this was one ugly red flag. The police "coverup," the officers drinking Crap-pucinos, the slowly beginning gentrification of downtown, the terse press conference, and now this, all suggested Bowden as the point man of some kind of larger scheme. Maybe one that spiraled, unfortunately, out of control and ended in three people dying. I suddenly wished I had bagged a sample of the stool on my car for DNA testing. Something made me feel the Police Chief was behind (pun always intended) that too.

With this information, I retreated to my office. It had been swept clean of books and back issues and the walls purged of hundreds of coffee-stained sticky notes. As I walked, without worrying about tripping, around the desk, I felt a draft, though there was no window within. My chair felt incredibly high, or maybe the junk removal had simply lowered the room. There was a pad and pens on the frighteningly clean desktop, and for a moment, I contemplated grabbing a Natty Ice while jotting down some notes. Suddenly, however, I was overwhelmed by a wave of apathy that rendered me unable to do anything but spend the next minute and a half contemplating what a good garage band name that phrase would make—if I had a garage, or was in high school, or ever played in a band, for that matter.

That pointless pondering complete, I realized I needed to get out of the office. I folded the paper with the numbers I was supposed to call and placed it neatly in the pen/pencil holder slot of the empty desk drawer. By this means, I convinced myself I'd actually take care of it later, whereas had

I stuck it beyond in the full drawer, I was preemptively admitting I was never going to do it. It was by such rationalizations, I got through my days. I felt satisfied, till I closed the drawer and a corner of the note stuck out, thereby launching a full-blown episode of OCD. I proceeded to position the note more carefully, then closed the drawer gently, only to see the paper catch on something, causing the corner to slide out again. I repositioned it a second time, and slammed quickly, but the air resistance shot the paper straight up in front of me. Catching it with my left hand, I folded it twice more, down to postage stamp size, and used my full palm to close the drawer, and simultaneously cover the area between the desk and drawer, so it couldn't escape.

Now I definitely needed a drink.

To that end, I summoned the strength to formulate an excuse, and bolted from my office toward the back door. I needn't have bothered. One boon of technology is that people are often too preoccupied with their devices to care about you. Teenagers didn't yell at you from car windows anymore, or kids mimic you singing "You Shook Me All Night Long" out of the back of a school bus, and there was virtually no clothing style so unhip, that it could tear kids away from their phones, or not seem ironic. Of course, I could've used this more as an insecure teenager, than as a "who-gives-a-fuck" forty-year-old, but it got me past the currently distracted Gladys/Derf/Hubbard triumvirate, so you take what you can get.

Once free, the Falcon sputtered through town like cars haven't sputtered since the advent of fuel injection. It was bucking and knocking, till it felt like it was one loud backfire away from being something Slip and Satch drove on The Bowery Boys. I turned left onto the main commercial drag. Johnny Java's loomed up on the right, and I noticed its plastic and neon juxtaposition to the rest of our so-called Strip. This consisted of the ubiquitous pizzeria, and Chinese restaurant, in between Morgan's Hardware, Henry's Shoe Repair, the Artfield Market, and a Feed Store, that also offered tattooing on Wednesday 4-8, and all-day Saturday. Heck, I thought, we were just a cooper and buggy whip dealer from being a mid-sized 19th century city, so to say the up-to-date coffee shop stood out like a sore thumb, would be an understatement.

    The one thing that struck me, as I looked upon this anachronistic commercial district, and then glanced in my rearview back at Johnny Java's, was the signs. The older stores had their names painted on the doors, or in plastic lettering bolted to wood above the display window. A few, like Morgan's, had taken up the offer of an itinerant, hippie sign painter (Is there any other kind?), who lingered in town a few summers back, and sported tasteful black-on-white clapboard signs, that hung perpendicular to the stores on simple, black wrought-iron brackets. Conversely, Johnny Java's featured a giant, blinking coffee cup topped by red and orange flashing light tubes, meant to indicate heat or steam or something, that frankly I found somewhat disconcerting. It also hung over the entire sidewalk, and nearly into the road, at least triple the size of any of the hippie's signs. This seemed like the kind of thing that would twist the pole up the butt of an old zoning stickler like Wes Willard, unless there was some incentive, fiscal or otherwise, to let it slide. I made a note to consult Miriam at Town Hall about that.

I also noticed while passing Johnny Java's, that the lights were on in the office of the Episcopal Church. That meant the rancorous Right Reverend Logan Brooks, who'd accosted Miss Iceland and me the day after the murders, was still in town. His knowledge of Curly Carson's state of mind, and what ax he had to grind with his neighbor Johnny Java's, would have to be probed. Yet with each additional piece of the puzzle, I felt more like the one being probed.

That's because, once again, this sounded like a lot of work on my part, and I hadn't even considered meeting with Barton and the teachers later, to see if they got into Sheehan's place, or finding out what info my sister had culled from my brother-in-law. I began wondering how those literary detectives, like Sam Spade and Phillip Marlowe, did it. Maybe a tougher name, like Mike Hammer, might help, but there was still the whiskey-drinking, bullet-dodging, doll-chasing, and wearing of shoes, that could crack a walnut. No wonder they were always on the surly side.

My mind was working overtime, as I pulled off the main drag, and I next began to stress over the inevitable interviews: Reverend Brooks, the State Police, the County Coroner. I hated interviews. As a reporter that seems counter-intuitive, and it is, but I just couldn't get past it. People exhausted me. That's why I quit Boston and took this gig. I craved comfort, people I know, and I wasn't embarrassed about it anymore. Lord knows, I'd never win a Pulitzer, hell, I may not ever get married, have kids, or even own a house, but I figured if those instincts hadn't kicked in by 40, they weren't happening. I was tired of chasing things other people wanted. What I wanted was to drink beer, read books, laugh with friends, and otherwise be left alone. Not lofty goals, but as the *Washington Post* horse racing writer and author Andrew Beyer once put it, "Why is it that a man studies the religious symbolism in the poetry of John Milton and he's a scholar, while another studies the symbolism in the numbers of *The Daily Racing Form* and he's a bum?" I was beginning to understand more and more, it wasn't what you enjoyed that mattered, it was your capacity to enjoy it.

    I turned right off the main drag, still waxing philosophic about the state of things, but knowing deep down I was really looking for an easy way out that just wasn't there. If nothing changed in about a month's time, I'd be a man with one somewhat marketable skill, scant drive, and a mountain of debt that left very little wiggle room, and no desire to wiggle anyway—something that most folks were fine never seeing. This in mind, I searched for some offbeat inspiration—because the normal kind bounced off me like bullets off Superman—and recalled the words of tennis great Martina Navratilova, who "ghost-wrote" in her autobiography (a library discard), "I wasn't so much driven by the joy of winning, as by the fear of losing." Of course, I reasoned, that if one had such a great fear of losing, one should just not play in the first place. Problem solved. Then again, that may not have been an option for an athletic pre-teen in Soviet-dominated Czechoslovakia—a place where, I'm pretty sure, my attitude would not have played well.

All this musing brought me to my apartment, where I took a spot directly in front of my door. There was nothing like doing nothing on a weekday morning. Empty parking lots, lineless supermarkets, kid-free parks, these are the little things that made life bearable. I went through the door, up the stairs and into a comfort zone where a ratty, brown futon never looked so enticing. No sooner had I retired to said sofa/bed with a Natty Ice and George Orwell's *Burmese Days*, then a text message came through on the flip phone. It was Miss Iceland.

*Gym opening total shit show smh   managing overly extravagant & cheesy @ same time lol like they added rumpus room on the Taj Mahal   good news** Rutland BOE meeting canceled   meet u in ur office @ 4*

I liked all the asterisks and ampersands better, when their primary function was to indicate curse words in comics, but time moves on. I was happy Miss Iceland would be there to help sort out what Hubbard, Gladys and Barton had gathered, and I immediately made such thoughts known by mashing down on the various number keys of my flip phone, 3 to 4 times each, in a text that seemed to have an inordinate amount of the letters c/f/i/l/o/r-s/v/y-z. It was really time to upgrade.

I knew I should be back at the office preparing leads for Miss Iceland's return, but I was nothing, if not a pro, at procrastination (actually I'm retaining my amateur status in case it ever gets into the Olympics). After going through the "recharging my batteries," "I'd only be in the way," and "I do my best thinking alone" school of excuses, I got back down to what I do best: reading and drinking. But no sooner had I taken a pull and tucked into another sweaty colonial scene (Is there any other kind in Burma?), then the flip phone went off again. This time it was Gladys on the other end, in a rare state bordering on animation.

"Got word the president of the construction company is going to be on site this afternoon," she began pleadingly. "Get up there and interview him today."

While I was fixating on Chief Bowden's involvement in the crime, Gladys had always maintained a belief the builders of the new development had at least a hand in the evil doings. That the president of R. James Home Builders, Inc. was a furtive, never seen character, only fed her intuition. To date this mystery man had unleashed a phalanx of lawyers on town planning meetings, as well as, teams of architects, foremen, carpenters, plumbers, laborers, and such, on the job site. But all the while he had stayed back in New York, pitching plots to the idly wealthy, early retirees, and tele-commuters, with stacks of cash, and a penchant for Fall foliage and good skiing.

"Goddammit," I let slip out, closing old Eric Blair. "Uh, I mean, what's his name? Will he be at that trailer? Go out there? What should I ask?"

"Did they just find you under a cabbage leaf?" Gladys sneered. "You went to school for journalism. You worked for one of the biggest papers in the country. You don't know how to conduct an interview?"

"OK, OK, I was coming out of a nap," I lied. "I'll go up around 3 and feel the jackass out. I don't feel as strongly as you about this one, but I'll do my best to see what he knows."

"And for God's sake put on a button-down shirt and a tie, or at least a sports coat. Let him know you're a professional."

"You're asking a lot of a sports coat," I cracked, but she was already gone.

I shot off another labor-intensive text to Miss Iceland, asking if she could meet me at the development by 3. She said she could, and eschewed my offer of directions, reminding me that cars and phones in the present come equipped with GPS, and hoping someday I might join her in that world.

Gladys's advice on presentation seemed sound, so I retired to the bedroom and slid open the lone closet door. As a child, I could recall my father putting on a suit and tie to take us to Arby's, but times had changed. While his closet was chock full of perfectly pressed vests, blazers, button-downs, ties, and assorted-necked sweaters (V, crew, turtle), I stared into what appeared to be an Appalachian dental x-ray. Four or five hangers of mismatched attire, liberally spaced, while shoved into a corner below, was a good-sized pile of yellow-collared dress shirts and wrinkled khakis, in need of cleaning. Unfortunately, I didn't own—or know how to properly work an iron, and dry cleaning always seemed like an expensive chore, what with the dropping off, picking up, and I'm no Joan Crawford, but enough with the wire hangers already.

Fortunately, one of the garments therein was indeed a sports jacket. Unfortunately, it had belonged to my much broader, stouter father so when I tried it on, I appeared to be a pair of horn-rimmed glasses, and a series of right-handed karate chops down my left forearm, short of breaking into a pitchy rendition of "Once in a Lifetime." Obviously, I'd been "letting the days go by" too often, without examining my vestments. When you're down to acid-wash jeans and an 8-ball jacket, and folks are asking "Who the hell is Frankie and why does he want me to relax?" then you've let things slide. In the end, I managed to scrounge up an outfit that even included a never-worn, pastel Jerry Garcia brand tie that Kayla gave me back in the days when she thought she could change me—bless her heart, the sweet kid.

I laid the clothes on my bed, which being a mattress on the floor seemed something of a lateral move and retired back to the futon. I drained the remnants of the Natty Ice and lay down with hands folded to contemplate my plan of attack on the building company president. I mulled, meditated, dozed off, woke, contemplated, rolled over, ruminated, and still had nothing. Finally, I resolved on saying we were from the *Burlington Bee*, since technically my paper was no more, and just get a general feel for this guy, good or bad, while hinting that we thought the whole murder/suicide thing was just a tragic misunderstanding, not a crime. Maybe a useful lead would slip out or, more likely, life would once again prove to not be a TV detective series, and it would all be a big waste of time. Well, at least Miss Iceland would be there.

A few hours and phone calls later, I stubbed out a nervous cigarette as Miss Iceland's wheels crunched over the gravel of the construction trailer's parking lot. She exited the Volks in her work clothes: a well-tailored black pantsuit, white blouse, low-heeled black shoes, and "K" pendant on a gold chain around her eminently bite-able, pale neck. I favored the relaxed, jeans and sweatshirt look of the morning, but that was probably only because it was less stunningly intimidating. Watching her tuck a strand of golden hair behind her ear, I was reminded of a campus visit to the University of South Carolina—a school I passed on applying to, for fear I'd get a rejection letter stamped: "Too Ugly."

"What's up?" I said, casually popping a slightly lint covered Altoid into my mouth.

"Thank God, a water pipe burst at the Rutland Town Hall," she blurted out. "If I had to sit through a BOE meeting after that soul sucking gym opening, I woulda friggin' shot myself."

Maybe not the kind of girl you necessarily were going to run right home to Mom, but as she shook out her ponytail and arched her back, it was not the direction I was leaning anyway—or ever for that matter.

"Well, aren't you the belle of the ball?" she continued, fingering my tie. Then added, "So how are we gonna play this?" as it came back to me, I still hadn't come up with a specific game plan.

The idea, as Gladys sketched it out, was for me to find out what I could about the builder and the development, without alluding to the murder/suicide in any overt way. Meanwhile, she was gathering info on the finances of the company, their other projects, and any litigation they may be involved in. Her theory being the traditional, "follow the money," and you're liable to find anything. The question was how to best go about it.

My default position was to step back and let Miss Iceland take the lead. Unfortunately, it felt too much like "Good Cop/Testosterone Patch Wearing Cop," and even I had my pride. Just then, what I assumed to be R. James of R. James Builders stepped out the trailer door gesturing for us to give him a second to finish a call.

Sizing him up he was a fairly tall man—6'2" or so—in his mid-30s, nattily attired in brown shoes and tan dress pants, topped by a lavender shirt and matching tie. His jet-black hair was molded into one of those fauxhawks, by means of enough gel to contaminate the groundwater, and his complexion was something Crayola might label "Tanning Bed Orange." On one arm, he wore a watch that was worth more than everything I owned, and on the other, a veritable rainbow of those stretchy wristbands that seek to inspire by combining multiple words into one: LiveStrong, BelieveAchieve, SuckADick and so on (though that last one I may have misread). Overall, he gave off the impression of the kind of guy who drank every kind of milk but what came from a cow (almond, soy, cashew,) and could tell you what "Steampunk" was, and why it represented the future somehow. In short, he seemed the consummate young, upwardly mobile entrepreneur, except for one thing. When seen in profile, one noticed a large, disproportionate paunch that gave him the appearance of a lowercase "b" or "d"—depending on which way he was facing.

Making his way down the temporary steps from the trailer, he continued a rather animated discussion. "Listen, do me a flavor on this one, will ya? Email me the approval, attach those docs and everything'll be copasetic, capeesh? OK, stay in touch with yourself."

Miss Iceland and I exchanged glances as if we hadn't heard right, but before we could synchronize our eye rolls, he was coming at us across the lot, hand extended.

"Hi, Richard James, president and head of sales," he said, pumping our hands and cocking an eyebrow. "But you can call me Rick." Here he cupped one hand over his ear, in a gesture that was last cool if you were MC-ing the *Amos and Andy Radio Hour*, and sang falsetto, "*She's a freak, a Super Freak, that girl is Super Freaky!*" Then looking up into our dumbfounded faces added, "Rick James? Super Freak? Get it?"

We did, yet it didn't make it any less creepy. I still had no clue how to conduct this interview, and tentatively opened my mouth to introduce myself, when he came to my rescue with a rapid-fire sales pitch unlike any I'd heard before.

"Listen," he began while checking his watch. "In a minute I gotta make like a baby and head out, but you look like a happy couple (Miss Iceland, I'm happy to say, didn't flinch at this) just the kinda folks who'd love it here—young, active, looking for a community to raise a family (obviously he hadn't been reading my blog). This is the place for you, close to skiing, hiking, good schools—and we're re-doing the whole downtown—recruiting upscale eateries: steak, Thai, Italian and a seafood joint just for the halibut, plus shopping—an outlet mall with the top names: Polo, J. Screw, Nerdstrom's, Tommy Middlefinger, all the best—here's a couple of brochures that detail the whole thing—prices start at 450,000 doll hairs—now it's tooth-hurty, I'm late for my dental appointment. Only kidding, but I gotta run—smell you later."

And with that, mercifully, he was gone.

"That guy's a piece of work," said Miss Iceland, as we watched him drive off in a tricked-out Cadillac Escalade.

"Oh, he's a piece of something alright," I responded, thinking we'd just found a new suspect.

Chapter 11: They're Off, You Lose

The office was quickly becoming my second home, which wasn't a bad thing with Miss Iceland in tow. A not-so-recent ex listed, among her litany of logic for breaking up with me, the fact that, in nine months, I had never once invited her to my abysmal abode. Of course, how enough recycled beer cans to make you think you missed a party (sadly, you hadn't), dust bunnies multiplying faster than real ones, and furnishings that could make the Kramden's apartment look palatial, was supposed to lengthen our liaison, I'm not really sure. So, having the office to return to after our interview with Rick James was convenient, and saved me from a bathroom project that, frankly, would take a team and untold amounts of cleaning products to tackle.

We seemed to have the place to ourselves, so I liberated a pair of Natty Ices from the gulag of their 30 pack, and we took up places across the desk in my office. I sat down gingerly—making sure to keep my feet on the ground and not roll the desk chair back and smash into the wall—like the pre-pubescent I usually am.

"So, you like Rick James for the murders," she began.

"Do I *like* him for the murders?" I replied, trying to raise an eyebrow. "Yes, I do, and after we prove it, you can 'Book 'em, Danno.'"

"Shut the fuck up, you know what I mean."

"OK, settle down Sipowicz," I answered, sliding a Natty Ice across the desk towards her.

"Hey, thanks," she said, eyeing up the can. "What, were they outta Schlitz?"

She opened the can and took a pull with a deftness that stilled my heart. Meanwhile, I fired up my computer and thought about her initial question. I still wasn't convinced I "liked" Rick James for the murders. Based on what I had seen, it was hard to like Rick James in any way, frankly. He was on the radar no doubt, but I'd actually done some research between naps earlier that day and was itching to show her the results of my efforts. Since, like most house parties I'm invited to, I brought little to the table thus far.

I opened two internet pages on my laptop. One was Miss Iceland's daily, the *Burlington Bee*. The other was for a political webzine called *Deeper Blue*. On both, I had called up recent articles by the hipster-geek reporter, who had been mysteriously talking with Curly Carson's ex at that morning's press conference. "Check this out," I beckoned and began to turn the monitor toward Miss Iceland. But before I could, she'd slid around the desk to look over my shoulder, one hand suggestively (so I thought) placed on my back.

"What am I looking at here?"

"Articles by that kid the *Bee* brought back to replace you on the Sheehan/Carson story," I explained. "On the right are his stories for your paper. On the left, is stuff he's posting at the same time, for the political blog he left the paper for."

"What the hell kinda name is *Deeper Blue*?"

"I think it means it leans far left," I explained, as she looked confused. "You know, red states are Republican, blue states are Democrat. Right?"

She scrunched up her face even more. "I just figured out which one was the elephant and which one the donkey—I got no freakin' idea. What should I be looking for?"

"OK, his name is Jeremy Martel, and he's listed as Associate Editor and Contributor for this site. Here's a list of his articles," I said, and began scrolling through links with synopses of his work. "Global warming, Russian hacking, immigration, Syria, and he's not playing nice. He rips everyone on the right a new one. Now look at the pieces he did on Sheehan/Carson for the *Courier*."

I closed the blog and brought up the newspaper page. Miss Iceland began reading. She leaned into page down, and I leaned back deeper into the palm of her hand, and to cop a little "shoulder breast," because I'm still a sexual 7th grader.

"What do you think?" I questioned, while guessing solid C-cup with my scapula.

"Well, I haven't seen this many participles dangling, since I worked the Patriots locker room during my internship with the *Albany Times-Union*," she replied not moving her hand or chest, I noted.

"No, I'm talking about the content."

"Not much there. It's basic boilerplate, Journalism 101 stuff."

I was so happy she was following my thread, that I actually sat up in a less erogenous position. "Exactly, it's bland as a backup catcher. It's the tofu on a rice cake of writing. It's the who, what, where, when, and why did he bother writing this crap!"

"You're right, I mean I could shoot this off in my sleep and they wouldn't have to pay him a stipend plus expenses probably," she said, pale blue eyes brightening.

"Not only that," I added, "but this kid goes from protest marches in New York City and D.C., to coming back to write this garbage for some dinky daily? Uh, no offense intended."

"None taken. I mean at least I have a paper," she said, smiling and staring into my eyes.

Without thinking (cause that's the only way I'm not paralyzed into inaction) I leaned in with my signature first kiss face—lips leading, eyes a quarter open to limit the effects of Mace, but still able to catch myself if she were to pull away. Miss Iceland, somewhat to my surprise, did neither. In fact, I sensed her also moving in, and while it wasn't as Kevin Costner's character in *Bull Durham* described, a "long, slow, deep, soft, wet kiss that lasts three days," that was OK—because, frankly, that sounds disgusting, and may be why he chose to make *Waterworld*—a case of mononucleosis delirium.

What it was, was good enough to want more. And when she seemed willing, I slipped one hand around the small of her back, buried the other in that silken blond hair, prepped my tongue for a tonsillectomy and—heard a door slam shut.

Gladys's rubber soled, sensible shoes squeaked a straight line for my office. Miss Iceland and I untangled; she was smoothing down her skirt and retreating to her previous seat; I was pulling in my chair, and sliding my legs under the desk, for obvious reasons.

Fortunately, Gladys was back to her no-nonsense self. And instead of asking questions about the fumbling noises she heard, or even exchanging pleasantries, she got down to business. "Did you talk to that guy?"

"Who? Marlo Thomas's brother?" I cracked, realizing I wasn't much better than Rick James himself. She arranged her features in a way that said, "I know that's some kind of joke, but I don't have time to decipher it, and you're an idiot," all in one look. "Yes, we talked to Rick James of R. James Builders," I told her. "He was running out, but we got enough to know he's a character, a bit of a clown. Not a killer clown, like John Wayne Gacy. Just a sad, pathetic clown like, well, all the rest of them really."

She knew I didn't share her enthusiasm about his involvement in the killings but came prepared to change my mind. "Yeah, well, a search of R. James Builders came up with four lawsuits against them in the past year." I wasn't sure if this was a lot or a little, so I pulled on my Natty Ice, and returned to my usual dim-witted stare. She continued, "And the plaintiff in each case began with a similar phrase—'The Estate of'…"

"You think Rick James killed these people for their property?" Miss Iceland blurted out.

I chuckled to think I was just kissing someone that young and naïve. Then I started second-guessing myself and added, "Wait, that's not what you're saying right?"

"Jeezus, maybe I shouldn't have spoken to you two, until the blood rushed back to your heads," she smiled, indicating she had an idea of exactly what we'd been up to. "These are civil suits. R. James is apparently up to something shady involving the purchase of big tracts of land owned by the recently deceased."

As a guy who was still trying to figure out whether Razzles was candy or gum, this was too much for me to wrap my head around. Miss Iceland apparently felt the same way and started to head for the exit.

"I'm gonna get going," she stated, a little too nonchalantly for my recently surging libido. "I have to meet with my editor in the morning, about setting up a high school graduation coverage schedule. Whoop-de-damn-doo. I'll also see if I can find out more about what's up with this Jeremy kid. Call you tomorrow."

With that she was gone, and my insecurity went into overdrive, reminding me just how relaxing celibacy could be. Gladys, on the other hand, was completely unfazed, barely uttering a goodbye to that tremendous, departing blonde hair and ass combo. I stood at my desk and leaned sideways to follow it across the main office area and out the door, until Gladys woke me from my erotic reveries.

"So, now that you're thinking with the proper head, tell me, do you have another interview set up with R. James?"

"No," I admitted, sitting back down, and finishing off my Natty Ice. "But I have his contact info, and he said he'll be around the site, so I'll catch him."

"I will say you clean up nice," she said, finally noticing my uncharacteristic duds. "Though that shirt coulda done with the business end of an iron."

"The shirt's fine. It's the body under it that's wrinkled."

She shook her head, and I believe I saw the merest whisper of a smile. She then took a minute to recap the results of the other efforts that day. Semi-intrepid reporter Sandy Molesworth, and comb-over photog Charlie Grissom, had struck out at Artfield High, where administration was looking to return to normalcy, such as that is in a 21st century high school. Barton and his fellow English teachers also found little at Sheehan's place, the police having covered their tracks well, I thought. He'd be back at work tomorrow trying to keep football players awake through a reading of *The Crucible,* if I wanted to go over what he did find. Finally, she circled back to the penultimate point, "So are you still gonna fight me on this Rick James thing?"

"Listen he's as shady as the ground around Chris Christie's feet, I'm not gonna lie, but I can't see any connection to him, Sheehan and the Carsons," I lamented. "Meanwhile, I'm still trying to figure out why Chief Bowden didn't bring in the State Police to investigate the biggest crime this town has ever seen, and then wrapped the thing up so quickly."

Not a fan of confrontation or deep thinking, I reached across the desk and took a long pull from Miss Iceland's half full Natty Ice. "That's disgusting," said Gladys, a long-time germ-a-phobe.

"If you saw what we were doing as you walked in, then I think you know the disgusting ship has sailed on that one."

"Touché."

"Yes, and I might be poking her with my metaphorical sword right now, if you hadn't shown up like a turd in my punchbowl," I offered, draining the dregs. "Plus, besides money, which he doesn't seem to need so badly, he'd kill three people? What is James' motive? It seems excessive."

She wasn't buying it. "And what's Chief Bowden's motive? You don't know the ends to which people will go, for a big payday, and this development is gonna be huge. It will change the whole tenor of this town."

I thought for a second about James telling Miss Iceland and I about the makeover of downtown, that was going to allow him to get the exorbitant prices he was asking for his units. "So, what do we do?" I asked, thinking, like with my relations with Miss Iceland, I was getting in over my head.

"I'll put Sandy Molesworth on it," said the ever efficient one. "Isn't her legislator in Montpelier a lawyer? If not, they must be knee-deep in the bastards up there. I'm sure he can hook us up, and we'll find out what these lawsuits against R. James Builders amount to."

As the anti-Harry Truman, passing the proverbial buck was just fine by me. I'd still have to talk to James again, to get Gladys off my back, but that was my goofy ass cross to bear. Still, I couldn't let Bowden go.

"What about the police coverup? You still haven't answered that."

Here's aGladys sighed, like someone who felt they had to do everything around there, which was spot-on—I have to admit. "That's if it is a cover up. Sometimes it is what it is."

"Profound," I answered, "but they shoulda still brought in the State Police."

"They did in a sense," she said, sniffing a strand of her graying hair before tucking it back behind her ear—the only real quirk she had, publicly at least. "The ballistics report is due tomorrow, and for all you know they have the preliminary results already, and it confirms everything."

I had to admit Bowden and Wes Willard did look confident at that morning's press conference. Then, like women all my life, when I thought I couldn't get any lower, she cut me down even more.

"Remember the robbery spree that happened around here right after you took over the paper," she began, in a slightly preachy tone I knew and loathed so well.

"Yeah, buncha bored kids from Burlington thinking they could outsmart the yokels," I answered, realizing just how old I'd become when I didn't give a second thought to using the term yokels.

"And remember how it ended?"

I longed for another Natty Ice, some P.G. Wodehouse, and Miss Iceland. Sadly, as concerns my laggard libido, in exactly that order. In lieu of those, I replied only half facetiously, "I've logged a lotta Little League scores since then, refresh my memory."

"When the police in the towns around here couldn't solve the B&Es, the State Police offered to help, but no one, least of all Artfield, took up the offer. All these stubborn, old Yankee farts run their towns like fiefdoms, and think the rest of the world should keep out," she concluded, folding her arms across her chest.

"Yes, but if I remember correctly, the break-ins weren't solved till the kids hit a summer house on Kenmore Lake. They don't have a police department, so the troopers came in and cleaned up in two days, all that Bowden and his buddies couldn't crack in two months. Yet you expect me to believe they wrapped up a possible triple homicide in under a week," I shot back a little too smugly.

The first six words of my last rant were ones that were never going to get you anywhere with a woman, in love or war. True to her gender, Gladys wasn't going to let me get off easy. And even truer to her gender, she chose to attack me personally.

"Listen, I don't mind you looking into Bowden," she began, rising from her chair and making for the door, "but you have to follow up on everything, if we're gonna figure this out, and maybe save the paper. You can't be disappearing all afternoon, and you might wanna cut back on the drinking, huh. You'll need to be at your best, especially if you plan on keeping up with Blondie MacBlondenstein."

"Hey!" I shot out, a little too defensively. Maybe I was feeling something more than lust, as unlikely as that was, for Miss Iceland. "Don't call her that. I mean she's not Scottish, uh, or Jewish—not sure where you were going with that. I think she's Scandinavian, so that's Blondie Blondufsson to you."

"Can't believe I've put up with you for years," answered Gladys, shaking her head and walking out.

"Yeah, well, I didn't exactly draw the long straw with you either," I said, but I couldn't keep the smile from my face. I did need to hold up my end for these next weeks. I'd start by eschewing a longed for third Natty

Ice, getting something to eat, and staying up at least long enough to devise a plan for tomorrow.

I set about this, by first creating space between myself and the 30-pack cooling a hole in the office fridge. I locked things up, went to the rear lot, and fired up the Falcon, to the extent that it could be. Earlier that day, Derf had sent a text indicating he conned his employer into approving a motel room, due to some imagined sausage emergency that needed tending in southeastern Vermont. Considering they hired Derf in the first place, one had to figure they weren't exactly running a tight ship back at Sausage Central. So, that problem solved itself.

I still needed to talk to him, so with this in mind, I tooled out of town onto Highway 5, headed toward the New York border, and the only place Derf could possibly be, Green Mountain Racecourse. Of course, Green Mountain was a racecourse in name only, as it hadn't been such for about seven years. Instead, the rusting hulk and dilapidated property was kept afloat, by simulcasting: The video transmission of tracks from across the country for the wagering pleasure of compulsives, like Derf, and those for whom internet porn just wasn't getting it done anymore, I'm assuming.

The present bleakness and devastating drear aside, Green Mountain was once an animal racing triple threat, featuring mid-level thoroughbred, harness and dog racing, on a nine-month rotating basis. It was a license to print money in the early 60s as a night out, with the added bonus of gambling thrown in. It was glamorous, classy—at least at the Clubhouse level and above—and swelled the state budget without even trying, until the ubiquity of TV halved the crowd, and sent the expensive thoroughbreds packing. The cheaper harness game carried on, till 70s cable TV and the proliferation of the lottery, halved the half. Dog racing then carried the flickering torch, until a *60 Minutes* hatchet job exposed the seedy underbelly of that business, or as Brian the Dog from *The Family Guy* angrily summed it up, "Dog racing? That's our Holocaust, man!"

Outside of glamor tracks like Saratoga or Belmont, racing in the Northeast is mostly propped up these days by slot machines or full-blown casinos, running simultaneously on site. Derf thinks this portends a historical type of Renaissance, but it more likely is the calm before the plague. As soon as developers like Rick James can convince politicians the multitude of land taken up by a racetrack, could better be used for development around the already existing casinos, then it's just a matter of working out the kickback deal, before another American tradition goes South in a fleet of vans full of taped together horseflesh and illegal immigrants.

I paid two bucks to get in, and five more for a program as thick and jam-packed as a New Jersey diner menu. It featured the past performances of hundreds of horses at eight different tracks, printed in font size 2, and with ink cheap enough to leave you with the hands of a West Virginia coal miner.

I found Derf standing slightly removed from one of the five or six groups huddled around banks of TVs, piping in racing from such bastions of equine talent as Sam Houston, Wheeling Downs, and Pompano Park. Derf alternated between peering into the program and gazing up at the odds on the screen. He did more of the latter and less of the former, his wagering driven more by what kind of payout he might get, than say form, pace, or speed figures. Or, as he was apt to say when a 3-5 shot romped home easily, "I'm glad I didn't have that." It was not a recipe for long term success, but Derf was of the school that felt the greatest thrill in life was gambling and winning, the second greatest thrill, gambling and losing. Grinding out a profit, limiting losses or, worse still, breaking even, wasn't going to provide him with the fix he needed.

"Funny finding you here," I cracked, sliding in alongside and beginning the same program to TV screen head-bob the rest of the crowd was doing.

"Yeah, well, everyone has their 'safe place'," he responded, mocking modern psychology while juggling odds, post times, and potential trifecta combinations, in his head. And Derf really was in his element. He loved the desperate gamblers, the challenge, the excitement, while all I saw was a place where the windows cleaned the people (metaphorically I mean—in reality the stench of BO was overwhelming).

"Been here long?"

"Since about three. I hit a dollar trifecta at Aqueduct early, and I've been working my way through that ever since," he answered.

Derf wasn't going to leave, till he'd given everything, plus what he came with, back, or won enough to pay off his ever-metamorphosing debt—

an astronomical amount owed to various entities that was collectively known as "The Bill."

"Not enough to cover The Bill, huh?" I rhetorically questioned.

"Not even close. I thought I could parlay it into something big, but it's been all chalk at the West Coast tracks. No prices. That's why I switched to playing Sam Houston."

I looked at the monitor. Ten minutes to the 4th race at Sam Houston. I flipped through the encyclopedic program till I found it. Two-year-old maidens (never won a race) at four furlongs, 14 horses entered and only one had ever taken to the track in anger, number nine, and he'd given the Winner's Circle a wide berth, never finishing closer than 18 lengths back in seven starts. And yet he was the favorite. "Who do you like?"

"Everybody, but the nine," he replied, focusing on a screen crammed with so many flickering numbers and names (odds, exacta prices, pools, scratches, jockey changes) that it looked like one of John Nash's conspiracy delusions. However, a "beautiful mind" was not necessary to handicap this race.

"Why toss the nine? He's the only horse to ever run," I asked, naively.

"The nine's already proven he's a loser. At least with the others you can hope they can run," he explained. "Plus, he's the favorite, if I needed any more disincentive."

"So, you take a sorta Schrodinger's Cat approach to these Maiden races?"

"You got a better theory? Now let's see if Schrodinger can pick the double," and with that, he lurched off to the betting windows.

I, in turn, shuffled off to the lone concession stand, where the assortment of cancer stick-hot dogs and hockey puck-hamburgers did not meet up to the standards of even my far less than discerning palate. Turning back, I noticed the crowd consisted of the usual All-Male Revue. Derf often fantasized of meeting the woman of his semi-twisted dreams at the track, but like a hot cashier at the Dollar Store, there must be something seriously damaged beneath the surface, for her to wind up in this place.

We made our respective ways back across the sticky linoleum floor, me empty-handed, Derf with one breast pocket bulging with tickets, like a transvestite at the beginning of a sex change installment plan. Then we met up in the exact same spot, with three minutes still to post at Sam Houston. "So, what did you do all day?" I asked to fill the time, while several backstretch workers, too big to be jockeys, tried to load thirteen skittish first-time starters into the gate.

"I was working," he started, "uh, you know, on the murders," he concluded, just in case I was thinking he'd been running around trying to sell sausage all day (I wasn't).

"How so?"

He reminded me he'd established the strange link between Chief Bowden and Johnny Java's, which reminded me I never followed up on what that link was, which reminded me Gladys was very much right about me needing to change my slothful ways. Fortunately, before I could continue this usual spiral of self-loathing, Derf went on, "And see that degenerate over there?"

"It's a Wednesday night simulcast, you'll have to be more specific than that," I replied, looking at the sketchy crowd surrounding the adjacent bank of TVs.

"The one with the curly hair and a little drool coming over his lip. Bouncing from foot-to-foot. That's The Jester."

The curly hair and drool only narrowed the search down to three, but the bouncing was unmistakable. The so-called Jester was about 5'7" and 125 pounds, with the sunken cheeks and hollow eyes of the star of a late-night Sally Struthers infomercial, and a case of ADHD that could fell a prized Canadian heifer. He hopped back and forth like he was standing over a mine fire, while delivering a monologue that sprayed saliva liberally down the front of his faded leather jacket.

"Who the hell is that, and what does he have to do with our matter?" was all I could respond as I stared half frightened, half amazed.

"The Jester is a New England racing staple. I've seen him at every track from Scarborough Harness in Maine to Finger Lakes outside Buffalo," he began, oblivious to how he was painting himself with the same degenerate brush. "He's got the best disability scam in the business."

"What's his disability?"

"Take your pick. It's not about collecting disability—Lord knows he deserves that—it's how he uses his status," Derf informed. Then with a touch of jealousy in his voice he continued. "Any payoff of $600 or more on a $2 bet is subject to immediate IRS withholding. Though it may not look like it, the crowd around The Jester there pushes a lot of money through the windows, and cashes a fair share of trifectas, Pick-4s and other big winners. They're also not the kind of people that like to pay 25% in taxes or fill out government forms. The Jester, though, is tax exempt, so he cashes their tickets for a 10% fee. As far as the IRS knows, he's the greatest handicapper alive."

Derf stared at the drooling dervish wistfully, with the rare—especially in the case of The Jester—"but for the *curse* of God, go I" look.

Feeling we'd gone astray, I tried to reel him back in, as several uneager equines refused the gate at Sam Houston. "So how does he figure into our escapade?"

"The Jester also supplements his income as a runner for bookies—collecting debts, making payments and such. When I told him my story about your Police Chief and the hundred-dollar bill, he said the guy's a full-blown compulsive. Owes money everywhere."

"I thought bookies were passé. That everybody bet with those online places these days."

"Passé?" Derf said, raising an eyebrow, then went on to enlighten me in the ways of his chosen subculture. "You have to have money on account to play online. Bookies give credit, so there will always be bookies. Anyway, The Jester's been trying to collect from him for months with no luck. Says it's gotten to the NWB stage."

"What's the NWB stage?" I asked, tentatively.

Derf did the prerequisite white guy head-swivel then informed me, "Let's call it 'Negroes With Bats' though The Jester doesn't put it quite so delicately."

I had more questions, but they were in the gate at Sam Houston, and Derf lost interest in all else. If Gladys wanted to play the "Follow the Money" game, in solving this, Derf's info just kicked Chief Bowden several notches up the suspect list. Of course, I was already a champion of Bowden's involvement in the murders, so this just cemented that conviction. The question was: how it led to Curly Carson, Ted Sheehan, and the girl. I thought about approaching The Jester, but with the race at Sam Houston off and several other tracks just minutes to post, he was hopping and spewing saliva at an increased rate. To try and talk to him now would be like sitting in the front row at a Gallagher show and not wearing my rain slicker.

Then suddenly a thunderous "Fuck!!" burst forth from the crowd in front of us, as they hit the wire at Sam Houston. A shower of ripped tickets followed from the same general area, and Derf, who had taken his own loss with a well-practiced equanimity, cracked, "Another satisfied customer." With that, he slid off to bet on the three other tracks that were under five minutes to post. And with nearly a dozen other hippodromes in full swing, I figured I'd gotten more than I could've expected from this rendezvous, and surreptitiously slipped out.

As I headed back home, I felt I could eat a horse as they say—probably one of those from the just concluded race at Sam Houston, that was one more 8th place finish from fast food filler. My choices were basically to go home to the dismal digestive choices therein, or venture to Pete's Pub, which my woeful wallet rendered pretty much a non-starter. Then, in a misleading moment of motivation, that occasionally drifts through the transom of my otherwise purposeless life, I considered returning to the office to write up some notes, remembering the frozen pizza my well-wishers had stocked for just such an occasion.

To that end, I took the car through Artfield. A light was still on in the office of the Episcopal Church, and a figure I assumed to be Reverend Brooks, was moving around inside. He may have been packing, in preparation to follow through on his promise of ditching this burg, and it reminded me that the distasteful duty of trying to interview said nut-job, regarding his hatred of Johnny Java's and anything he had on Curly Carson, probably had to take place toot-sweet. Tonight, was neither toot nor sweet, so I continued to the office, and turned on as many lights as possible, so as not to let the rare occurrence of my working late, go unnoticed on the off-chance Gladys passed by.

As the toaster oven was busy turning two frozen slabs of cardboard into something resembling pizza, I was actually writing up a to-do list for tomorrow:

1. Check in w/Barton-Artfield High

2. Talk to Rev. Brooks re: Curly Carson, AA meetings, Johnny Java's

3. Contact Miriam at Town Hall re: Johnny Java's ownership

Then I heard a car pull up, and someone came in the rear entrance. Though I'd had a beer at the track, and was working on my second Natty Ice here, I hadn't gone around the bend enough to be paranoid. They weren't exactly stealthy in their arrival and shut the back door loudly. My first thought was Gladys, so I stood and took up my schedule proudly, like some over-eager schoolboy in a Dickens story. Next, it crossed my mind that Miss Iceland might be back for a little more sugar, which made me grimace, not over Miss Iceland, but at the thought of me even thinking of myself as "a little sugar."

Unlike characters in a Victorian novel, those were the only thoughts that could pass through my head, in the three seconds it took for the person to reach my door. A knife-like shadow crossed the threshold, and in the next instant Curly Carson's ex-wife, Debra Townes, was standing across from me.

"I was hoping it was you here," she stated, demurely. She was wrapped in a knee-length black raincoat, that looked like it was a sturdy tug away from going around her rail-thin figure again, and her lank black hair was tied back, revealing an expanse of forehead so vast, she could've been the bastard offspring of a drunken Tom Hanks/Christina Ricci/Martina Hingis three-way.

"Hey, Ms. Townes, can I help you with something?" I asked, in a way I thought was innocent enough. And that is when things got WEIRD!

Chapter 12: Disappointing Women And Other Things I'm Good At

It's hard to button one's shirt sans buttons, and as I glanced down my shirtfront, I noticed mine were MIA. Debra Townes had attacked me with such vehemence, some were on the desktop, some on the floor, and until she flossed, we may not know exactly where the rest wound up.

"What the hell was that?" I half-shouted, as I tried to cover my rapidly graying chest hair like a 1950s actress caught in her slip.

"I'm sorry," she muttered, overwrought.

Still shaken, I was not at my most erudite and fell back on another, "What the hell was that?"

"I'm sorry," she repeated, and it looked as if we were about to fall into one of those "Delete file in printer queue and try again" loops, when she added, "They're going to write an article about Curly, about my daughter, unless you stop poking around into this thing."

Now I was never very quick on the uptake, the down take, or any other kind of taking. Giving—I had that down—taking not so much, but even I could see where she was going with this. Still, I wanted to hear who "they" were from this horse-face's mouth.

"It was Jeremy," she continued, referring to the hipster reporter. "He called me over at the press conference. I thought he just wanted to say hello. Then he started in with it. Said he had dirt on Curly, which didn't really bother me much. He drank. He hit me a few times. It's a small town.

Everyone around here knew. But when he started talking about Monica, I couldn't take it."

I am many things: a decent writer, a functioning alcoholic, the last card-carrying member of Members Only, but a discerning detective apparently, I am not. I had never looked at her expression when I caught her talking to Jeremy at the presser. As one who lives his life by the mantra "just because your paranoid doesn't mean they're not after you," I simply assumed she was in on the conspiracy to cover up the murders, and tangentially shut down the paper.

As I stood in what was fast becoming my go-to position—dumbfounded, mouth agape, brain slowly processing—she pulled up a superfluous bra strap over her bony shoulder and continued. "He said Monica was having an affair with Ted Sheehan that went all the way back to high school. The police chief is trying to keep it under wraps, but you've been asking too many questions, and they might have to release it, if you make a big deal of this. I had a few drinks at Pete's Pub trying to figure out what to do. On the way back to my motel room, I noticed the lights on here. I stopped, hoping I could persuade you to drop the whole thing, let them just rest in peace. I didn't know what to say, I'm drunk, so I just acted like they do in the movies and threw myself at you. It failed, obviously."

My first thought was that this was not the most ego-boosting of come-ons, but I've had worse. My second thought was, "Did I just pass on sex?" As an average guy with little to no "game," I always viewed sex like mothers of young children view vegetables. Just as there was always someone "starving in (insert Third World nation) who'd kill for that broccoli," I always assumed there was a nerd in a dorm room somewhere, who'd kill for a piece of what I was being offered, so I shouldn't look a gift twat in the mouth, to twist a phrase. Besides, I'd done a lot more with a lot worse than Debra Townes over the years (I like my beer, you may recall), and usually I was on the begging end of getting that. Was this growth? Old age? The influence of Miss Iceland?

Fortunately, I didn't have sufficient time and/or alcohol for such self-analysis. So, I reset the old bean and suddenly realized, there it was, evidence that Police Chief Bowden was involved in a cover up. Barton, the teacher at Artfield High, had confirmed that Sheehan was not only a committed educator, but a "Friend of Dorothy," as they say. No way he would switch teams for Monica Carson, if not from general morals, then at least from the standpoint of possibly scuttling an already rising career. Bowden also had a motive—his rising gambling debts. And, who around here had the money to buy him off? Rick James, of course, but why?

"You don't believe that do you?" I queried, knowing Debra Townes already knew of Ted Sheehan's sexual leanings. She was almost fully dressed and ready to depart but nervousness tended to loosen lips and right now she was shaking like a Shih Tzu in Saskatchewan.

"No, but they have evidence, text messages and things. Jeremy said the police showed him everything, off the record. Besides, once it's out there people will believe it. It happens all the time these days."

The last part was sadly true. I even researched one of these stories during my time at the *Boston Globe*. I recall doing a Google-image search of teachers who slept with students. You could have gathered the women together and made a pretty good swimsuit calendar. Meanwhile, the men looked like headshots at 1970s porn casting calls, replete with cheesy mustaches. No one would have trouble imagining a good-looking guy like Ted Sheehan would have any difficulty manipulating a vulnerable 17-year-old into bed if he played his cards right.

Something else caught my attention as well. I noticed this was the second time she called the hipster reporter by his first name. "Do you know this kid from somewhere?" I asked, feeling as if I was finally getting the hang of this sleuthing thing. Though realizing that, akin to my seven seconds of rollerblading glory or the week of anxiety after that Dollar Store Pregnancy Test, it could be a false-positive.

"He was at Bennington College with Monica. They dated."

Well, I'd be dipped in shit and called "Stinky." I asked, "For how long?"

"About eight months," she replied, searching for a shoe. "But they stayed friends after."

OK, so nobody stays just friends with a girl as attractive as Monica Carson, unless they're trying to get back in, so to speak. Hell, Bob Dylan couldn't even get through the first chorus of "All I Really Want to Do (is Baby be Friends with You)" without laughing (check the original).

"Is this Jeremy from around here?" I questioned, thinking he might be known to Chief Bowden beyond his newspaper work.

"No, he grew up in New York City," she answered, while cinching up her overcoat to a tightness that suggested regret. "They met at Bennington. In an Environmental Science class, I think."

My first thought was lamenting that I might have to drive all the way across the state to Bennington to check out the history of the unhappy couple. I mean it's not like we live in Montana, but still I kept coming back to how this investigation was already putting a big dent in my comfortable reading/drinking/watching sports on TV lifestyle, and I was more the type to get OUT, as opposed to GOING, when the proverbial "going got tough." Yet if the paper went under, I'd be in even more dire straits reading/drinking/sports on TV-wise. That is, I'd have to get a real job, and if past experience was any indicator, there'd be no winners there.

During these desperate deliberations, I failed to notice Debra Townes had completed dressing and was making her way toward the backdoor. I stepped out of my office, with more questions germinating in my mind, only to hear her utter a final "I'm sorry," that seemed more directed at herself than me. Then the door slammed behind her mercifully cutting off my habitual, "Call me," and she was gone. God, I miss her already.

It took a few minutes, and a cold Natty Ice, to wrap my head around what just happened, but once I did, I realized—unlike David Foster Wallace's *Infinite Jest*, or how points are tallied in Roller Derby—this was starting to make sense.

Now, if watching reruns of the many *Law & Orders* (I mean I own a TV, how could I avoid them) has taught me anything, it's that to qualify as a suspect one needs means *and* motive. I now had two folks with the latter: Bowden-Money, Jeremy-Love. But as for means, as was usual with another definition of that word, I was lacking.

I needed to track their movements in the days before the murders, and their access to the triggerman, Curly Carson. The whole thing was starting to get me depressed. But considering I've turned around, blew off work, and crawled back into bed, because I screwed up trying to tear open and secure back the little sip tab on the plastic lid of a coffee cup, the bar for such things wasn't very high. With that in mind, I had a tot or five of Natty Ice and read a few pages of Solzhenitsyn's walnut-crushing *Gulag Archipelago*, that I'd been working through on-and-off for the last three years. Pretty soon, between the alcohol, and the fact that I wasn't building a stretch of the Trans-Siberian Railroad in cojones-contracting weather, while wearing burlap sacks for shoes, I felt my spirits were buoyed enough to crawl onto the office sofa and fall asleep.

Dr. Joyce Brothers, who I believe in real life specializes in diseases of the pancreas, said, "A positive self-image is the best preparation for success."

Waking up the next morning and looking in the mirror, it was immediately clear that ship had pulled up anchor. My clothes were rumpled and stained. My aching back left me with the posture of a jumbo shrimp. And my hair was simultaneously doing a William Henry Harrison in the front, and an Art Garfunkel in the back. Success? I'd be happy to just break even.

With this in mind, I brushed my clothes semi-unwrinkled, wet down the back of my head, poofed out the front, and found the to-do list I'd made yesterday among papers swept to the floor by Debra Townes' amorous advances. My mouth felt like I'd just licked clean the floor of Eli Whitney's workshop. So, I figured a little "coat of the canine" was not out of order and popped another Natty Ice, before getting down to work.

Derf had once commented during our cohabitation, there was no better feeling than "giving notice." With my name on the lease, this had an ominous ring, but now scratching my head and looking at the list, I could see some merit in his mantra.

Reflecting back, my father was of the belief, if the kid was afraid of the water, throw him in the deep end of the pool, and he'd have to learn how to swim. Of course, this often resulted in only learning to dog paddle the four yards or so to the ladder, climbing out of the pool, and never setting foot near any body of fluid greater than one's own toilet, ever again. And depending on the child's emotional stability, perhaps winding up one day in a bell tower, with a towel and a 12-gauge, trying to wipe off "Dad's dirty water," between taking potshots at passing pedestrians. (Don't worry my mom taught me to swim).

So de-sensitization was the watchword for me, if I wasn't going to get overwhelmed, and ditch this thing faster than a gym membership, or one of those "12 albums for a penny" record deals. The to-do list, I noticed, featured three interviews for today. As someone who gladly submits to the irony of paying a postage fee to order stamps online, I was not a fan of this much human contact all at once. Fortunately, in the office cleanup, Gladys had replaced my well-thumbed 1978 Sports Illustrated swimsuit calendar with a current one, Cheryl Tiegs in fishnet be damned, and I noticed it was Saturday. Artfield High would be closed, so with all the relish of Derf and Johnny ("Take This Job and Shove It") Paycheck combined, I crossed my meeting with Ted Sheehan's teacher friend Barton off the list.

This left Reverend Brooks and the builder Rick James as my interviewees. With his church closed, and plans to leave town imminent, sitting down immediately with the maniacal minister was unavoidable. As for James, my only contact with him had been with Miss Iceland by my side, where he had seemed more open to her comely concerns than anything I had to say. I was hoping she was available to come with me, when my flip phone began vibrating, in a not unfriendly way, in my front pocket.

It was Miss Iceland texting, of her own volition no less, to say she'd meet me at Pete's Pub at one o'clock, followed by an emoji that was either a palm tree or an outline of the country Laos, I'm still not sure. That meant we could reconnoiter over a cocktail, before heading out to the sales office to pump Rick James for info. Suddenly I felt better having cut my interviews from 3 to one and a half. I'd also have along the woman I gave up a bounce on the blotter with Debra Townes for, or so I was telling myself, in building a story of supposed growth that Gladys had shamed me into.

I noticed I had a little "teepee" working, as I now recounted the events of last night, only with Miss Iceland in the Debra Townes role. For a second, I considered retiring to the bathroom and strapping a stranglehold on the bald-headed champ to relieve said wigwam, but decided I might best be served channeling that frustrated energy into my interview with the crazy cleric Brooks.

When I accepted that I wasn't going to look or feel any better, I stumbled out the back door to the Falcon. It must have rained overnight, for I noticed the red expired inspection tag was showing on the lower, driver's side front window. I scooped up some mud on a leaf and slapped the whole thing over it, taking a second to make it look like it had just fallen there naturally. I slid in, it started—never a guarantee—and I was off downtown.

I pulled onto the main drag, such as it is, to find it, relatively speaking, hopping. It may have been city/suburb folk dropping in on Rick James's sales office or some sort of spring-fling, family-fun, I'm-glad-I-don't-have-kids-days at the ski resort. But the street in front of the square, two-story Episcopal Church was a mob of Saabs. I parked my shame a few side streets down and made my way toward the huge Johnny Java's sign that now dominated the block.

There was a bin overflowing with trash outside the church, but I knew the Reverend was inside. I saw him raging about within as I passed. No doubt packing up final belongings, so this might be the last chance for an interview. Thus, I quickly weaved through the North Face-attired sidewalk strollers and entered the church vestibule.

I immediately heard Brooks down the hallway to the left, ranting to himself against his perceived enemies. I made it down to an open door where, as I guessed, he was going through the last remnants of his office. The furniture was gone, and in its place were boxes piled high with unfinished writings, and books never to be opened again, and suddenly, I got that "vuja de" feeling–the opposite of déjà vu–where I realized I would be in this same situation in the future.

"I'll be right with you," growled the Reverend, sensing I was there without looking. He was bent over a box of God knows what, shuffling through it with a purposeless intensity. He wore a heavy, white cardigan, though it was in the mid-50s outside, and the thicket of brambly curls that grew on his neck made it hard to determine where the sweater ended, and his hair began.

I lingered in the hallway preparing myself mentally to enter that small room, and the steel cage match of an interview that would ensue. Fortunately, I was too broke and cheap, for that matter, to have stopped at Johnny Java's and brought an offending beverage with me. I looked around the hall and could see it was truly the end. Geometrically plotted indentations in the carpet, indicated where furniture had once stood, and rectangles of dust served as chalk outlines for the pictures that used to live on these walls. I picked up a wooden cross, Jesus included, off a pile of the Book of Common Prayers. The Son of God, I noticed, had a great set of abs, but considering what he had to go through to get them, I suddenly was more comfortable with my paunch. Reveries, such as these, were broken by a coarse bark from the office, "You still there? Whaddya want?"

I timidly dipped a toe in the room still clutching the cross. "You can't have that," he snapped, pointing at the crucifix. "This isn't a stinkin' estate sale, though they wish I were dead, those sons-of–oh, it's only you from the local paper. Where's the blond girl?"

Apparently, he at first, thought I was a parishioner, and I noted, if that was the way he talked to one of the flock, it didn't bode well for my hungover ass. "She's off today," I lied, for the same reason I minored in history in college, none. I noticed the veins on his neck protruding and pulsing, as if he was about to say something, but nothing came forth. The silence only seemed to make him madder, so I filled it, what I thought was, innocuously, with: "So, it's packing day, I see."

A-a-a-a-and that set him off. "Packing day? It's a goddamned tragic day that's what it is. This place is a goddamn institution in this town," he began, at which point I stepped back unsure if lightning was about to strike him down, but apparently there's some sort of special dispensation on damning God for men of the cloth. "An institution in this town dammit. But does anybody care? No! They'd rather have their good for nothing coffee bars and who the hell knows what else."

Johnny Java's was obviously still a hot-button issue, so I tried to turn the conversation, if that's what you would call it, to Curly Carson. "Actually,

I came here to talk about Curly Carson. Had he been attending the AA meetings here regularly before his death?"

"Yes. Uh...I don't know. I've been fighting with the diocese in Burlington. Had to go up there a few times, so I let the boys run it themselves–same eight to 12 every week–didn't need me. Now Curly's gone, the meetings are gone, and nobody cares. This place is an institution, but that don't matter to them."

Apparently, it was grammar that was damned, as well, in this congregation. However, it raised the question, "Who is 'them'?"

"Them, them," he spit, pointing wildly. "The coffee shits, the bullcrap builders, the city asses and their little sons- and daughters- of bitches, that's them!"

"I've had the coffee shits before. They have a pill for that now." This was obviously going nowhere.

"An institution, that's what this place is–an INSTITUTION!" he screamed, turning a pair of crazed Marty Feldman eyes on me, and waving his arms expansively.

This guy belongs in an institution, was my only thought. As a youngster Reverend Brooks was scarier than lawn darts, now I realized he was just a pathetic old man, having the last thing he cared about in the world torn away from him. I wasn't going to get an answer from him on Curly's sobriety or who bought the Church building. Then, fortunately, a phone rang somewhere in the myriad of boxes, allowing me to quietly slip away, while thinking I would've given 3 to 2 against the poor guy ever finding it.

I stepped out onto the street and the crowds had thinned a tad. It was still warm, but there was a cool breeze indicating, as was the case in Vermont in early spring, winter was still lurking. There must have been lead, asbestos, and God knows what other dense and carcinogenic material in the ancient church building, because the old flip phone (Are there new ones?) sprang back to life out on the sidewalk with a series of beeps.

Now, to paraphrase Buddy Hackett, there are two things that burn my ass: a flame about three feet high and multiple text messages. As the owner of outdated technology, I assumed I was discouraging communication. Thus, I opted for the cheap (I prefer thrifty), non-unlimited messaging plan. Others, however, refused to get on board with this, so that every worthless "LOL" or "K" in response or, worse yet, as part of a group text, was costing me a quarter a pop. So, it was with anger mixed with trepidation that I opened my phone to see "what fresh hell," as Dorothy Parker would lament, cellular/satellite advancement had brought me now.

It was three text messages, all from Miss Iceland. Suddenly, I liked her just a tiny bit less. I stepped over to a spot between Johnny Java's and the church and stuck my hand with the phone into the narrow, impassable alley between the two buildings, to hide my phone from 12-year-olds scooting by with their iPhone 9s or BlueTubes or whatever the latest tech was. It seemed my shame (car, phone, clothes), knew no bounds.

I quickly decided these messages could yield no good. It could be that Miss Iceland was texting to cancel our "date," which could only lead to doubts and recriminations, no matter how valid the excuse (Explosive diarrhea? I've had worse dates). Almost certainly, she was wanting info about my morning interviews, one of which (Barton) I blew off. Was Curly Carson drinking again? What was his mood leading up to the murders? Who bought the church building? Were they connected in any way to Johnny Javas? To Rick James? The answers were, like whatever happened to Richie's brother, Chuck, on "Happy Days" --I hadn't a clue.

Standing between buildings, debating whether to open or ignore the messages, I recalled a story about there being an old-timey advertisement painted on the side of the church wall. As kids we'd stick our heads between the buildings trying to figure out what it was. As an adult, apparently, I wasn't any smarter, so to kill time while deciding whether to read the messages, I poked my now much larger cranium into the void. Immediately, I realized this was an idea right up there with my bets on the Cleveland Barons (look them up) and Walter Mondale ("Minnesota is a bellwether state," I claimed). However, like most of my sexual encounters, I was in, so I'd try to make the best of it.

I tried turning my head, but instantly felt a pressure at the back and front that foretold a potential Three Stooges moment. So instead, I tilted back and tried to look up and in, simultaneously. Never one to be known for being limber, my "up and in" was limited and, no, I'm not talking about my sexual encounters again. What I could see, was some indiscriminate, chipped red and yellow paint that extended farther up the wall, and nearer to me, the words "Whitey was here" scratched into the brick. Now in the 1930s and 40s, you couldn't field a sandlot baseball team or shout across a Sweet Shop, without coming across someone named Whitey. Post Civil Rights movement not so much. If my thinking was correct, that made the church building at least 70 to 90 years old, but in an area where every other farmhouse sported a plaque, saying Ethan Allen and the Green Mountain Boys slept there, this hardly qualified it as an "institution."

From this dis-advantage point, the advertisement looked like Mick Jagger with a feather boa around his neck. I started to determine if the Rolling Stones could be that old but found Keith Richards' exact age to be incalculable and gave up. I had no idea what all this was accomplishing. I wasn't a detective, I wasn't even a very good reporter and the feeling that I should give up the ghost—on the paper, the murders, Chief Bowden—was overwhelming. Derf's oft-fantasized idea of us moving to Reno and becoming blackjack dealers, was suddenly palatable; that's how bad things had gotten. So, I turned my head slowly, eased it out from between the buildings, and looked up into the smiling, well-groomed face of Rick James. Yeah, Reno, blackjack, it was looking better by the second.

"I think you're going to have to go around—or lose a lot of weight," he chuckled, while tilting his head toward the narrow alley.

I really wasn't in the mood for his cornpone humor and made note to be on the lookout for hand buzzers, squirting flowers, and if told there was a spot on my shirt to not look down—though chances were better than even money, he would be telling the truth on that one. Nonetheless, I patted my beer gut and tried to be sociable. "Well, losing a few pounds, in general, wouldn't be a bad idea, I'm sure."

"Actually, you're in luck. I've been negotiating to put an LA Fitness in here, once enough units are sold," he said, grinning too widely.

"If the LA stands for 'lard ass' I'm in otherwise," I let the thought, and inevitable snarky finish, trail off when I realized, as annoying as this chance meeting was, it was an opportunity to redeem myself for the all too familiar sloth and failures of this morning. I could practically hear my mental gears grinding as, against my better judgment, I tried to change tack, "You're looking sharp. Got a haircut?"

"You know I was there, I had the money, I said what the hell let's get 'em all cut. How's it going with you?"

I respected the way he'd put a spin on the old 'I got 'em all cut,' so I decided to return serve. "Oh, you know. it's going. I wish it were gone, but it just keeps on going."

He laughed into the big crazy straw coming out of some kind of iced coffee frappe-thing in a clear, plastic Johnny Java's cup, complete with whipped cream, under a dome lid.

"Nice coffee. What does your husband drink?" I cracked.

"Very funny. I told the girl no whipped cream, but I think the dozen earrings affected her hearing."

"Yeah, that would've made it all better," I deadpanned.

"Man, it's packed in there," he said, pulling hard on the giant straw.

"They do a nice business with the touristy crowd. They got the skiers passing through in the winter, now the foliage-fetishists in the spring. You must be happy 'bout that."

His demeanor changed, and it wasn't a brain freeze from sucking on his girly-drink. "Happy? I'm pissed. I wish I had a piece of that deal. That's the best location in town."

I recalled how he had mentioned to Miss Iceland and me, how brokering these deals with big name franchises was one of the perks of redevelopment. Probably money that went right to him, without having to pass through the business and related taxes. I was no William Levitt, but I noticed he was right about the spot; anyone on their way north to the Sugarbush Resort had to travel right past here. It was the only thing that kept the town going over the years. So how had this big-time, well-connected New York City developer missed out on the "best location in town"?

"Then who owns it?"

"I don't have a clue. It took so long to get approved by those old bastards at the Planning Board, that by the time I got around to other matters, it was already vulture-d. It happens."

The crowd on the sidewalk was picking up again, and the ubiquity of phones in hands had me concerned that my "head between buildings, ass in the air" moment was already going viral somewhere. I'd swung and missed on who bought the church building. I'd swung and missed again on who owned Johnny Java's. Behind in the count seemed to be the self-inflicted story of my life. So, this is usually where I took a backdoor slider, in both the baseball and prison metaphorical senses, and retired to my dugout/apartment with cheap beer and frozen pizza. But with Miss Iceland's and Gladys's inquiries, waiting on my phone and at the office respectively, and the distasteful prospect of job interviews in my future ("Where do you see yourself in five years?"; "In a shallow grave by the highway—why do you ask?") I figured it was time to swing for the fences. Maybe I'd hit something.

"So why are there so many lawsuits pending against your company?" I confronted Rick James, throwing caution to a stiff breeze.

Now, when one detects privately, as events thrust me into doing, one needs certain skills. Such a skill is the ability to read faces. After all, every episode of *Dateline* features the reporter asking the inevitable, "Did you kill your wife/husband/girlfriend/boyfriend/parent?" And no one has answered yet: "Whoa jeez. Yeah, you got me." However, unlike most things I say and do, one does bear repeating, and that is—I am not a partisan of people. Due to this, I really don't even like to look at most folks' faces, unless, of course, they look like Miss Iceland's. Even then, I'm thinking they're reading the dirty thoughts that must be written all over my visage, so I generally end up averting my eyes there as well.

Thus, it took a concerted effort to look into Rick James's peepers, where I discerned a look that may have been concern or constipation, which only confirmed further that I was in over my head. Surprisingly, though, no infantile insult, corny quip, or ribald riposte sallied forth. His brow furrowed, and his eyes raised upward, and I thought perhaps I'd caught him off guard, searching for a plausible response. However, I also realized my brow was furrowed, and my eyes skyward, as I tried to figure out how to follow this up to maximum benefit. Just then, he reached inside his sports coat, and despite the broad daylight and surfeit of pedestrians, I still flinched a little. Fortunately, only a cell phone emerged, he grunted twice, muttered an "OK" and now fixed me in the eye.

"Gotta run. Sales office is jamming," he remarked, as he put a hand on my arm and eased past. Over my shoulder I heard his standard, "Stay in touch with yourself," and, I thought, that is all I'll be doing after I report my myriad failures back to Miss Iceland.

As I staggered back to the Falcon, I took out the flip phone, and debated whether to look at the three text messages. It had long been an axiom of mine, that when waiting on a call/text, good news took forever or never arrived, while bad news was as punctual as one of Mussolini's train conductors. These messages had been two things I seldom was—bright and early.

I reached the Falcon, found a non-rusted patch, leaned against it, and opened the mailbox. The three messages stared at me, no doubt wanting to know where I was, and what I'd accomplished—and to think, just when I'd almost forgotten the little joys of the male/female relationship. The first two were as suspected. What happened with Barton? What happened with Brooks? The third in this Trio of Gloom was a cryptic, "Big news. Tell you later," from Karina (we were meeting in a few hours, I needed to practice her real name). I trashed all three unanswered and got in the car.

I drove away wondering what I would report to Miss Iceland during our rendezvous at Pete's Pub, or if I should cancel the meeting altogether. The office was not an option for mulling it over, as Gladys was there awaiting info on her favorite suspect, Rick James, no doubt. Instead, I drove around aimlessly looking for an out-of-town gas station that had coffee and was reminded of the words of Lawrence Durrell, who wrote in book one of his Alexandria Quartet, "as well as displeasing myself I had displeased another; ...alone I have only myself to displease. Joy!"

At first, this gave me resolve to cancel with Miss Iceland. But sipping a 24-ouncer and eating a Little Debbie's at a Phillip's 66 just outside Brattleboro, I remembered Lawrence Durrell was a bit of a prig, who took four books to wring his metaphorical hands over his unrequited love for the flighty (and frankly fairly slutty) Justine. Conversely, all I wanted was a piece of ass. So, filled with caffeine, I headed back to Artfield and Pete's Pub, to see if I could find a way to get Miss Iceland to give up some.

CHAPTER 13: Love In The Time Of Sarcasm

There were a mere four cars in the lot at Pete's Pub, but I parked in the back and waited for Miss Iceland. Not that it would have been hard to find my vehicle had the lot been full. There aren't many 1965 model cars on the roads these days, and those are usually clean and pristine. I, of course, was working on a whole other level: Rust and Dust.

I had little for her regarding the murders, but I had a thing for willowy, borderline anemic blondes, and I felt we'd gotten to the point where I just might get to show her that thing. Though we'd been working together, and even fooled around some, this meeting was akin to our first date, and I wanted to make a good impression. Even if I couldn't produce any strong leads, I wanted to look cool OR confident; both being too much to ask.

I removed myself heavily from the bench seat of the Falcon and shoved open the door with an unearthly groan—the door, not me. Miss Iceland texted she was minutes away, and I tried to position myself suavely in wait, though the backdrop of the car, and my ubiquitous dishevelment, made this a Sisyphean task. First, I leaned against the trunk, arms crossed, legs akimbo—too aggressive. Then hands in pockets, legs crossed—too Springsteen Tunnel of Love-y. Next, I looped my thumbs through my belt loops—too Kingfish Huey Long. Finally, I tried arms crossed, legs crossed, with face pout, and a slight upper body lean to the left, until a stiff breeze kicked up nearly blowing me over. At that point, I gave up the ridiculous ghost just as Miss Iceland's Volkswagen turned into the lot.

Faded bootcut jeans—worn, but not factory-ripped-Mexican serape-style, hooded sweatshirt, and a pair of dirty Chuck Taylors on her feet, she looked like she just walked out of a hippie's dream. You know, the good kind, where Abbie Hoffman almost started a revolution, every acid trip was a spiritual awakening, and Woodstock was actually fun—not a soggy, traffic nightmare, germ-fest with bad sound. Wisps of blonde hair fell in her eyes, and that, along with girls in baseball caps, always made me hot—Veronica Lake, Chrissie Hynde, heck, I'd get turned on watching *The Addams Family* every time Cousin It appeared—uh, Cousin It was a woman, right?

"Am I late?" she asked, as if it mattered. I had nowhere to be till the Tricentennial.

I pushed up my sleeve and consulted my bare wrist. "I can't tell off hand," I replied, instantly regretting my defensive jokiness around attractive women.

"You don't wear a watch?" she asked, in a tone that reminded me of one of those Victorian-era, class-conscious clashes, out of, say, *Great Expectations* ("He calls the Jacks knaves." Good heavens!).

"I don't accessorize," I said in defense. "I prefer to be unencumbered." At this point though it didn't matter, as she was busy sizing up our meeting place in a manner I'd describe as pensive. Pete's Pub wasn't that bad, but its future wouldn't require the donning of shades, to paraphrase that 80s Timbuk 3 song—something I never thought I'd do.

The paint was peeling, the masonry crumbling, and the sign on top of the one-story structure was a monument to understatement, reading only "BAR." Of the four vehicles in the lot, I recognized three, the odd one being a new-ish white pickup with ladders and heavy tools in the bed. We walked close past a salt-stained panel van with a faded Grateful Dead bumper sticker that read, "I'm One of Jerry's Kids."

"Jeff 'Fucking' Jensen's here," I muttered, giving the van an open-hand slap, thereby releasing a reek of stale pot smoke from the half-closed passenger-side window.

"You don't like this guy?" said Miss Iceland, dwelling on the expletive.

"No, it's not that, uh....You'll see."

Inside Pete's was, in a word, dank; in two words, very dank. Direct sunlight came here to die. The two most popular shots of barflies, who spent extensive time here, were Jack Daniels and Vitamin D. Entering on the left side of the building, Miss Iceland, a person of light and beauty (at least in my lust-filled mind), blinked several times to adjust her vision. I, on the other hand, was fine. To our left, along the wall, was a row of two-person tables broken up in the middle by a 35-year-old, never updated, 45-RPM playing jukebox, on which the most popular titles were "Turning Japanese," and "My Sharona."

"So, this is where you hang out?" Miss Iceland asked. She gave the place the once-over, but I didn't worry. I figured if she'd gotten past my car, my clothes, and my corny jokes, she had a pretty high threshold for trashiness. Besides, cocktails waited within, and could do nothing but work in my favor on this date, or whatever it was.

"I used to," I answered, realizing there was no way to deny it, since I was featured in various states of inebriation in the holiday photo montages that decorated the walls. "Though now I only go out often enough to remember that staying home is preferable," I added, truthfully. Not exactly saving the situation but dealing with it in a 'lesser of two evils' sort of way.

To our right, ran a parentheses-shaped bar on one side of the long aisle, and we took up seats across from it, about halfway down a row of booths that ran along the permanently shuttered windows.

Several slugs were adhered to the far end of the bar and barely acknowledged our entry. Farthest away was Beer Gut Buddy, looking about a bacon-cheeseburger away from needing one of those long grabber things to reach his beer, like some sort of perverse boardwalk crane game. Considering his standard "last call" order was three beers, a burger, and a plate of wings, it could happen tonight. To his left, was Four Drink Frank, with a beer, Screwdriver, and White Russian, in front of him (and later he'd add a black coffee to the lineup, as if that would sober him up for the drive home). His left elbow rested on the back of an empty chair with a spent shot glass and the dregs of a short beer in front of it, indicating a recent appearance of The Fleischmann Flash. An old-timer, the Flash would appear several times on a given day, order a shot of Fleischmann's whiskey, a short beer chaser, and drink them standing up, before returning to his still-running car, where his wife was waiting for him to continue chauffeuring her on errands. Finally, there was Liquid Lenny, so-called because he had never been spotted consuming solid food. Of indiscriminate age, with an 80s perm, and a complexion that fell somewhere between that old Procol

Harum song and an E.L. James novel (A Whiter Shade of Grey?), Lenny was most noted for bringing mini bottles of his favorite brand of tonic water and lining them up on the bar like terra cotta soldiers, as a substitute for whatever generic swill Pete's was mixing in his gin/vodka tonics. These he consumed in such quantities; it was a safe bet he'd never contract malaria. Cirrhosis of the liver, on the other hand, was a distinct possibility.

    Nearer to us at the bar, sat two half-finished beers and a pack of Salem Lights, before the empty stools of Jeff "Fucking" Jensen and whatever derelict du jour he'd rustled up to assist him in his itinerant painting business. Both, no doubt, were in the back abusing the facilities. Looking back over my shoulder to the dark end of the bar, I noticed the mystery pickup must belong to a pair of burly, brown coverall-clad types, engaged in a discussion over one of their iPhones about an ongoing battle of Fortnite, Black Ops, or some other combat video game I knew nothing about, preferring to escape reality the old-fashioned way, with alcohol. I assumed they weren't employees of Rick James's crew. The latter had clustered at Pete's for the first couple of weeks of building, until they realized Sunday through Thursday at Pete's was, what we jokingly referred to as the All-Male Revue, with not a woman in sight. Even on the weekend, the women that attended were spoken *for*, and the ones that weren't were of the type that were rarely spoken *to*. Instead, the framers, carpenters etc., of R.L. James Construction, spent their time up at the bar at Sugarbush, where at least occasionally, was heard an encouraging word, and one could listen to music produced in the current millennium.

Behind the bar, I noticed Serge was filling in for Pete himself, who probably took advantage of the good weather to partake in his two passions: hunting and fishing. In fact, so engrossed was he in these activities, that we'd often have to beg him to switch away from Animal Planet, Outdoor TV, or the Redneck Channel, just to watch a Red Sox playoff game…or the Super Bowl. Though I must admit, an occasional episode of Meerkat Manor could be entertaining.

Serge, in contrast, couldn't care less what you wanted to watch, or drink, as long as the former didn't feature a Kardashian, and the latter was beer, wine or a mixture of no more than two liquids. At 5'9" and 235 pounds, with a jaw you could teach grade school geometry on, he was a no-nonsense, French-Canadian, bull of a man, who did not suffer fools or Long Island Iced Teas lightly. The apocryphal story about him being, the night a gaggle of college coeds wandered in and ordered a pitcher of Daiquiris, only to be sternly informed there was no blender on the premises. When they pointed to one behind the bar, just inches from Serge's right elbow, he promptly picked it up, dropped it in the trash and told them there was a Houlihan's (he pronounced it Hooligan's) on Route 7, should they wish to take their perky patronage elsewhere. This was much to the chagrin of several regulars ready to pounce on them like a puma on a porkchop.

The waitress, if there was one, was MIA, so I sallied up to the bar (yes, I occasionally do sally) for a pair of menus and some drinks. Serge was his usual surly self, so I took the cautious liberty of ordering two Coors Light drafts, figuring Serge wasn't about to be mistaken for Mr. Boston this afternoon, and after the Natty Ice in a can she had in my office, this would be the equivalent of Dom Perignon in a Pimp Cup to Miss Iceland.

Returning to the table, it was time to face the proverbial music, and it was already playing in my head like a Jim Morrison poetry album. True to feminine form—at least the 'feminines' I've known—Miss Iceland wasted no time in turning up the volume. "So, what did you find out today?"

"Ah, well," I, less than eloquently, stalled. Then I remembered my abortive fling with Debra Townes, and produced a clue without revealing my sordid source, "Uh, I did find out Jeremy the Reporter and Monica Carson dated in college."

Now, I'm not one to rest on my laurels, but what happened next felt like I'd been kicked in them. Instead of praising my sleuthing skills, or even questioning how I'd come across such a choice morsel, Miss Iceland showed all the emotion of Dolph Lundgren in *Rocky IV*. She took out her reporter's notebook, jotted down the fact and moved on to what she apparently thought was my real assignment: interviews.

"Did you speak with Barton, the teacher?" she questioned, as I tried to re-descend my testicles.

There was no avoiding the answer to this so, I tried a dodge. "It's Saturday, school's closed," I said, prevaricating.

She was having none of this, and shot back so sternly, I was finally convinced we were in a real relationship or something close to one, "Well, you have his phone number, don't you?"

I honestly didn't know, so I tried moving on. "I did speak with Reverend Brooks," I began.

Again, her forceful questioning brought me up short, in more ways than one. "What did he say? Why did the church sell the property? For how much? Who bought it? Was Curly still in AA?"

"Not much. I don't know. I don't know. I don't know, and, uh, I don't know," I answered all too truthfully.

I felt like Derf, who once informed me on coming home from one of his plethora of internet dates, "Women aren't interested in a compulsive gambler with no job and no money."; "Yeah but she doesn't know that yet," I retorted. "No, she does, I told her." It was his way of not wasting time on those likely to be intolerant of his, shall we say, quirky lifestyle. The one caveat being, if the woman in question met a certain level of beauty, at which point he would hold his self-defeating plan in abeyance until he "threw her a chop," as he so gracelessly put it. He once drew a chart on the back of a racing program that displayed in linear graph form, the balance of lies to truth he would reveal, as a ratio to the attractiveness of said date, that ended up looking like something Elon Musk was planning on taking to Mars. So, considering Miss Iceland was the equivalent of an eHarmony homerun, I started backpedaling immediately.

"Well, he did say the whole thing was handled through the archdiocese in Burlington."

She brightened a tad, though I wasn't sure if it was from the info or having finally concocted her exit strategy. However, when she started scribbling again, I stopped calculating the angle and distance to the rear exit and went on.

"I also spoke to Rick James."

"Without me?" she interjected, quickly. I wasn't out of the woods yet.

"He ran into me coming out of the church," I partially lied, leaving out the part about my head in the alley as being superfluous–she already knew I was an idiot.

"What did you get out of him," she asked, with all the confidence of Derf with a horse up on an INQUIRY.

"Well," I was nothing if not hesitant about my next move, and with each fall and tuck of her blonde hair behind her ears, I was starting to sound like King George VI at an IRS audit. "Uh, he doesn't own the coffee shop or know who does. Said it was the best commercial spot in town, but somebody stole it while he was still finalizing the deal for the development."

She suddenly sprang to life, which is the only way to spring, I believe–"suddenly" and "to life"–that is. Writing furiously, she seemed to brighten for the first time since we entered. Though alcohol and poor lighting do have a way of making Pete's and my charms, as well, look better by degrees. I signaled Serge for two more beers.

"So, I pushed him on the lawsuits, and he seemed to turn pale. Then again, it's Vermont and everyone's pale, so I may have lost my ability to judge. Plus, he had enough layers of spray tan on to make George Hamilton jealous."

"Is that the guy from The Beatles?"

God, I'm old, was my first thought, but decided it was best to forge ahead. "I'm just saying, he flinched like a guy caught with a dildo in his bag at airport security, at the mention of the lawsuits. Then he said he had a call coming in, though there was no ringtone, talked quickly into his phone, said he had to go and took off without answering."

"Maybe it was on vibrate?"

"Uh, the dildo thing was a simile."

"Not the dildo, stupid," she said, shaking her head, but smiling, "his phone."

"Oh. Ah, right," I sloughed it off.

"That's great," she added, unexpectedly. I searched her for sarcasm, patronizing and/or condescension, found none, and felt better.

"Yeah sorry 'bout not seeing Barton or getting anything from Brooks, but..."

She cut me off with praise—the equivalent, in my dealings with women, of finding a bald Native American. "This is good stuff. Not great, but it's a start. We have to talk to the diocese in Burlington about the church sale—who bought it, how much, why sell it now, that type of thing. Plus, now we know Rick James is out on the coffee house, we can focus on those lawsuits. And, by the way, how did you find out about Monica and Jeremy dating?"

Ah, my laurels were back, so I ran with 'em. "Oh, you know, I have my contacts. Sometimes you gotta beat it outta them. Sometimes you gotta charm it outta them," I sniffed, then extended my arms across the back of the booth, striking my most confident pose.

"Hey, numb nuts, your beers are ready!" It was Serge snapping me back to reality.

I picked up the beers, while she continued scribbling, and I felt relieved. She was a trained investigative reporter. No wonder she was ticked at being pulled off this story and made to cover elementary school Tricky Trays. I also liked a woman who took charge and knew what she wanted, as opposed to those who wanted to be entertained, then judged me by the results, like I was Julie on *The Love Boat*. Somehow playing softball, stopping for a couple of beers, and eating Chinese takeout in front of the Bruins game, didn't constitute a dream date. I blame *The Bachelor* for setting the bar too high. It seems women these days like romantic hikes and long walks on the beach but ask them to go to the kitchen for a Natty Ice, so you don't miss the power play, and they bite your head off—but I digress.

At this point Dot, the waitress, turned up reeking of cigarettes, and tossed a pair of one-page laminated menus down, like they were Kleenex, and we were $5 whores. She was short, late 50s with hair and skin too orangey to be just as God made her. Unfortunately, years of hard living had left her bitter, lonely, and at this moment, angry that we'd come in for a late lunch, when she assumed she'd just cruise until her replacement showed up for the dinner shift.

She frowned at our drinks, no doubt thinking about how this would impact her tip. Then she pulled out her pad, expecting us to order, before anyone short of Evelyn Wood would have time to speed-read the choices. In my case this was expected, since I'd been here enough to memorize the Bill of (threadbare) Fare, that last changed when they overfished Orange Roughy.

"I'll have the bacon cheeseburger," Miss Iceland announced, decisively, and my loins gave a flutter. A woman who knew what she wanted and ate like a man. This WAS a find. "No bun, and he can have my fries," she added, but it was too late for my loins to turn back now.

"You know Dr. Atkins died at 41," I quipped, suspecting she was watching her carbs.

"He did?" she replied, trying to gauge my truthfulness.

"Yeah, he was hit by a bus." She looked relieved. "On his way to an angioplasty," I added. "So, who knows really."

"Huh?" Now she was thoroughly confused.

"Never mind. I'll have the Turkey Club." She didn't fully get me, but then again, no woman did, or wanted to, it seemed. Though if she could stay above The Mendoza Line (see, it ain't easy) as far as jokes were concerned, we just might have something here.

Dot moved off toward the galley kitchen, just as Jeff "Fucking" Jensen and Dennis Trevino came up the aisle from the men's room, conspicuously sniffing and twitching in stereo.

Jeff was squat, nondescript, with a pudgy, round face that belied the fact he could procure for one, any illicit substance from marijuana to methamphetamine to "goofers," as my father used to say. Dennis, on the other hand, was a character of the type that could cause you to sleep with the light on. At 6'3" and weighing a buck forty post-Thanksgiving, he looked like Ichabod Crane had his stomach stapled. This was due, he claimed, to having every digestive ailment known to WebMD, which he wasn't afraid to describe in Med School-like detail. Particularly, a case of perpetual acid reflux so violent, it had burned his back teeth down to mere nubs. Though, based on the strings of greasy hair falling out the back of his strictly ironic, dirty Middlebury College-hat, hygiene, no doubt had a hand, as well, in that dental disfigurement. He owned more flannel shirts than John Fogarty, and he had one on under the ever-present down vest with fishing license pinned to the back, that he wore everywhere, including to play softball in the middle of August.

As they returned to their bar stools, they sized Miss Iceland up from behind, and gave me that lascivious "way to go" look that was meant to make me feel proud, but just made me uncomfortable. All paint splattered clothes, twitching hands, and goofy grins, they sat facing us and waited for introductions.

I was in no hurry, however, to have what I saw as fast becoming my past life, intersect with my potential future, so I slow-played it. "Dennis, longtime, what ya been up to?"

Never a raconteur, Dennis opened his mouth, but before his brains could force the words down Jeff, coked to the gills and shaking like Robert Kraft at a Geisha House, jumped into the breach.

"I'll fucking tell you. Been fighting with fucking Artfield Police over fucking parking fucking tickets. First, they fucking send me to fucking jail in fucking Rutland on fucking possession charges. Then when I fucking get out, they fucking send me a fucking summons for fucking parking violations. I told the fucking town fucking judge, 'How can I fucking get parking fucking tickets in fucking Artfield, when I'm in fucking jail in fucking Rutland'. I mean what the fuck?" he ejaculated in a breathless stream-of-consciousness that sounded like Jack Kerouac with Tourette's.

"Uh, that's fucked up," I deadpanned, then turned back to Dennis. I had always had a soft spot for Dennis Trevino, ever since he lost an eye in some sort of backhoe incident on his family's dairy farm back in high school. It wasn't the loss of an eye that bothered me—I'm sure he was high, or his father was drunk—it was my idiot friends and I, telling everyone to take the yearbook survey, white-out the "s" and vote Dennis "Nicest Eye." He won, but fortunately, less immature heads prevailed in editing.

"What's up with you?" I turned to Dennis as Miss Iceland wrapped her head around Jeff Jensen's story. "How ya feel?"

I regretted this immediately, remembering we had food on the way. He turned his head as if looking at the front door, fixed me with his one good eye and said, "Not bad, considering. My doctor says I get less than 10% of the nutrients in what I eat. It just passes straight through my digestion system and is excreted as bile."

I made a mental note to hold my bathroom needs till home.

Then I had an epiphany, which I learned one Valentine's Day was not a cheap, knockoff jewelry brand sold on the internet, "Did either of you see Curly in the week before the murders?" I addressed them both. "Was he drinking, do you know?"

"That was crazy," said Dennis, reflecting on the murder/suicide. "Curly was a good guy. I wonder what set him off?"

"Fucking tragedy," from Jeff. "We were just fucking there for a fucking estimate two days before it fucking happened."

Miss Iceland had her notebook open again. She took a long pull on her beer, then began writing. "So Curly was fine, not beating up the Budweisers?" I reasserted, invoking the dead man's beverage of choice.

"No way. Sober as a judge," said Dennis and, I thought, if anyone he should know, having been in front of his fair share over the years. "We even asked him for a beer, but the place was dry."

"And we fucking checked his fucking hiding places from when he was fucking married. Fucking nothing."

I knew I wasn't in the presence of a pair in the know, but I asked the question anyway, "So was Curly attending AA meetings at the church regularly?"

I may as well have been asking a couple of Crips about a Klan meeting. They looked at each other dumbfounded until Dennis glanced down the bar to his right and said, "Let me ask Lenny."

That was my cue to be dumbfounded. Liquid Lenny in AA? My jaw hit the ground like a turkey in a *WKRP in Cincinnati* Thanksgiving promotion. "Lenny's in AA?" I stammered. "The last non-alcoholic thing he drank was Similac."

"It's terms of the probation from his last DUI. He shows up late, adds a little Irish to a coffee, then sits in the back till it's over, and Reverend Brooks, or whoever's running it, signs off he was there."

Since I broke up with Kayla, I hadn't been attending Pete's regularly and obviously I'd missed a lot. "Lenny?" Dennis shouted down the bar, disturbing Serge from his newspaper. "Was Curly Carson at the last AA meeting?"

Lenny looked up from his whatever-and-tonic, turned his perpetually sleepy eyes to us and answered casually, "Yeah, every week for the past month, month-and-a-half. I talked with him a few times. Tried to get me to join the discussions, but I told him, 'Curly, good for you but I'm just marking time. I'm no quitter'."

Coming from a man who never held a job for more than six months, that seemed an odd statement, but I chalked it up to a case of selective stamina. "And he hasn't been coming 'round here?" I shouted down the bar, further annoying Serge.

"I haven't seen him," Lenny replied, then turned to the other slugs as if passing the question along. They all shook their heads in agreement to coin a contradiction in terms. Between the four of them, plus Dennis and Jeff, I figured they had probably covered every open hour of Pete's since Hands Across America, like some sloshed surveillance squad, so I was satisfied.

"In that case I should've sold my Anheuser-Busch stock," I quipped to Miss Iceland, who gave me a smile that certainly wasn't for my wit. I could see the full-blown investigative reporter she longed to be, kicking in now.

"Curly's not drinking, Sheehan's never been fooling around with his daughter, and he's forward-looking enough to have Drunk and Drunker here," she tilted her head at Jeff and Dennis, who'd gone back to their cocktails after I remembered Miss Iceland's real name (Karina), and finally made brief introductions, "come over for an estimate. And nobody's thinking about going through the guaranteed ass-ache of painting or renovating, if you're planning what Curly did."

"OK, but who drove him to do it? Chief Bowden has gambling debts, but Curly and Sheehan weren't 'making book' or loansharking, and what's Curly's connection to Rick James?"

"Why does it have to be one of those two? And who says Curly did anything? Maybe it was staged to look that way."

"And the Artfield police are dumb enough to buy it?" I said, and then added, "And the State Police took their word for it?"

"Look around," she said, again nodding at the backs of Dennis and Jeff, then half-turning to take in the bar slugs and Serge with his paper. "The cops here ain't exactly chasing down Keyser Soze. They've got it easy and when they're in over their heads they're happy to accept the obvious. This isn't front page news outside your paper, which suddenly is no more, so the State Police have no reason to not accept the locals' conclusion."

Son of a bitch! Nothing is ever easy. Here I thought Gladys and I had it narrowed down, and then Miss Iceland comes out of nowhere with her pasty pulchritude and rational reasoning, and craps in my Count Chocula. I mean I liked *The Usual Suspects* reference, but just two weeks ago I had a moderately failing local paper, no entanglements socially, a fridge full of cheap beer and Bagel Bites, and a living room scattered with "Books to Read" like bodies on the battlefield at Gettysburg. Now, I had to solve a double-murder-suicide (if that's even what it was) before penury set in, and a pseudo-girlfriend/partner, who was going all *Dateline* on me. Seemed I was caught between the proverbial rock and a hard place. Fortunately for her, the hard place was in my jeans, so I let her Woodward and Bernstein fantasies play out a little longer.

"So, who do you suspect?" I was forced to ask, though I knew I wouldn't like the answer.

"I have a coupla ideas, but we have a lot more leg work to do first."

"Son of a bitch!" this one was audible. "But we only have two weeks until the money runs out," I said hopefully, such was the depth of my laziness. Immediately I felt bad: there were three good people dead with no real closure, several jobs on the line if the paper closed permanently, and a fine, little New England village descending into corruption and/or greed. I had the means to possibly do something about it if I didn't, for once, take the easy way out.

"So, then I suggest we get to work," she answered, breaking my tortured ruminations. Then she held up our empties, found Dot dozing over a cup of coffee, and called out. "Two more here," and I fell in love all over again.

The rest of the afternoon was why my GPA in college never topped 3.0. We talked, laughed, drank and but for the lack of bong hits over a game of Yahtzee, I might have suggested we blow off Poly Sci to play Ultimate Frisbee on the Quad.

We went over the evidence again while we ate, and I was impressed with her organizational skills and deductive reasoning. She clearly didn't belong covering church bake sales and high school performances of *Brigadoon*. She'd be off to a big city daily someday, and I'd be left behind, which wasn't a bad thing. I was not exactly marrying timber or anything near it. A mere dalliance with a woman of such beauty, energy, and ambition, is all I could handle. Anything more, and they'd be picking me up with a stick and a spoon.

Of course, this wasn't the growth I was looking for, but one thing at a time. I promised myself I'd stay with her on the investigation until it was completed. Completion of difficult problems never being my strong suit, so that was something. Besides, I was feeling for the deceased, and the town as a whole. When I had walked into Pete's, I looked around and had one of those "You mean this is my life" laments, as I surveyed the assembled. But they were good folk for all their quirks and, hell, who was I to judge. They came through with some key info, and if the paper ever had a chance to get back on its feet, they'd be here for Max Lipper's proposed fundraiser. And that, I realized was maturity, in and of itself, but before I tore a labrum patting myself on the back, I recalled I was forty and should have come to these realizations many a year ago.

After the meal, the afternoon continued to degenerate easily, culminating in a tour of Pete's history, via the special occasion photo montages on the wall: St. Patrick's Day, New Year's Eve, Super Bowls, etc. It also dovetailed, sadly, with my romantic history. If one cared to search me out, one arm drunkenly flung around the 'Lush O' My Lust' at the time and Miss Iceland, sadly for me, did care.

"Who's this?" she asked, pointing to a buxom brunette, several sheets and a couple of pillowcases to the wind, leaning up against me in a Polaroid.

"That's Crazy Mary," I replied, reflexively cringing. "We were friends since high school, tried dating, and long story short, we don't acknowledge each other's presence anymore."

"Why go out with her in the first place? Isn't that kinda ending implied in her name?"

"You mean 'Crazy'?" I countered. "Hey, sometimes crazy is good, uh, but you're right it has a short shelf life."

The construction guys at the end of the bar were getting loud over the games on their phones, and Serge peremptorily served them with their check. Meanwhile, Miss Iceland and I returned to our table. It had turned to dusk outside, and a few families drifted in for an early dinner, before the heavy drinking crowd took over. The construction workers settled up and exited with a leer at Miss Iceland, and I signaled to Dot for our own check, though it wasn't delivered with the alacrity Serge brought to the task.

I seldom courted "moments of truth." In fact, I spent the better part of my life trying to avoid them. Unfortunately, as we approached our cars there was no place to hide. Not necessarily a spot where I shine.

As we approached our vehicles, I placed a hand on the small of her back, and she turned to me surprisingly easily. Behind her bumper, we shared a beery kiss as I tried not to burp in her mouth—it had happened before on almost this exact spot.

It seemed too late, and we were too buzzed, to chase down any leads, so I steadied myself, looked into her forehead—as she had meanwhile listed forward—and delivered my most eloquent ultimatum, "So?"

At that moment I looked down, she looked up, and somewhere in the middle she gave me an awkward kiss: all noses, teeth and chins banging.

"Let's go to your place," she mumbled, into the general vicinity of my left ear. My loins leapt, and I was actually giddy–something I hadn't been since I quit doing "whip-its" off whipped cream cans in college–but before I could suggest I drive, she had hopped into her Volks and started the engine. She seemed to be in a rush to get to my humble hovel, which is something, as regards women, that had never happened. Coaxed, coerced, begged, and bribed being the more standard ploy. But fearing I'd be left behind and/or run over, I fumbled for my keys while heading at a quick stagger to the Falcon. The state Miss Iceland was in, vis-a-vis my attractiveness, being like the career of Right Said Fred; fleeting and capricious.

Now, nothing quite makes one sober up, like a giant chrome spotlight through the rear window, and a boxy vehicle with an audible V-8, bearing down on one's bumper. At that point the cherry-top is inevitable and as I appeared to witness this happening to the trailing Miss Iceland, my emotions took an immediate roller coaster ride:

    Sobered up Miss Iceland   Bad
    My knowing all the cops in town   Good
    Police Chief not happy with me   Bad
    My brother-in-law on the force   Good
    In debt to my fat-ass brother-in-law   Bad

Before this Olympian over-thinking could get any further, I noticed the VW quickly inching up on my bumper. I realized there were no flashing lights yet, so I grabbed the unglued rearview mirror from the dashboard and tried to get a better look at what was going on. At approaching 70 MPH this, as expected, failed spectacularly. I turned back to my sideview mirror and saw that the vehicle behind us was taller and wider than the sedan-sized cars of the Artfield PD.

Suddenly, there was a crunch, a crack, and the realization something bad was happening; the same thing that happened the last time I'd bitten down on a handful of Skittles. Miss Iceland was now right on my ass when, ironically, I thought that's where I'd be on her by now. Then there was another clash of metal, and when her Volks banged into the Falcon's bumper, even I knew it was no time for crass wordplay.

Looking back, I saw a full-sized pickup with its brights on, dropping back and then accelerating, for another run at the Volks. Fortunately, the road had some semblance of a shoulder, and I slid over giving Miss Iceland the opportunity to speed past me, without having to cross completely into the oncoming lane, on this quickly darkening, rural Vermont night.

The truck followed her path, but the fact that it was wider than her compact gave me an idea. Now I've been known to rehearse my order before going to the fast-food drive-up window, so quick thinking is not necessarily my forte. However, between adrenaline and seeing my tumble with Miss Iceland going by the books, both my heads for once worked in sync. Moving over alongside the Volkswagen, I took my foot off the gas and let the rear passenger side bumper of the Falcon smash into the front driver's side bumper of the pickup.

The impact was a stalemate, allowing Miss Iceland time to move out of harm's way. Luckily, the Falcon was constructed with the densest metal this side of the Monitor and Merrimack. It made Old Ironsides look like one of those toy balsa wood gliders, and the crunching of the pickup's fiberglass bumper was the sound of chalking one up to 1960s environment-be-damned technology.

Miss Iceland sped ahead, and I accelerated, leaving the truck in a non-catalytic converted cloud of trachea-scorching black smoke. The pickup, its headlights halved, began to drop back. At a junction, Miss Iceland made a hard right, and I followed until we both slowed down, when we saw our pursuers continue straight. I pulled alongside the Volks, and we nodded an "Everything's OK," since reaching across the seat, finding the pliers that substituted for the missing handle, and manually rolling down the window, seemed a waste of seconds in our still potentially precarious position.

We turned around, her in a deft semi-circle, me in an unwieldy forward-and-reverse turn that resembled a script capital Q, and pursued a circuitous, back road-sy route to my apartment. As we did, I felt guilty when I caught myself not thinking about Miss Iceland's well-being, the damage to her car, or by whom and why we were attacked, but instead worried how this would affect the likelihood of sex. This surprised me in that, as an average-looking introvert in rural America, I could go months, even years, without female contact, all the while standing on my head, whistling the theme song to *The Patty Duke Show* until cousins, indeed, started looking pretty good. So much about these last thoughts made me think women were wise to avoid me, but before I could mull this into a fine powder, we had reached my parking lot.

We pulled into adjacent spots, and Miss Iceland was out of her car and coming around my driver's side, as I emerged gingerly, such as I knew how to do anything in that manner, squeezing the bridge of my nose.

"Are you alright?" she asked, immediately.

Her concern was touching, but I was incapable of playing the hero. "My nose banged the steering wheel when he hit me," I half whined.

"Were you wearing your seatbelt?"

"Uh, no. But that's my father's fault, he always said he preferred to be 'thrown clear.' In case of fire or what not. He'd have been 70 last month," I fake lamented with a smirk. "Besides, it's hard to get parts for this thing. I think my unlicensed mechanic used the driver's side one as a fan belt last time she broke down."

Miss Iceland surveyed the rear of our cars, as I followed surveying the rear of her. From behind, it looked like we'd just had a run-in with the Malachi Brothers, while in no way exhibiting the cool of Pinky and The Fonz. In fact, we were experiencing a case of not unexpected gender role reversal, with me shaky and weak-kneed, and Miss Iceland angry and vengeful, and here I thought she wouldn't feel that way till after we'd slept together.

"Who the Hell was that?" she seethed over her chewed up fender and deeply dented trunk. "I'll bet it was those construction guys that looked at me when they were leaving."

"In their defense everyone was looking at you in Pete's. You just happened to notice them. Did you get a plate number or a description of the truck? I remember a white Dodge in the lot when we arrived."

She turned on me like a badger, or at least in a way I thought of a badger turning, since outside a University of Wisconsin football game, who the heck ever sees a badger. "Sorry, I wasn't taking copious notes, while they tried to ram me up your ass, like a gerbil on Fire Island."

I let the homophobic remark go because, first off, she wasn't that and, second, she, at that moment, ran her two hands through her spectacular blonde hair causing me to think of the word "cascade," which, having never owned a dishwasher, was not one I used or thought of often, if ever.

As I watched the gilded locks rain down over her shoulders, she regained her composure and said evenly, "But, you know, this does mean we're on to something. Whoever came after us was trying to send a message." At this she smiled, and I blanched. I barely liked people coming close to me let alone after me.

We moved over to my car to assess the damage. However, determining so amongst the dents, dings, and chipped paint was futile. Then she shifted emotional gears yet again, and looked as if she was about to cry.

"You saved me," she stammered, looking into my eyes.

I was trying to placate these varying feelings, but it was like those novelty birthday candles, blow one out and another lights up. "'Save' is a powerful word," I started before finishing torturously. "Let's just say I, uh, un-prolonged your, ah, vulnerableness."

This checked the tears, and she drew me near, delivering a uvula rattling kiss that woke up Mr. Peabody, so to speak.

As soon as I was able to extricate my keys from my left-front jeans pocket—I tended to lean to the portside—we were upstairs, with clothing trailing behind us, like a horny Hansel and Gretel. As I mentioned, it had been a long time between amorous encounters, but I fell back on the old cliche about riding a bike, to see me through. Of course, some women are tricky like a unicycle, some are easy like a Schwinn 3-speed, and some are like those gay-90s bikes with the giant wheel in front—just climbing on them is such a feat, you had little energy left for anything else. Miss Iceland, though, was like a sleek 10-speed, and though I'd never been good at riding those, she put *me* up on the handlebars and did all the work. This was fine with me. When it came to sex with a woman like Miss Iceland—top, bottom, watching from outside through a window—it didn't matter. Like a boil on Scarlett Johansson's butt, I was just happy to be here.

In a lip lock, we passed the bedroom door, which was a good thing, since the "bed," was two stacked mattresses on the floor, and the possibilities linen-wise were my childhood NFL team sheets or nothing. Meanwhile her shirt was off, and I ran my hands slowly over the curves at her sides and the small of her back—so pronounced and smooth were they, it felt like I was driving a freshly paved Lombard Street. We veered toward the kitchen table, as I tried to undo my pants to the point of easy removal, but not so much that they'd fall, and we'd tumble over backward. Sex was harder as you got older, so I was overjoyed she didn't want to climb up on the table. Not that I didn't enjoy a little kink, but it took Kayla and I 15 sweaty minutes to get positioned there once, only for her to immediately start yelling, "Get off, get off me please!" And I looked down to see I was kneeling on her hand.

Finally, she stopped the bike—to continue the metaphor—at the living room sectional, threw me down, and slipped off my jeans. She then mounted a different kind of banana-seat (hence the metaphor continuation) and when she leaned over me, all golden hair, full breasts, and creamy skin it was over. Uh, I mean in my heart, not the other way.

So, I laid back and enjoyed the sweet beginning. Of course, the middle is where I screwed up, leading to an inevitable end, but for now I was going to take it one screw at a time.

Chapter 14: Clues For The Clueless

If every new relationship does start with a sweet beginning, then this one should've come with an insulin pump. We arrived at my place early Saturday evening and didn't emerge until Monday morning. Thereby establishing a new Women's Record for consecutive hours in my apartment, made even more impressive by the fact I was present the entire time.

Coming out, I noticed my neighbor, Housecoat Helen, peering through her blinds in disbelief. I clasped my hands around Miss Iceland's lower back, and posed with her for Helen's benefit, like models in an advertisement. She looks like the naturally beautiful, outdoorsy, Eddie Bauer catalog type, and I, like one who should be modeling socks on the radio.

We lingered that way on the walk (heck, I didn't want only Helen to get a look), to go over the plans we'd worked out over the weekend, in between tumbles between my theoretical sheets.

She began authoritatively, "I'll go up to Burlington to check on the Archdiocese; why they sold the building and who they sold it to. Then I'll swing by the State Police barracks up there. I still have my press credentials and I'll try to see why they took the locals' word on the murder-suicide theory. Meanwhile you…"

"I know, I know go to the high school and see what Barton found at the house. You don't have to nag," I moaned, semi-facetiously.

"I don't nag," she said, in a tone that seemingly made my point. But I was too experienced to get into that little Circle of Hell. Besides she didn't nag, really. Heck except during meals (I ordered in, my fridge containing only beer, pickles, and ketchup), we hardly conversed the whole weekend. On Sunday, the true journalist that she was, she consumed the entire Boston Globe, while I sat on the sofa and finally started Rebecca West's 1158 page classic travelog *Black Lamb and Grey Falcon*, that I had previously employed for crushing bugs (it was bought at a garage sale for 50 cents, when I realized on a cost per page basis, I couldn't pass it up). Unaccountably, from her standpoint mostly, we just enjoyed being together to the point I was having a hard time getting a pause in edgewise.

I felt this was maturing, so when she leaned in to kiss me goodbye, I avoided reaching for that plum of an ass, so as not to stunt the growth (though, it now occurs to me, writing that about that segment of her anatomy may have killed the effect, in and of itself). I could have stared at her pale visage all morning, but she broke my reverie with an all too real-world question.

"How is the money situation?"

"That's Gladys's department," I deflected. "But if I had to pin it down in a word I'd go with—'bleak'."

"Hmm," she breathed, wrinkling her nose as she thought.

"Hmm, indeed," I said, pretending I was thinking as well.

"What if we start, like, one of those GoFundMe pages—uh, have you ever done one of those before?"

"Actually, I have a page like that in my name, but that's on the 'Go Fuck Me' website created by a coupla ex-girlfriends," I cracked. "Don't think we want to hit them up for help."

"Well then, this is gonna be a problem."

"Ya think..."

Sarcasm was reflexive in me. She broke free and began walking away which, in turn, seemed reflexive in women privy to my sarcasm.

Suddenly, something that got lost in the weekend's exchanging of mucosal fluids, popped into my head. I called out trying to save the moment, though speaking has never been my best option in such instances, "Hey, you texted on Friday that you had big news. You never told me what it was."

"Oh yeah," she said, entering her car and putting the window down electronically, as if to taunt me and the Falcon simultaneously. "I quit the paper. Now I can devote myself to solving this thing full time."

She blew a kiss, which I pretended to catch and put in my pocket, before switching gears, pulling out the waist of my jeans and miming dropping it down there. With that the window went up, the car pulled away and I stood there dumbfounded. It was like being in that Franz Kafka story, where the protagonist wakes to find everything changed and can't figure out what's happened, which, come to think of it, is pretty much all of them. One second, I was wrapping Miss Iceland in my arms. The next second she was wrapping me in a cocoon of commitment. Now we could work together, play together, even, good God, live together. My only thought was. Where can I get Febreze?

By the time I waved, she was halfway to Canada, so I quickly pulled my hand down and looked for any witnesses. Spotting none, I made my way around to the driver's side of the Falcon. There I was confronted by an

8.5" x 11" manila envelope plastered to the window. I pulled it away carefully—the Demolition Derby of Friday still on my mind—but instead of the tearing sound of tape breaking free, I had the distinct feeling the envelope was adhered with some kind of paste. Looking over the missive, I saw a viscous brown substance had been used, and it was then I realized, with ironically sphincter-tightening distress, that the Mad Shitter (from Chapter 5) had returned.

I happily found my dented trunk still opened, pulled out a sweat-stained softball shirt that declared I was a member of the 2002 Businessman's B-Division Slo-Pitch champs—no wonder Miss Iceland couldn't keep her hands off me—and returned to the package. First, I inhaled deeply through my mouth and held my breath. Next, I separated said package from the window gingerly—a mode I never knew I had—and wiped the window and back of the package with the t-shirt. Finally, I laid the package in the trunk, looked right then left, saw no one, dropped the t-shirt on the ground, hopped behind the wheel and pulled out.

I'd look at the contents of the envelope at the office, after calling around for a Hazmat suit. Actually, I was glad the Mad Shitter was back. Not just for the potential clue, but to possibly meet the man with such bowel control.

Fifteen minutes, and a tollbooth collector's shift worth of gas fumes later, I pulled the Falcon into the rear lot of the office. The engine shut off with the automotive equivalent of an exhausted groan. Hopefully Miss Iceland had a savings account, I mused.

Inside I was met by my staff, such as was left of it, wearing the combined look of folks pulling up to the DMV inspection line on the last day of the month. Gladys sat at her desk; her mouth pursed into a web of wrinkles. Sandy Molesworth had a flank hoisted up on one of the new desks that hadn't gotten much use, filing her nails. Our photog, Charlie Grissom, leaned against the counter stirring coffee, his comb-over looking like he had slapped a dozen strands of whole wheat angel hair pasta across his head.

No sooner had I stepped into the room then they pounced. At least they hadn't bothered to notice the envelope I carried well out in front of me and stashed inconspicuously on a file cabinet. Such was their enthusiasm to rip me a new one.

"Where have you been all weekend?" Gladys started in.

I didn't have time to open my mouth—probably a good thing—before our lone reporter Sandy Molesworth answered. "I heard he was with his bleach blonde floozy all weekend."

Considering Sandy had enough spray tan and hairspray on, that she walked around with her own private hole in the ozone above her, like a climate change denying Schleprock, the hair remark was uncalled for. I passed it over to focus on the second insult though. "If we're gonna talk in 1930s slang I prefer skirt, dame or hotsy-totsy. But she has a name you know, it's, er, um, Miss Iceland," I finally blurted out.

At least Charlie Grissom thought this was funny and snorted into his coffee cup. The women, on the other hand, were having none of it.

"We're going under here and you're out there playing doctor," Sandy cackled, getting on my nerves.

"Doctor, really? How freakin' old are you?" I shot back. I didn't care about Sandy Molesworth. She delivered some decent copy, and the fact she was banging half the legislature in Montpelier, gave us an in up there. Mostly, though, she just liked to put a pencil behind her ear, don a pair of those Ashleigh Banfield rectangular glasses, and prance around town playing reporter. "Besides, what have you been doing?"

"We've been brainstorming."

"In your case it's more like a drizzle," I countered, and turned to Gladys. "What's the state of our finances?"

"Bleak at best," Gladys responded.

"Hey, that's exactly the word I used to describe it."

"Oh great, now I'm thinking like you. We really are doomed."

I had had enough, and not only because I'm always amazed "had had" is proper English. I snatched the package off the file cabinet, grabbed a beer from the fridge, and with a nod to my only seeming ally, Charlie Grissom, I stormed into my office. I tried to slam the door, but the cheap, hollow plywood caught against its own wind, and I had to back kick it shut. Just one more thing to piss me off.

Sitting at my desk, I was relieved to notice the envelope didn't smell. I might have cried if it had. All the weight was at the bottom where a compact, rectangular object resided. I squeezed but there was no give. So, unless it was a petrified turd, this was something the Mad Shitter wanted me to see. A clue? At this point, I wasn't sure I'd know a clue if Colonel Mustard hit me over the head with one in the conservatory. Nonetheless, I held my breath and opened the package.

Halfway down was a once-folded piece of paper, which I removed, revealing a gun-metal gray object I was all too familiar with—a cell phone, more precisely a flip phone. Opening the note, I found the message: "Is this yours?" in childish, lower-case letters across the fold, like a ransom letter from e.e. cummings. Now, I never won any penmanship awards in school—that capital script "Q," that looked like a big number 2, tripped me up every time—but this shaky correspondence seemed to come from a 5-year-old with Parkinson's.

Looking down into the envelope again, it obviously wasn't my phone. Not to brag (as if I could), but mine was a sleeker, antennae-less upgrade in classic black. This one was the kind I had prior—gun-metal gray and thicker. I opened it and pushed the red END key to turn it on, but the battery was dead. The fact that I had a flip phone was a running joke around town. Even in this semi-rural burg, everyone but the oldest of timers had iPhones, and the old bastards, like Wes Willard and his gang, had nothing. Whenever my cell rang with its generic, default rock song in Pete's Pub, someone would snatch it from me, answer and say, "It's 2003 calling to say get a freakin' real phone." I countered by claiming they could put their kids off constant upgrades by stating, "Look at poor Mr. Williams, he still has a flip phone," like I was analogous to the "poor (insert Third World Country) kids" our parents threw out at us when we wanted ColecoVision.

So, anyone could have left it. Someone either playing a joke, or actually finding this phone, and thinking it could only be mine. But why the unsigned note and why attach it to my car as they had? Was it the Mad

Shitter? Or, like the Kennedy Assassination, was there a mysterious Second Shitter? Maybe there was a Crap-ruder film out there? —OK, I'll stop now.

It was all too much. I sat back, took a swig of the Natty Ice, and pondered my future. At this point, I couldn't work for anyone else. That lazy ship sailed long ago. There was my idea for a Procrastinating Writer's Workshop, but then everyone would attend the "next" meeting and write me a check "later"—so that was a no-go. I considered again, querying Shark Tank about funding my Elf on The Shelf-like marital aid, Whore in The Drawer—find the correct drawer and get a bedroom surprise that evening. But my major character traits—snark, sarcasm, self-deprecation—didn't play well in a sales environment.

To Hell with it, I thought, I'd just keep plowing ahead and throw myself on the mercy of Miss Iceland—and her couch—if the whole thing went bust. With that, I chucked the note and phone back in the envelope, snapped it up under my arm, like a German Field Marshal with a riding crop, and headed off to Artfield High to meet Ted Sheehan's friend Barton.

Exiting my office, I tossed the empty beer can in the trash, and in keeping with the day's theme, Sandy Molesworth was right there with a wisecrack.

"What happened? Your 'Brain Juice' didn't induce any bright ideas?"

"Screw you and the whore you came in as," I snapped back. Gladys gasped. Sandy was, for once, speechless. While Charlie Grissom snort-laughed again, which was nice to hear because I was non-confrontational overall and wasn't sure, in my new-found anger, my comment made any sense. I opened the screen door to the parking lot, stepped out, and this time, due to a perpetually broken spring, was able to slam my way out.

I was just easing myself into the Falcon when Grissom came out and called to me. "Can I tag along? Too much simmering estrogen in there for me." I motioned for him to get in, so he tossed his coffee cup in the dumpster, and jogged around to the passenger side.

"Where're we going?" he inquired, but I don't think he cared.

"Artfield High," I said through gritted teeth, and was pleased when Charlie didn't ask why. As a retiree, he was just happy to be out of the house and away from his wife. The office had provided no solace, so like a dog, he jumped in the open car door and was just thrilled to be there. Hell, I think he would have stuck his head out the window if it wouldn't have blown his comb-over all to crap.

We arrived at the school in a blissful silence that allowed me to calm down. Inside, we went through everything short of a body cavity search, before we were issued Visitor passes—thank you Trench Coat Mafia and other trigger-happy punks for that—then Charlie went to the faculty lounge to poke around, while I set off for Barton's room.

Surprisingly, I found the room through the labyrinth of identical hallways, and peered into the vertical window that ran from the top of the door to just above the handle. I could see Barton's head just above the shoulder of a gangly kid in a long t-shirt and lounge pants. He saw me and motioned me in, as he finished with the student. Surveying the class, I noticed something looked different, but like my parents when I was in high school ("...maybe just once you could wear a collared shirt, even open-necked..."), I had no clue regarding today's fashion. Then the student stepped away, and I saw Barton, in a terry cloth robe and slippers with silk pajamas peeking out at the chest and ankles.

"It's Pajama Day," he offered, noticing my confusion. "I used to not participate, but then I'd feel like an orderly in a mental institution. I mean more so than usual." He smiled at the class, who obviously had never seen *One Flew Over the Cuckoo's Nest*, so I ditched my Chief impression ("mmm, Juicy Fruit"), as they used the distraction to surreptitiously ease their phones out of pockets and pencil cases.

"Well, I guess I fit in, since this is what I slept in last night," I half-joked.

"At least you don't sleep in the nude, like your friend Max Lipper threatens to do, before these events."

I suppressed a laugh by asking, "What are you teaching them today?"

"Well, these seniors were about to continue with *Hamlet*, until someone said we left off at Act 'eye-eye,' Scene three, so we transitioned to a mini-lesson about Roman numerals," he said, indicating the board.

"Yeah, you gotta know your Roman numerals."

A fat kid in the front row, wearing pajama bottoms and an 'I Beat Anorexia' t-shirt, immediately spouted, "Why?"

"How are you gonna know which Super Bowl it is?" I deadpanned to some nods and chuckles. I thought I could get into this teaching thing. It was like doing stand-up comedy without heckling, since the audience counted on you for good grades. I filed it away as an option, if/when (we were getting to that point) the paper went completely under.

Barton had moved to his desk, no doubt anxious to be rid of me and my possible impression on developing minds. He pulled a manila folder, like the one the phone came in, from a bottom drawer and handed it to me. I took it by a corner, which I'm sure Barton thought strange, but once shit on, twice shy, was the motto I never thought I'd have to live by.

"Police pretty much cleaned the place out," Barton whispered, so as not to alarm the kids. "It was in a locked file drawer in his basement office. I had a key. Just papers, but maybe it's important."

The fat kid was jamming a pencil in the electric sharpener over and over, in a way Freud could have written a dissertation on, so I barely heard Barton's words above the drone.

"That's enough Brendan," Barton mildly scolded. The kid pulled the pencil out and admired a point that could be used to dress a deer. Meanwhile, I headed to the door looking for the old manual sharpener that invariably went dull on one side and left students in that "sharpen, pull out point, sharpen again" conundrum. Kids are soft these days.

In the hallway, I debated looking for Lip in the gym, when Grissom wandered around a corner, coffee affixed to hand. "I just saw a kid wearing overalls," Charlie mused. "Is that in style again?"

"Either that or he's in a Dexy's Midnight Runners cover band," I listlessly joked. Too tired for Max Lipper's perpetual exuberance, I motioned toward an exit. "Come on, let's get out of here."

Crossing the students' parking lot, I noted the preponderance of muddy pickups and thought those would be joined, incongruously, by BMWs and Mercedes, once Rick James' development was fully populated.

Unless the rich still sent their kids to boarding schools, like in those Evelyn Waugh books that claim to be "Uproariously funny," but only deliver a few pissy, British "Gee, that's clever," moments.

Charlie Grissom was going off about some well-endowed co-ed wearing lingerie, but I steered clear, thinking once the paper went belly-up and Miss Iceland inevitably grew weary of me, I'd be substituting here to pay the rent. In the car, I opened the envelope, and as Barton said, it was full of miscellaneous paper. There were letters from state and federal agencies, with acronyms I didn't recognize, and pamphlets depicting houses like you'd see along the beach in Newport, Rhode Island. There were also several dozen chicken-scratched Post-It notes that kept falling onto and, considering the state of disrepair, nearly through, the floor of the Falcon. So, I shoved everything back inside, fastened the clasp, and tossed it in the backseat.

I sighed, which is something I rarely do, and sadly I didn't know what it meant when written out in *Peanuts* comic strips until I was twenty-two (why is Snoopy always saying 'sig-hah' to Woodstock? I pathetically thought). Then I became very chagrined (can one be a little chagrined?) as we drove off. With the acquisition of the phone and this packet of miscellany, plus whatever Miss Iceland brought back, it seemed we had gone from too little to too much evidence in one leap. I often had trouble seeing the proverbial forest for the trees, and now I felt as if I'd been dropped in an Amazon jungle, or warehouse—whichever is harder to get out of—it's probably a tie.

Charlie, sensing my unease, offered up his unsolicited advice. "Well, when I was at the *Albany Times-Journal*," he started. This was usually my cue to tune out, like my sister and I used to do when our grandfather would start a story, "Back when I worked at the foundry" a place that produced what, I'm still not sure, and seemed to employ an inordinate number of fellows named Smokey and Dutch. Grissom went on, "I worked with the investigative reporters on, you know, political scandals, corruption, that kinda thing. Anyway, at some juncture, they'd lay out all the evidence, their notes, my photos, and try to make out the big picture. I think you've reached that point."

I thought about it, and he was right. We had a couple of weeks left on the office lease, a couple of days left on the money front, and no one was stepping forward to pony up more. We had evidence, suspects, motives, and theories, but never tried putting them in any coherent order. So, I realized, it was time for me, and only me, to lay them all out and make a bold, decisive move. God help us all.

After dropping Grissom at the office, I headed home. On the way it all seemed so simple: spread everything out, list the suspects, columns for MOTIVES and MEANS, notebooks, index cards, heck, I'd even break out some colored highlighters, if I had, or could find them. Miss Iceland would be so proud. When she showed up, I'd put on a show.

Then I got home, cracked a Natty Ice, and it was a show alright —A Shit Show.

First, I sliced my finger on a box cutter I never knew I had, while scouring my junk drawer for colored highlighters (uncovering one, orange, dry). I found all of two index cards, then rummaged through a stack of notebooks, each containing failed attempts at the Great American Novel, plus a few disturbingly erotic doodles. I did manage to locate three pencils larger than miniature golf size, and a pencil sharpener from grade school, housed in a tiny, plastic Buffalo Bills helmet (the old one with the buffalo just standing there taking a dump).

I took the beer, pencils, sharpener, and least salacious notebook, to the sofa. I laid them all out on my plywood plank across two milk crates, passing for a coffee table, and stared. I figured I'd start with suspects, and I turned the notebook landscape—er, portrait, no, landscape, uh—with the binding at the top. I wrote three names and crapped out, with three-quarters of the page left. So, I erased what I'd written and turned the notebook back, um, 'normal-ways' and started again: CHIEF BOWDEN, RICK JAMES, REPORTER JEREMY, CURLY CARSON (because it could actually be as the Artfield PD said)—and finally REVEREND BROOKS (just because I needed a name to balance the page, and he was nutty enough to be involved somehow).

At this point my beer can was empty, and I found a random Cheese Doodle (puffed, not crunchy) of indiscriminate age, poking out from under the sofa. I knew I should throw out both the can and the Doodle, but I was too tired. So, I pushed the beer to the corner of the makeshift coffee table, ate the Doodle when it wouldn't fit in the top of the can, swung my legs up, and took a nap.

Maybe I didn't want Miss Iceland taking over my life, but it was looking more and more like I damned sure needed it!

204

Chapter 15: On Crotch Shots And Gordian Knots

I napped the kind of nap that makes ambition seem ridiculous. I dreamed of Hail Mary TD passes, game-winning home runs, and buzzer-beating baskets. It didn't take the combined minds of Carl Jung and Dr. Phil to discern, I knew we needed a miracle. So, when I awoke to find Miss Iceland sitting on the edge of the couch sorting through the clues I'd assembled, she looked like Tom Brady, David Ortiz and Larry Bird rolled into one with a pale, blonde downy neck I wanted to kiss passionately (I mean, of course, Miss Iceland, though I'm sure Mr. Bird's neck does resemble that description).

Suddenly, she turned to me confused and said, "What the Hell is all this?"

Not exactly the "Eureka!" moment I was hoping for, and if this were a football, I might have suggested we just punt. Unfortunately, that was not an option at this point.

"It's the stuff we gathered about the murders," I said tentatively, like the first time, or to be truthful, all the times I've ordered at Starbucks ("uh, is Venti a size or a type of coffee?"). "I thought if we laid it all out, between the two of us, we could make something of it."

"Freakin' hell!" was her only comment, I think, for at that moment she ran her hands through that long, straight, golden hair, and suddenly the situation's desperation was fighting my ever-present sexual desperation for center stage.

I fought back my amorous attraction long enough to ask, "What did you come up with in your travels?" At this point, I tried to innocuously rub the sleep from my eyes, but she caught me and looked disappointed.

"Not much," she stated. "My contact at the State Police said, as far as he recalls, investigators reviewed the locals' theory, and from crime scene photos, ballistics, and some messages the Artfield PD collected, it all checked out. Monica Carson was having an affair with Sheehan, her father caught wind of it, confronted them at Sheehan's house and shot the place up."

"But we know that's not true. Sheehan was gay!"

"Listen, homo-, hetero-, bi- or pan-sexual I don't care. I'm tellin' you what they said."

"Pan-sexual? Is that like doing it on the stove?"

She looked at me like I was in my early hundreds, and said, "Jesus, you gotta get outta this apartment and this town more."

That wasn't my plan at all. Though I'd often made jokes about Artfield, this whole ordeal had finally made me appreciate this town and the folks in it, despite the flaws. I'd gone away to college, I'd worked and lived in Boston, I'd traveled a little, partied often, dated many, and had my fun. But as a philosophic Derf once put it, "Fun? It's not all it's cracked up to be." It wasn't, compared to finding a home, and this was mine. It was too late, and I was too tired (read: lazy and/or broke) to start over again. So, whether this community was being destroyed from within or without—and I felt in my bones something was being done to change it for the worse—I was going to find out, or become a jaded, disenchanted, manic depressive with a growing alcohol problem if I didn't. Heck, but for Miss Iceland, I was practically there.

The State Police were obviously a dead end, so I turned my questioning to her other fact-finding mission. "Were you able to find out who bought the church building?"

"Yes," she began while taking a cursory look through the mess I'd made on the table. "Some investment group–stupid name, something with a bird in it."

"Who are the principals?" I queried gently. My questions, or my napping on the couch with a beer can beside me, seemed to be pissing her off. Based on experience, probably both.

"I had to call Montpelier to get the info. They said it was a private LLC and they aren't authorized to give out the names of the principals. The address is a P.O. Box in Burlington."

"A private LLC, it figures," I said, as if I knew what those letters stood for. Watching her profile, Mr. Peabody stood at Parade Rest, as they say in the military, but any chance of his receiving the "Ten-Hut" command, quickly went by the boards.

"Oh, and I got an estimate on the damage to my car," she said, in a tone that precluded anything good following. "It'll be $1800. That's all I have in my savings. Did you ever find out who owns that white pickup that rammed us?"

My plan to be a gigolo, a prohibitive longshot at best, dead, I began to stammer until a plausible lie came to me, "Uh, no, but I got some guys down at Pete's working on it."

Realizing such a feeble defense couldn't hold long, and not being the most quick-minded around beautiful, or any women for that matter, I began to sort through the items on the table. In particular, I pushed her way the phone and the packet of papers from Ted Sheehan's house Barton had found, as those were the two things, I did accomplish on the case today. I hoped she was buying my Potemkin efforts, when my flip phone rang. It was my sister, and I walked to the kitchen, debating whether to answer. Seeing as Miss Iceland hadn't softened, but Mr. Peabody had, I picked up and regretted it immediately. She wanted a favor.

"Can you come over and watch the kids," she blurted out over crying, wailing and general mayhem.

"I'm kinda tryin' to save my livelihood right now," I said, without much conviction. I could never muster up drama at will. "Can't someone else, do it?"

"Oh, you're probably out with your Peroxide Princess, I bet."

"Why is everyone so fixated on her hair?" I questioned. "She's got tits and an ass, you know!"

"Yeah, and so does my husband, but you don't wanna hear about those. I gotta run Old Lady Murchison to the vet. Her cat's been dying for three months now and with any luck this'll be it. She's out in the driveway sobbing, so I'm leaving now. Get here before the kids burn this shithole down."

She hung up, and as the last part was no idle threat, I grabbed my keys. Miss Iceland had pulled the brochures and paperwork from the envelope Barton had taken from Sheehan's house. I was anxious to see if she could make something of it, and as my presence was only serving to distract and annoy her, I was at the stairs before I told her I was leaving.

"I've gotta go watch my sister's kids. I'll be back in about an hour," I said, one foot on the stairs.

She didn't seem too thrilled about this, but asked, "Do you want me to go with you?"

"No, stay here and go through the info. Besides you might wanna have kids one day, and one hour with my sister's brats and your ovaries'll seal up like a mayonnaise jar on Funk & Wagnalls porch." I knew she wouldn't get the reference (Johnny Carson's Carnak), but the subsequent confused look gave me just enough time to sneak out and leave the heavy lifting to her. As I descended the stairs, I tried to think if it was safe to leave her in my place alone, where she could snoop around. Then I considered: no porn videos, no nudie mags, no sex toys. Maybe she was right, I should get out more often.

I entered my sister's house about eight minutes later and heard my nephews barreling towards me from two rooms away. I immediately covered my testicles. Maybe I should rephrase that: my testicles were covered clothes-wise, but I struck a pose like soccer players taking on a penalty kick. That's because said nephews were in a pro wrestling phase, or more dangerously a pro wrestling video game phase. Now I don't like to brag, but I'm kind of a squared-circle savant and could believably "sell" a blow, as they say in biz. Unfortunately, at their height and limited reach, these callow clouts all seemed to cluster around my tender parts, and with the accession of Miss Iceland, I currently needed those parts in relatively functioning order.

Huey, Dewey, and Louie, for an inability to remember and/or care about their real names, came charging into the kitchen screaming. "Uncle Luke! Uncle Luke! Uncle Luke!" they exclaimed in ear-piercing stereo.

"Yeah, what?" I said, sternly. This brought them up short, sock-sliding to a halt on the linoleum floor. I'd heard an elementary school teacher say, the best way to control a class is to not smile until November. The tone having been set, I removed my hands from my aforementioned testicular region, and grinned at them. I mean I'm not a monster.

A couple more stifled "Uncle Luke's" were released before Ryan (I think) spoke, "When are we going to get to stay at your home?"

He was playing fast and loose with the word home, but as they all chimed in, I cut them off again. "My house is filled with fire and broken glass. Kids aren't allowed there." As they pondered this, I considered whether they were too young to know any better, or thought I was the kind of person that might live in such a place.

"How 'bout Halloween? Can we come over then? Do you give out candy?" asked the middle one (Ryan II, I'll call him).

"Yeah," I said, pretending to wet a pen on my tongue and then write on my hand. "Note to self: Get razor blades. OK, see you then."

At least I was having fun.

"Who wants to play the wrestling video game?" I said, since this was the only bonding experience I could think of, with them not the type to enjoy a reading from Dostoyevsky, say.

"Me. Me. Me"

"OK, go set it up and I'll be there in a minute."

"I'm gonna be John Cena," said Ryan I.

"I wanna be Goldberg," cried Ryan II, and they ran off pulling Ryan III in their wake.

As I moved into the dining room and took off my coat, I had to laugh. While living with Derf in Boston, Bill Goldberg was in his wrestling heyday. Walking in one day, Derf pointed at the TV and asked, "Goldberg, do you think that's his real name?"

Never one to look gift sarcasm in the mouth, I replied, "No, I think he changed it to that for wrestling. Probably thought 'Let's see they have The Rock, Stone Cold, The Undertaker—I'm thinking something Jewish might work'."

Then, as I went to hang my jacket over a dining room chair, something caught my attention. It was a note written by my brother-in-law Andrew to my sister. It wasn't the content that was of interest— 'hon, pick up steak and burgers i will grill tonight.' It was the style: child-like scrawl, no caps.

Immediately, I pulled out my phone, flicked my wrist, and flipped it open (I don't care, I still think it looks cool) to call Miss Iceland.

After exchanging pleasantries, I began tenuously. "Hey, what's going on?"

"Just trying to sort out this pile of crap you left me," she replied, testily. Then on a positive note added, "I think I figured out what's in this packet the teacher, Barton, gave you."

"Great. Do you have the note that was with the flip phone there?" I asked, hurriedly.

"Yeah, and you're welcome," she replied, with a trace of exasperation with me that I shrugged off as inevitable. Papers shuffled, then, "Wait, what note?"

"The one that was in the manila envelope with the phone. I found it on my car this morning after you drove off. Didn't you look inside?"

"I did. I just assumed you forgot your phone in the rush to leave me here with everything."

This was not going well. I pined for a Natty Ice. Fearing the bloom was bidding farewell to the proverbial rose between us, I took a deep, not nearly as satisfying, breath and spoke calmly. "Why would I leave my phone in a manila envelope?"

"Based on the state of your car and apartment, I figured you were marching to the beat of a whole different drum corps, so I chalked it up to your, uh, idiosyncratic nature, shall we say?"

"OK, you got me where the hair is short there, but now dump that envelope and look at the note," I said.

"That's disgusting," she sneered, regarding the first half of my statement, but carried out the second half as I heard the envelope crackle and the phone hit the plywood with a thud. "OK, I have the note. You want me to read it to you?"

"No, I read it already. Just tell me is it all in lowercase?"

"Yes."

"Does it look to you like a 3rd grader wrote it?"

"To be generous, yeah."

I examined the note to my sister again. "Are the T's crossed low so they look like plus signs."

"There's one T and it could be a plus sign or a crucifix for a midget."

"Freakin' Andrew," I blurted out.

"Are you done playing CSI, and mind telling me what this is about?"

"My brother-in-law Andrew, I told you, he's a cop in town. Based on the writing, he's the one who left that on my car," I informed her.

"Wait, didn't Monica Carson have a flip phone on her, or near her, at the crime scene? That fat cop at the door told us about it."

"Fat cop? This is Artfield you're going to have to be more specific," I wisecracked. My inveterate jokiness out of the way, I saw she had a point. "Yeah, that's right Woody Maynard was there keeping people away. He mentioned that when I pulled out my phone."

"I always thought that it was strange why anyone under 60, um, present company excluded, let alone a 24-year-old girl, would have a flip phone," she pondered. "I meant to check that out, but then the newspaper pulled me from the story."

I heard more "Uncle Luke's" from the living room, and figured I hadn't long till the three snotnoses dragged me away. I couldn't figure out why Andrew would give me such a potentially explosive piece of evidence, but Miss Iceland, without such complacent thoughts rattling around her head, had already moved on.

"How do you turn this on?"

"I tried, no charge. Go into the kitchen. Try my current charger. It's on the kitchen table," I said.

"You didn't try your charger?" she growled slowly, in a voice I heard Gladys, girlfriends, my mother, and assorted others of the distaff set, use all too often. "How friggin' lazy are you?"

"In grade school, whenever we did a report on a President, I chose William Henry Harrison. So don't be afraid to set the bar real low. Are you at the kitchen table?"

"When it has a hole in the center for an umbrella, it's a patio table. All I see are newspapers."

"If you're going to criticize my decor, we'll never get this case solved," I lamented. "Now look under the newspapers. Got it?"

"Yeah, it's no good. The phone has a female end and so does the charger. We need a male end to stick in the female end of the phone," she claimed, rather graphically, I thought.

"That's the second worst phone sex I've ever had," I declared.

"What was the worst?"

"Let's just say it was non-traditional and involved a free *Sports Illustrated* helmet phone, and copious amounts of Neosporin. Quick, go to the linen closet. There should be a box filled with junk on the floor there." For once, I thought, my laziness and hoarding instinct may have combined for something positive.

"You have linen?" she answered, starting to enjoy herself now. Suddenly I realized what it was like dating me, but without the good looks.

"It's a figure of speech. The closet by the bathroom."

I could hear her footfalls and the squeaking of the 60s era hardwood floors. "Yeah, yeah, I'm there. I pulled the box out. What am I looking for?"

"I may have the charger to my old phone in there," I answered. "It might work on this one."

I heard rummaging and then she released an exuberant "Oh my God!" making me think we really were having phone sex. "What is it?" I asked with trepidation. "Is there a big bug living behind the box? Kill it now before it hides somewhere else. I'll never sleep if that happens."

She pulled me back from what was not my finest moment, by incredulously asking, "You played minor league baseball?" She had uncovered my memories.

"Yes. One year with the Lake Havasu Gila Monsters in the Arizona Rookie League. The scouting report on me was 'He's small, but he's slow.' Undrafted free agents with that label are destined for the slo-pitch softball circuit," I informed her. "Now, look underneath and…"

But it was too late, and since she was having fun after our testy exchanges previously, I let her go on. "Wow, you graduated with honors from the University of Vermont?"

"Wow? You don't have to act so surprised."

"I wasn't acting," she said with added snark.

I responded with pomposity, "I'll have you know I also won the prestigious Biederman Scholarship in Journalism which I didn't use, but, alas, that was one score and 7000 beers ago."

"And what's this in the plastic sheet?"

"Don't touch that," I pronounced a little too forcefully. "That's my ticket stub from the '80s Palooza' event I attended in 1999 at Boston

Garden, signed by two of three members of Bananarama and a Thompson Twin. That could be worth something someday."

"You're kidding, right?"

"Hey, you don't know, one of them could freak out and kill a bunch of people, and I'll be laughing all the way to eBay." At this point I had enough of playing *This Is Your* (Pathetic) *Life* and decided to give her the abridged version, so we could get on with what I really wanted her to find in the box. "Listen, the program's from Game 1 of the 2004 World Series, the matchbook is a memory from a couple hours spent at the Fountain Motor Lodge, 'nuff said, and the legal release papers stem from a night in the Drunk Tank at Lake Placid Spring Break 2001, where some local named Tweety and I banged on the bars, singing Dylan's *Hurricane*, till they dropped charges and kicked us to the curb at five in the morning. He still sends me a Christmas card every year."

"Well, seems like you've lived a full life," she cracked.

"OK, now take that crap out, and see if you can find my old charger, among the wires and cords at the bottom."

"What the____?," she stopped short of the expletive out of shock and not decorum I believe. "This is worse than when I had to help my dad with the Christmas lights every year." She was talking about the plethora of wires I'd accumulated over the years and left in a tangle, which made Cobble's Knot in Jerry Spinelli's *Maniac Magee,* look like the twist-tie on Wonder Bread.

"It is a Gordian Knot, but I have confidence in you," I said, trying to summon something that sounded remotely like confidence.

"Do you even know what the Gordian Knot was," she spat. My silence indicating ignorance, she went on, "The Gordian Knot was tied by the god equivalent to Zeus and could not be undone for over a thousand years, until Alexander the Great chopped it in half with his sword in 333 BC."

"Uh, well, let's call that Plan B," I stammered. "You know, maybe see if you can work a finger in there first, or something."

She sighed so deeply, I could feel her breath bouncing off a satellite and coming through my phone. "I'll work on it," she said, in fading tones until the last thing I heard before she shut her phone off was a faint, "Freakin' Gordian Knot—what an ass!"

Well, I've had worse girlfriends, I thought. That's when the sound of sock-covered footsteps came padding down the hall, and stopped closer than anyone would want their kids to me. Another chorus of increasingly annoying and shrill "Uncle Luke's" later, I put my phone away, returned the note to the center of the table, and agreed to follow them to the den to take them on, in Greco-Cyber wrestling. That is, until my sister returned, and I could get back to my apartment, where I planned to take on Miss Iceland in some catch-as-catch-carnal excitement of our own.

Distracted by the thought of Miss Iceland's pale pulchritude, I dropped my guard long enough for Ryan 2.5 (not sure if it was II or III) to catch me with, what my high school baseball coach referred to as, a shot to the "cubes." It was my own fault, for suggesting we play a game that had a button labeled "Crotch Shot." As I hobbled knock-kneed off, to lay the proverbial smack down on some Ryan's ass in the game, suddenly sex was the last thing on my mind. However, unbeknownst to me, I'd be overwhelmed by it, in a way I never thought, when I finally got home.

Chapter 16: To All The Shitholes And Mine

"Jeezus," I screeched, looking down at the phone, and feeling dirty all over. Reading the text messages Miss Iceland had unearthed, I went through a gamut of emotions in seconds: embarrassment, anger, titillation, shame. Like your middle-aged neighbors showing you their sex tape, or watching Gorgeous Ladies of Wrestling–the original, not the Netflix comedy. "I need a friggin' Silkwood Shower after reading this!"

Miss Iceland was shocked. "Don't tell me that actually turned you on?"

"No," I began, then stopped. I was too tired for a history of 1970s cinema and the No-Nukes Movement, and frankly, she'd probably already broken it down to its component parts–Silk, Wood, Shower–so it was going to be a tough save anyway. "This is disgusting."

Miss Iceland had charged the flip phone Andrew had left me, and the messages on said phone were like reading *Penthouse* Forum without the bothersome storylines. I didn't know 80% of the acronyms used, but they seemed to have a lot of 'Fs' in them and I was able to deduce a few by context.

"No way Monica Carson wrote these texts," I stated, confidently. "This reads like the censored sections of *50 Shades of Grey*."

"Yeah, like you read *50 Shades of Grey*," Miss Iceland chuckled.

"How do you know what I read or didn't read?"

"So, what did you think of it?"

"Didn't like it," I facetiously lamented. "The plot had too many holes."

"Funny," she deadpanned, then had a thought. "Do we know Ted Sheehan's number? Are these texts from his phone? Could someone be trying to frame him for setting this whole tragedy in motion?"

I could see where this was going. I didn't have Sheehan's number, which was plausible, but I knew who had it. I had even met with him—Mr. Barton at Artfield High. That I didn't have his number was, uh, not so plausible. Exchanging digits, as they say, is an invitation to contact each other—something my misogyny wouldn't support. Hence, I owned a small-town weekly, while others wrote columns for the *Boston Globe*.

It's been said good things come to those that act. They didn't say anything about acting smart, as far as I recall. So, before she asked me for Barton's number, I reached across the sofa and tweaked Miss Iceland's breasts like I was an Amish kid on Rumspringa.

"What the heck are you doing?" She wasn't so much mad as confused.

This, surprisingly, was just what I was hoping for—an entry to sex would have been better, but that was more dreaming than hoping. Her train of thought broke, and I changed the subject. "You said you figured out what was in this envelope," I said, stashing the phone beneath some papers, and dumping the contents of the envelope Barton found in Ted Sheehan's desk, on the table.

"Fucking-A," she cried. "I had that all organized."

I tried putting it back as it had come out, but that seemed to make it worse, as is generally my M.O. with, what I sometimes think of as, the (un)fairer sex.

"Fucking-A again," she exclaimed. "Just don't touch it. Didn't you hear me?"

"I heard you. I just thought you were just reciting the official alphabet of Brooklyn—you know, Fucking-A, Fucking-B, Fucking-C."

As usual when I'd screwed up with women, my humor beaded up and rolled off Miss Iceland's back like she'd just bathed in Turtle Wax. At this point, I clapped my hands and held them up palm out, like a blackjack dealer at the end of a shift. She then sorted and organized things into two neat piles.

"OK," she began seemingly calmed, as I mentally filed a note on someday comparing our strains of OCD. She pointed to the smaller of the two stacks. "This is paperwork from The National Historic Register in D.C. The larger pile is from the Vermont Historical Society. The latter contains Determination of Eligibility Form #A3223-1, which is the first step toward getting a building put on the state list of historic sites. Sheehan had filled his name and address in at the top of five forms, but the rest of each form is blank."

While she was spewing this officious rhetoric, she had tied her hair up and stuck a pencil through the resultant bun. Wisps of blond hair that had eluded her grasp, fell about a neck that was so creamy, I was afraid I'd have to pop a Lactaid tablet before kissing it.

"Are you listening to me?"

"Yeah," I lied, while really wishing she wore glasses so she could tear them off and reenact Van Halen's "Hot for Teacher" video with me in the role of Waldo.

"Stop being a perv for two seconds," she'd caught me staring, teeth bared, at her neck, "and think about what this means. Ted Sheehan and Monica Carson were trying to get a building put on the Vermont or National Register of Historic Sites."

"Sheehan's house was built in the 1970s," I said. "I could see the shag carpeting through the windows."

"Well, they were trying to get some house on there, and maybe that pissed somebody off. You told me Monica Carson majored in Environmental Studies in college. It's just a hippie's hacky sack toss from there to historic preservation."

She said "hippie" in such a way that I felt my hair in the back. I could use a trim. She was obviously angling to the builder Rick James, as the mastermind behind a scare tactic gone horribly wrong. After all, he was in the business of buying up properties, and getting sued for it over and over, but I didn't see how this fit.

"If you're insinuating, they were trying to screw Rick James, they couldn't have been, and it's too late anyway," I began, authoritatively, which is not an adverb that is in my proverbial wheelhouse. "All the buildings, the home, barns, silo, on the Old Man Hillman's Farm, where James is constructing his McMansions, were torn down before the old Yankee bastard was in the ground. Besides, there was a fire at the main residence, and it was rebuilt all new, uh, I'd say 21 years ago. The underwear I'm wearing is older than that. Wanna preserve it too."

I thought I went too far with that last line, but she shocked me by saying, "I'm hungry. Let's get something to eat." Not the response I was expecting. In fact, whenever my undergarments have entered a confab previously, they've acted as an appetite suppressant. But I have to say I was pleasantly surprised. We might have something special here.

Outside I headed for my car, but, apparently, while talk of my skivvies made her hanker for a pastrami on rye, another frolic in the Falcon was where she drew the line. Instead, we hopped in her Jetta, which I was happy to note, was only a fraction less messy than the Falcon. Clean cars rub me the wrong way, though it was nice to have a door panel, and a side window, that could be adjusted without the need of a torque wrench. I immediately began to poke around, as was my custom, through the desultory distributed detritus—receipts, Post-It notes, fast food wrappers, the usual flotsam and/or jetsam of the working reporter.

Looking around further, her car had myriad features of which the Falcon could only dream: tripmeter, CD player, spare tire (I'm assuming), intricate temperature adjustment instruments, a functioning defroster, and various compartments our relationship wasn't established enough for me to stick my nose in, though, Lord knows, I felt the urge. In a well in the console, I found three CDs. As she backed out, I looked at them nervously, knowing if there was The Starship's "We Built This City," or some Brie-eating pantywaist like Michael Buble amongst them, it might irrevocably taint our relationship. Derf once had a girl break up with him because he threw her cassette of the Steve Miller Band's *Greatest Hits* out the window of her car upon noticing the phrase "funky shit" in the song "Jet Airliner" was dubbed over with "funky kicks," and I backed him in the matter. So, this was big.

The first CD was Norah Jones. I could live with that. Next was the soundtrack to the play *Hamilton*, some catchy tunes, and it played to my history buff side. The last was *Slowhand* by Eric Clapton, not my favorite by him, but I had to give her kudos.

"Nice. Listening to a little Clapton, I see," I said, smiling and waving the CD around like it was a tambourine, and I was Davy Jones on crack. It's just that I felt this relationship needed a sturdier foundation than our mutual fondness for sarcasm. Though I had ones that were built on less. "I like his stuff with Cream better, but this is a good entry point to his music. I played my nephews "Tales of Brave Ulysses" once. They had nightmares for a week. You can work your way up to that."

Not sure why I was rambling like Lester Bangs, but Miss Iceland was fast mastering the art of tuning most of me out, which could only work in my favor. "I just like the song 'Wonderful Tonight'," she replied. I had feelings for that song, as mentioned previously, but didn't this was appropriate time for my "3 Meanest Songs" rant.

I finally looked to discover she had had an ulterior motive (Am I the only one who thinks that should be "alterior?"). We were at Rick James' development, but mercifully the trailer/office looked closed. Miss Iceland continued past the gravel parking lot, and as is my wont with women, both mentally and physically, I had no idea where she was going.

"Where are we going?" I asked, prosaically. "James isn't in."

"I know, I called ahead. Reporters do things like that."

"Someone has quite the acid tongue," I replied, a little turned on for some reason. "Then what are we doing out here? Pete's Pub is on the other side of town."

"We'll get to your favorite shithole, narrowly edging out your car and apartment by the way, soon enough," she answered, turning up the Ph-level on her tongue several degrees. "Look around, are any of these homes old enough to qualify for the Historic Register?"

She had slowed to a crawl once we got past Rick James' development. The simple 1950/60s suburban-style houses were well-spaced, with good-sized yards filled with toys, swing sets and jungle gyms. I could, at last, see where she was going with this. If Rick James could have bought up some of these properties, even if they weren't contiguous with his current development, he would dominate the area—maybe put condos up that the upper middle classes would keep, or rent as weekend retreats, during ski and foliage seasons. Or, if he could get the town to agree, put up a commercial center with shopping, restaurants, and assorted other places I'd never patronize, and they wouldn't care. However, a few strategically placed, historically protected homes, could throw a monkey wrench in James' plans, and perhaps, that is what Sheehan and Monica Carson were up to. The problem was I couldn't tell a Cape Cod from a real cod, and I once lived in Gloucester, Massachusetts for 15 months.

"I don't know, uh, maybe that one," I said, pointing at a faux-Victorian.

"That house has vinyl siding, central air, a three-car garage, and is less than 25 years old."

"How do you know that?"

"It's on the realtor's sign," she exclaimed, shaking her head. "You ran the local paper; don't you know anything about this area."

"I believe I mentioned Pete's Pub is on the other side of town," I offered in my defense.

She sighed a sigh of frustration–or disappointment–or most likely both.

"Listen, I'm an apartment guy," I stated, foolishly. "I never wanted a house with a yard. That just means grass cutting, hedge trimming, painting, and all that crap."

"And you say you've never been married? Huh, imagine that!"

I hadn't tossed a softball like that to a woman, since I wore a Dead Kennedys "Too Drunk to Fuck" concert shirt to Pete's Pub when I was 25, and least 5 girls came up, read the printing, and said, "Good!"

Speaking of which, I was getting thirsty and hungry, so I directed Miss Iceland to the aforementioned watering hole. There I downed a pitcher and a plate of wings, while Miss Iceland combed her reporter's notebook trying to find I knew not what. To see my contented visage against her furrowed brow, one would think she was the one about to lose bed and business, not me.

She finally looked up from her notebook, eyed the pile of chicken-less bones on the plate and rolled her eyes (she should know me better by now, it'd save eye strain). As the waitress brought a new pitcher of beer she began, "About the phone, it must be Curly's. No self-respecting person under 60 would have that phone."

"Hey," I interjected, meekly.

"I said 'self-respecting'," she replied.

"OK, then go on."

"So, who sent Curly those text messages, that were clearly supposed to be between Sheehan and his daughter?"

"Why don't we call the number that sent them."

She shook her head like I knew nothing, so I refilled my glass, assuming things couldn't get any worse if I had half a bag on. "Like my father used to say, 'You're as worthless as tits on a boar'," she exclaimed.

"He was a man of letters I see. Erudite, even genteel, if you will."

"Listen, we can't just call the number," she continued. "If we use our phones, they can trace our number and they'll know we have the phone. That phone is our only advantage at this point."

"We'll use someone else's phone," I said, proudly. Tits on a boar, my ass.

"Three people are dead. Someone tried to run us off the road and make us numbers four and five. Do you really wanna get someone else involved?"

I took a glass-draining pull on my beer and tried to picture a boar with tits but wasn't even sure I knew what a boar looked like anyway.

"But wait, what if those messages came from Sheehan's own phone?" she started.

I stopped her. "Sheehan's gay, remember."

"Yeah, I know that doofus." I hadn't heard "doofus" in a while, it was refreshing, even if directed at me. "Somebody could have stolen or hacked into his phone or something. I'm not sure what those computer geeks are capable of, but either way, if Curly called the number, he would have gotten Sheehan and that set the whole thing in motion."

The phrase "computer geek" got me thinking, to the point where I almost knocked over my beer in my haste to finally add something constructive to the discussion. "Glenn Hubbard, the reporter, said that kid that's on the story now, uh, Jeremy something, is a big phone guy. Plus, he dated Monica Carson at Bennington College. Maybe he hacked Curly's phone."

"Not bad," she said, putting it down in her notebook. That she used a non-condescending tone, also had me feeling pretty good, so I sat back, crossed my arms, and smiled smugly.

And then it happened. "You know what we could do," she said. I hadn't a clue, but if it started with another pitcher, and ended with us naked, we would be on the same wavelength. It did not. "You can call Barton and see if the number on those texts is Ted Sheehan's."

I had Barton's phone number like tofu has taste. Combine that with the fact I was on the San Andreas Fault of shaky ground about my performance so far on the case, and it didn't bode well for "prospects de amore," so to speak. Fortunately for Mr. Peabody and my libidinous desires, the backdoor opened just then, and Miss Iceland's attention was drawn away, mercifully, from my stammering self.

"Here's that 'tall drink of drunk' from the other day," she spat, "and he's coming our way." She dropped her gaze as I turned to meet my savior.

It was Dennis Trevino, and fortunately, he was not in the company of Jeff "Fucking" Jensen. He was, oddly, followed in by Liquid Lenny, two humble souls that didn't have a car or driver's license between them. But to paraphrase Alexander Pope, "Hope springs eternal in the human liver," and I wasn't about to look a dipsomaniacal deity in the mouth.

I slid over to make room for him saying, "Dennis, my man, have a seat."

He tore his eyes away from Miss Iceland to give me a quizzical look, like I'd never asked him to join me before, mostly because I hadn't. Sitting down he smelled like Pepe Le Pew with a pack-and-a-half a day habit.

At a loss for, well, almost everything, I re-introduced Miss Iceland, getting her name right (Karina) but stumbling over our relation to each other. I seem to remember the phrase "gal-pal" landing with a thud, but I can't be sure. They shook hands, and while she discreetly wiped hers on her jeans, I groped for a topic that seemed even mildly plausible and led us away from Barton's digits.

Stumped, I reached into my pocket and produced the flip phone in question. "Hey, 2005 called, they want their phone back," cracked Dennis, thinking it was mine.

Miss Iceland laughed a little too heartily, and Dennis beamed at her, a little too brightly for my taste. "He's starting to grow on me," she said, still chuckling.

"Yeah, me too. Like a tumor," I shot back.

Miss Iceland took the phone from me, held it up in front of Dennis like a tennis ball to a Golden Retriever, and said, "It's not Luke's, but we were wondering, could it be Curly Carson's?"

Attention from a pretty woman straightened Dennis's posture like a scoliosis brace and sharpened his focus. He removed the phone from her hand and studied it. He mulled, he pondered, he ruminated, he brooded for what seemed longer than it took me to look up those synonyms in a thesaurus. Then he, sagely, replied, "No."

"Gimme that," I wailed and snatched the phone from him.

"What? I had to make sure. But to tell the truth I don't think Curly even had a cell phone."

"Not even for his job," Miss Iceland interjected, incredulously. She was of the generation where this was impossible.

"Nah. Curly was a lineman for the phone company," Dennis answered. "They still have radios in their trucks."

If he wasn't going anywhere and he wasn't, Lord knows not from lack of me trying to nudge him out of the booth, I figured I'd run one more thing past him. I went to the message list—I didn't want him to see the actual messages, he'd be here all night—then asked, "Do you know this number at all?"

He went into mull-mode again, so I elbowed him in his too-prominent ribs, "Yes, or no?!"

Miss Iceland held her napkin up to her mouth, trying to hold back her laughter, at me trying to parry with this drunken dolt (I'm certain he and Lenny probably shared a pint of something on the walk over). That's when

Dennis pulled out his own phone and started scrolling through his contacts looking for the number.

I shook my head at Miss Iceland, but she was still stifling her merriment at Dennis's antics. So, I took a moment to contemplate how I was going to get her blanched, bloodless beauty into my bed later, when suddenly she looked at me wide-eyed and terrified. My first thought was "she's reading my mind," but then she dropped the napkin from her mouth and squealed, "He's not dialing the number, is he?"

Sure enough, Dennis had stopped scrolling and now was punching in a number. "Dude!" I yelled, but it's hard to invoke fear into another when using the language of surfers and stoners.

I reached for his phone, but he fended me off with one long, bony arm and stunningly sharp elbow. "I'll find out who it is," he said, looking directly at Miss Iceland, and I realized, for once, her sallow sexiness was working against us.

She reached for Dennis's phone to preserve the secret of our only piece of physical evidence.

I reached for it to preserve my chance of getting in Miss Iceland's knickers that night.

And then something strange happened—the flip-phone in my hand started ringing.

Chapter 17: It's Almost Over, I Promise

Miss Iceland woke me at 5 a.m. I hadn't seen that time since my mid-20s, and that was coming around to it awake, with a full bag on. My head didn't feel any better meeting it this way.

"What? Why are we getting up?" I said, groggily.

"We're starting early. This is the day we solve this thing, remember?" She answered, commandingly. The whole mattress on the floor thing had its disadvantages. She clearly held a position of power, and I had a long, aching way to go, to obey her.

"Why 5 a.m.? What can we do now?" I countered, propped precariously on an elbow.

"High school starts at 7:30 a.m. I want to question Barton first."

"At 7:30 a.m.?" I tried to think if in my day high school started that early, but a couple of Natty Ices, on top of the pitchers at Pete's, left me only able to focus on the trivial. "What time is lunch, 10 a.m.?"

"I knew I was gonna have a problem getting you up," she mused, hands on hips.

"Funny, you had no trouble with that last night." She looked down at me with that Johnny Winter, white-blonde hair framing her–fortunately not Johnny Winter–face, and Mr. Peabody, at least, was wide awake. I thought of reaching up and pulling her down for another tumble. But the look on her face advised against it, and besides, if I had that kind of energy, we wouldn't be 17 chapters in now would we.

"I see your sense of humor is already in high school mode," she cracked. "Now I need the rest of your lazy ass to follow." She kicked the mattress violently. I put a pillow over my face, as she reached into the back pocket of her faded jeans and dropped her reporter's notebook on my gut.

"Ow. What the Hell?"

"It weighs six ounces, you baby, and it's open to our itinerary for the day. Look at it, while I search the floor for what you're going to wear."

In large, bold, capital letters that looked like they meant business she had written:

HIGH SCHOOL
JAMES'S TRAILER
OFFICE
TOWN HALL
COFFEE SHOP

Other than getting agitated by the "S'S", which I find superfluous (I also throw a hissy-fit if the Zamboni misses a sliver of ice at an NHL game, so the problem is probably mine), I had to admit it was a tight list. It encompassed all the places we had found clues, and for the stop at the office, she'd already ordered lunch, and booked the staff for a brainstorming session. Our lease was up in a week, my bank account and blood pressure were going in opposite, unhealthy, directions and I was looking at joblessness, homelessness, and the prospect of moving back in with Derf, dead in the eye. Needless to say, that got me out of bed, Toot Sweet!

Problem was, something about an itinerary rubbed me the wrong way, as opposed to the right way to rub me, which Miss Iceland wasn't offering at present. The last time I had an itinerary was the last time I went anywhere on a plane. Considering my ideal vacation spot is my couch, that was back in the days when air travel suggested businessmen in suits and attractive stewardesses.

Nevertheless (I love 'Bargain Words,' 3-for-1) Karina wasn't taking nei ('No' in Icelandic) for an answer. Lifting myself out of bed with the groans of a much older man, I began the day earlier than a day should ever begin. A knee, shoulder, and other miscellaneous bones cracked, as I put on the clothes she'd thrown on top of me, and I was off—in one sense or another.

More groans and cracking accompanied my *toilette*, as it were, and we were in her car by 6:15 a.m. This gave us enough time to make an important, impromptu stop. I directed her to Sadie's Cafe, a diner on the road between Artfield and Warren, where the ski resort was located.

Sadie's is a Jersey-style diner with a menu like a Tolstoy novel. Though, if anyone ordered the foie gras, they would probably need an auger and chisel to unearth it from the back of the walk-in freezer. It was more a breakfast/lunch type place favored by the hands-dirty, working class.

Besides getting coffee and pastries, we were here to find my "muscle," such as they were, Bean and Tombs. Between them, they weighed seven bills and a pocketful of change. But what they lacked in muscle, they made up for in menace. Bean, with a Fu Manchu mustache so thick you'd need a machete to locate his lips, and Tombs, sporting a beard that seemed to be growing out of eyes, and an epic Jew-fro that could make the harmonica player in the J. Geils Band jealous.

I figured if we had "pulled the goalie," I should call in all my favors. One of those favors was covering our asses, lest an incident like our little Demolition Derby of a few nights before should take place.

Sifting through the truck drivers and landscapers, I found the pair in their usual spot–the large, round table in the rear, backed by a banquette– the only seating that could hold their gargantuan girth. After the grunting out of pleasantries, I got to the point. I needed them to be "on-call," if any difficulties of a physical nature arose. We were going to be confronting Rick James and Police Chief Bowden directly. If either was involved in the double murder/suicide, I wouldn't put it past them to start something my sorry ass couldn't run and hide from fast enough.

They expressed their consent, while never looking up from platefuls of grease that fortified them for their jobs as grave diggers at the big non-denominational cemetery in Warren. To seal the deal, I fished through the sea of dishes for the bill.

"I got this," I said, not knowing how. They nodded, or so it seemed, but I felt like it didn't take. I headed to pay, hoping there was no trouble that would require me to call on them. A roadside hot dog truck could sink the whole investigation.

As I weaved through the tables, I looked down to see $68.46. But my musings on how poor people can afford to get obese, were interrupted by Miss Iceland approaching the register. I didn't have $68.46 to my name if you sold all my belongings, so I was down to my Blanche Dubois moment– relying on the kindness of strangers.

"What is this? I have our bill right here," she said as I handed her the check, face down, with eyes I usually used for begging sexual favors.

She picked up on this look instantly—probably because she had seen it less than twelve hours ago—and immediately flipped it over with an expression that said she was about to be reamed again, only this time, in a less desirable orifice.

"$68.46! What did you get a blow job in the kitchen while you were gone?" she spat.

I winced at the sexual vulgarity. But graphed on curve with her hotness, it was well shy of a dealbreaker. "Uh, I'll explain in the car. Can you cover it?"

"Yeah, yeah." And she whipped out a credit card which was impressive and, at the same time, disconcerting. Like seeing a young, attractive couple on *My Lottery Dream Home*. People should not get that lucky twice.

Still, as before, it was not a dealbreaker. Hell, looking at her blond hair bouncing above her tight faded jeans on the way back to the car, I had to admit she could have three bodies in the trunk, and we could still negotiate an accord.

"It was to secure us back up if anyone, uh, you know, throws down." I was trying to justify the bill I had Miss Iceland pay back at Sadie's. Suffice it to say, unlike Bean's and Tombs' breakfast, she wasn't buying.

"Why can't you protect us, if someone, as you put it, *throws down*?" she questioned. And I found out contrary to Baby in *Dirty Dancing*, I, apparently, could be put in a corner.

I stuffed my mouth full of a bear claw to delay answering and, mercifully, in that time we came up on Artfield High School.

AT ARTFIELD HIGH SCHOOL: Spring in Vermont could be a full 3 glorious months redolent in color (thank you carbon emissions); or two rainy weeks at the end of May, giving way immediately to the heat and humidity of Summer. Usually it trended towards the latter, but this year it was more of the former, and the girls of AHS were taking advantage by donning their skimpiest fashions, bringing out a previously unseen prudish side of Miss Iceland.

"You're not fooling anyone," she scolded me, as I tried to surreptitiously peek at a healthy co-ed in cutoffs so short, they could make Catherine Bach and Dawn Wells blush. "If I tried to leave the house with my butt cheeks hanging out like that, my parents would have wrapped me up like Ralphie's brother in *A Christmas Story*."

I paused for a moment trying to picture Miss Iceland in Daisy Dukes, then, not wanting a bulge in my pants to be misconstrued, snapped back to reality. "Well, they tried to have a dress code here, but it was the parents that went to the Board and sunk it," I explained. "We devoted a whole front page to it. Besides, you know what they say, 'Sun's out, buns out!'"

"Nobody says that" she said.

"I'm tryin' to make it a thing," I admitted.

"Let me rephrase: *Don't* say that!"

She shook her head and laughed. "Why did I get myself caught up in this? Let's go to the office and find out where Barton is."

Barton had just gone into a meeting with the principal, so we retired to the gym to find Max Lipper. Six half-court basketball games were in progress, while Max and three other Phys. Ed. Teachers sat on the front row of bleachers, talking and twirling whistles around their fingers—the latter being a prerequisite for gym teachers and pool lifeguards. As he approached, he looked tanner than ever, one might even say polychromatic.

"What the hell happened to you?" I asked.

"I was cleaning out my medicine cabinet, and used the last of three different bronzers," he lamented. His face was a leathery brown, his arms burnt orange, and his legs, what I would describe as, liver disease yellow.

"Christ, you look like a Terrorist Threat-Level Chart."

Miss Iceland laughed with me on that.

"This is Karina," I said by way of introduction. "She's helping us out on the case."

But, as I was patting myself on the back for remembering her real name, Max was quickly giving her his usual creepy once over. Knowing I'd be the one to pay for that with an earful later, I pulled the phone in question from my pocket to move things along.

"Hey, 2003 called they want..." Lip began.

"IT'S NOT MY FREAKIN' PHONE!" I stated emphatically enough to stop the game nearest us.

"Play on," Max said, as Miss Iceland laughed AT me this time.

"Sorry, but we already went through that with Dennis Trevino last night," I apologized. "Listen, could this be Curly Carson's phone?"

"No," Max answered quickly. "Curly didn't have a cell phone."

"How do you know?" Miss Iceland queried.

"Cause, I run five softball teams and Curly played on three of them. I'm always looking for bodies to fill out a lineup. I have every softball player in a four-county radius on my phone. For Curly, I have only one number, a landline."

Lip scrolled his phone down to "Curly C.," and a single phone number was listed. It didn't match the number of the flip phone.

"What about Sheehan?" she continued.

"Sheehan pulled out his phone at the staff meeting the week before he died. He read some dates off it, assemblies, deadlines for grades, that type of thing. It was an iPhone. Your boyfriend is the only one that still has a phone like that."

There was a flinch at the "BF" word, and it came from me for some reason. Not wanting to dwell on my feelings at this time—or, uh, ever—I got back to the phone.

"So how do we track this," I said to Miss Iceland, not expecting her to know, or she would have revealed it already.

Lipper interrupted this holding pattern with a suggestion. "Whenever I have a phone question I go to a student. Their whole lives are their phones. Hold on, I'll take you to my go-to tech girl."

He picked up the phone on the wall, talked to someone and with a "Cover me," thrown over his shoulder to no one in particular, he led us into the hall.

"Man, I should have become a gym teacher," I thought aloud.

We went down a hall that didn't exist when I was a student and ended up in the Music Department. Max looked just as lost as us. Ultimately, we stopped in front of a door, from behind which a powerful, female voice was running scales. Considering I fall somewhere between Tom Waits and Kris Kristofferson in terms of vocal range, I was impressed. So, when Max knocked on the door, I felt we were interrupting, doing something wrong. Though to be honest around high school girls I always feel that way.

A petite, attractive brunette appeared, and Max introduced her. "This is Caitlyn, my personal tech support."

"Nice to meet you," I said. "Luke Williams from the Artfield Press. Caitlyn? Did your parents name you after Bruce Jenner?"

As an icebreaker this was awkward. To get everyone to roll their eyes it was spot-on.

Miss Iceland had had enough of my shenanigans. She grabbed the phone and thrust it at Caitlyn. "Hi, I'm Karina. Can you tell us anything about this phone? Where would you get a phone like this? Can you hack into it? Do you know the company that makes it?"

Caitlyn held the phone like a Hindu holds a hamburger. Embarrassed, lest anyone should see her with it. "This is a burner phone."

I'd heard that term before. Probably on the *ID Network* or as my grandmother used to call it "The Murder Channel." "What's that?" I asked, seriously, for a change.

Caitlyn looked at Max, judged his authority and ability to care. Fortunately, he was wearing shorts and a t-shirt that proclaimed, "Bun's

Gentlemen's Club," with the "B" of Bun's formed by the ass of a woman lying on her side, and complete with the tagline "Bun's, this ain't no bakery!" (Man, I must get a certificate to teach gym!!) Concluding both were slim or, more likely, none she continued, "Kids that sell vape pipes or pot, sometimes use them. They're untraceable and there are no plans. Just prepay and toss it in a dumpster if someone is on to you, then buy a new one."

"Is there a brand name? A way to tell where it was bought, at least?" queried Miss Iceland.

Caitlyn turned on the phone, clicked on the "Menu," and worked her way through pages that were still virgin territory on my phone. "That's strange. There's no identification that shows up anywhere. This is really professional." Then looking up at Max added, "Uh, or so it seems, I mean."

Miss Iceland appeared chagrined, but for me suddenly something clicked. Not a knee or elbow like usual. It was something that energized me, like Derf walking into a casino, or Winona Ryder when the Saks security goes on break. I was not any closer to solving the mystery, but I recognized, clearly, the wrong path, which is something I usually don't do till I'm miles down it. In my gut, I was starting to believe Rick James and Police Chief Bowden were false flags. They may have been involved to some degree, but there was something bigger we were missing. Then again, maybe I ate that bear claw too fast. Still, I was going to see how it played out.

"Well, thanks. That was helpful," I said, as she handed the phone to me. "By the way, you have a beautiful voice, and I know. I toured for three months as one of the Celtic Women."

On the way out of the school Miss Iceland wanted to stop in the office again. "Why?" I asked.

"To get Barton's number from the secretaries."

"Oh. Wait, how did you know I didn't have it?"

"What did they just find me under a cabbage leaf, yer not a good liar." She playfully slapped my cheek, and we were off to Rick James's Trailer.

In my new, and unusual, animated state, I was full of questions—or full of something—as far as Miss Iceland was concerned.

"Could you shut up for a minute and tell me if we're going the right way to get to James's trailer," she spat.

As previously noted, I never cared for that "s" apostrophe "s" deal, but I sensed now was not the time to quibble about pet peeves. "Yes, stay on this road till it ends, then go left," I informed her. "Are you upset because you didn't get to talk to Barton?"

"No. At least *now* I have his phone number. I can call him anytime."

I'm no Dr. Ruth, but that "now" sounded like I was on my way to not getting any tonight. "I thought this was the full court press. We were gonna wrap it up today or die trying."

"What are we, *Rizzoli & Isles*?"

"Oh, can I be Rizzoli? Wait, which one is Angie Harmon, and which one is, um, you know, uh, the other woman?"

"Listen, doofus," she began, and I felt we were back on familiar footing. "You and I aren't judge, jury, and executioner. We're just reporters. But if we can prove a coverup, we can take it to the State Police, and they can catch the bad guys, and maybe save your piddly-ass paper in the process."

"So, I didn't have to get up at 5:30 a.m.?" I asked, incredulously.

"That's what you took from that?" she said, shaking her head. "I was trying to light a fire under your ass. You're a professional procrastinator! Go left here?"

"Yes, left. And for your information I'm not a professional procrastinator. I'm maintaining my amateur status in case procrastinating becomes an Olympic sport."

AT RICK JAMES'S TRAILER: We crunched onto the gravel lot of the sales trailer, but something appeared askew. There were sounds of work in the distance: hammers, nail guns, prevalent profanity. But in the sales lot, there was no one and nothing except for Rick James's Suburban parked at an odd angle. Up the steps the door was locked, but retching noises could be heard inside.

With a slight effort, that I made sound harder for Miss Iceland's sake, I shouldered in the door. Inside papers were strewn about, chairs knocked over, and an empty Jack Daniels bottle was broken on the floor, while a quarter-full Absolut bottle seemed to taunt it from the off-kilter desk above.

Rick James, himself, was on all fours in a tiny bathroom to our right. One shoe on, one shoe and an adjoining sock off, he was dry heaving into doll-sized toilet–boxer shorts with subsequent plumber's crack, staring us in the face. Taken in total, it looked like a rough night for Rick James, or a slow Tuesday at Caligula's palace.

"Sales office is closed," he managed to say between attempts at orally giving birth to his duodenum.

As stupid questions go my, "Are you alright?" wasn't in first place, but it was securely in playoff position.

He shakily stood, hiked up his underwear, and turned to us. A piece of gauze tied around his head showed a big red spot near his right temple. It looked as if he were either about to fly a kamikaze mission or limp off to the Battle of Yorktown playing a fife. It seemed ridiculous to maintain the charade that we were a couple in the market for a house. So, after another, "Sales office is closed," directed at Miss Iceland, I interjected.

"No. We're reporters."

Between his temporarily addled, and permanently self-absorbed state of mind, I could see James thought we were there to interview him about the break-in, beating, orgy—or whatever happened last night. Figuring we might get something out of him that we wouldn't under normal conditions, Miss Iceland took out her reporter's notebook, and we played along.

"So, I guess the moral of the story is don't hire non-union workers to do a union job," he began. "Ah, but that's off the record. Anyway, I was with this woman I met at the bar at Sugarbush—but don't put that in, I have a wife and kids. Anyway, we were in the middle of making out, when I heard crunching in the parking lot. I untangled myself and looked through blinds to see who it was. Next thing I know, the door bursts open and a guy—or two, or maybe three—bursts in and starts pounding me. Though don't put it that way. Make it seem like I put up a fight."

"Any description of this guy and/or guys?" Miss Iceland asked.

"No. It's a blur. Maybe it will come back to me later."

"What happened to the woman?"

"She made like a sheep and got the flock outta there. She didn't seem to know the guys and they were only concerned with me. She gave me a fake name, no phone number."

"Well, I think you've given me enough to go on," she added, eyes in full spiral.

"Why do you think it was union guys–or, uh–a guy?" I interjected.

"Just a hunch."

"Of course," Miss Iceland concluded, closing her notebook with nothing written on the page. "You've been a virtual wellspring of information."

"No problem."

"Wait, one more thing," Miss Iceland was apparently doing her best *Colombo* impression, or maybe she did have another question. She pulled her phone out meaningfully, swiped a few times, and showed James a picture. "Did they have a truck like this?"

"Hard to tell, it's kinda dark in that shot," he replied as Miss Iceland showed a picture, she took on the night we almost got run off the road.

"Was it a Ford? Did it have a dent on the passenger's side fender?" she queried.

"Yeah, yes it did," he confirmed. "I was thinking one of guys got into a fender-bender, but I have all Dodge Rams and it was definitely a Ford."

He started to clean up around him, and I decided we had gotten one clue why not go for another. "Maybe it was someone sending a message, regarding all those lawsuits you have pending."

He considered this for a few seconds, made a face and uttered, "Nah, not a chance."

My shoulders sagged (more than usual). Miss Iceland made for the door, but I wasn't taking "Nah" for an answer.

"Then what are those about?"

He leaned in as if he was going to share an E.F. Hutton stock tip. A powerful smell of whiskey and Paco Raban hit me squarely in the nostrils. "How do you think I find prime properties like this?"

"Multiple Listing Service?" I asked, like it was my first week on the job.

"Obituaries. When a person dies with a nice chunk of land in a desirable area, I swoop in before it hits MLS. I make a low-ball, all-cash offer, and put on the hard sell. There's always one black sheep heir, with a drug or gambling problem, that gets the others to go along."

"Where do the lawsuits come in?"

"When they figure out, they got screwed. Collateral damage, I call it," he said proudly, while feeling the bandage on his head. "I'm waitin' out an old bastard near the Finger Lakes region that's on life support. There's a ne'er-do-well son with a stripper fixation I'm working on. I said, 'Isn't there a plug you can trip over? You're sloshed half the time; it'll look like an accident.'"

"You should get to a hospital," Miss Iceland stated, as his bandage oozed an eggnog looking substance.

"No, I just need to self-medicate." He staggered to his desk, opened the bottom drawer, and drew out a flask.

That was enough for me. We had our clue- the guys who tried to run us off the road were union workers of some sort. Rick James was off my suspect list, though I was sure Miss Iceland and Gladys would not scratch his name so easily. "Well, you look like an alcoholic with places to be, so we'll just leave you to it," I said, joining Miss Iceland at the door, and before James could say, "Smell you later," we were in the Volks and headed to the office.

AT THE OFFICE: The usual gang was gathered, in what I can best describe as awkward sadness. Like a balding youth seeing "Before and After" pictures of Andre Agassi and being told they were taken only a year apart. Sandy Molesworth was jealous of Miss Iceland from a reporter standpoint, Miss Iceland was jealous of the receptionist Winnie (we were not paying her, yet she kept showing up—not that I am complaining) from a mammary standpoint, and Gladys sat giving off a Native American on a reservation thousand-yard stare. Meanwhile, photographer Charlie Grissom sipped coffee, and even Derf showed up, no doubt manufacturing some urgent sausage business, so he could hit the simulcast races at Green Mountain Park.

Sensing a leadership vacuum, I immediately took control, shocking everyone into attention. The mere fact that I was the one taking charge of this crap fest displays how desperate things had gotten. Having nothing to open with, I was pleased as punch—not something I see as having animate qualities, but such is the saying—that Derf spoke up to confirm racetrack contacts from here to Boston had fingered Chief Bowden as someone who owed money to everybody. No one bill added up to much, and even taken in total it did not seem like enough to kill three people over. Also, how was the money to be made by the Chief offing Sheehan, Curly and Monica?

I thought this would set off a discussion, but was met by a silence I hadn't heard, since I deleted my eHarmony account. Then my newfound "nothing to lose" attitude kicked in, and I began barking out orders.

"Sandy, see if your wannabe cop in the legislature can track down this phone number," I said, with what passed for me as authority, while handing her a piece of paper. "It's a burner phone. See if he can find out where it was purchased."

"Yessir, boss," she uttered, sarcastically. It was all I could do to not return in kind.

Out of the corner of my eye, I could see Miss Iceland was impressed by my assertiveness, so I continued.

"Charlie," I began in my best "coach from every football movie I ever saw" voice. "Contact the State Police. Tell them the *Artfield Review* has new information regarding the Sheehan-Carson murders. After they finish laughing, try to track down the detective that signed off on the Artfield PD's investigation. Maybe this goes all the way up to Montpelier."

"You got it."

That left Derf, Winnie, and Gladys from our dwindling crew. Relative to expectations, Derf had done yeoman's work so far. I knew how to reach him, and where he would be, so unless some urgent kielbasa crisis should arise, he was superfluous. Winnie, conversely, I had plans for and, no, not in the way you are thinking. She offered her cell number, but I knew better to take that in front of Miss Iceland. Though I could see the latter thinking, "Yeah, like he's got a shot." Still, better safe than sexless.

That left Gladys. Sad Gladys. Seeing her there in front of her uncluttered desk—at least the desk she'd chosen to nest in after the cleanout—not directing the comings-and-goings of the office and everyone in it, made me sad too. It was then I realized, like me, Gladys was seeing her town changing as well. She, of course, had more years invested in it than me. Maybe that's why she clung to Rick James as the mastermind of some nefarious plot that left three townsfolk dead. It could not be anyone from Artfield, anyone she'd known all her life.

I couldn't bring myself to tell her James wasn't involved. Already the unnerving effect of seeing me as the point man of our last-ditch effort to save the paper, and solve the murders, had rendered her virtually catatonic. So, I kneeled next to her and said, "Keep on working the lawsuits angle. I feel like something's gonna break there."

Then, feeling like everyone was looking at me and thinking, "Christ, that blonde chick has turned him into some brie-eating pantywaist," I grabbed a hunk of the six-foot sub, Miss Iceland had ordered (and which Derf, I was told, had worked through two-and-a-half feet of), shoved it in my mouth, said a garbled goodbye, while spewing bits of lettuce everywhere, and made for Town Hall.

AT TOWN HALL: One favorable thing about living in a small town is parking. We pulled up to the Municipal Building/Police Station, and though relatively busy, we found a spot right in front. It was a "high sky," as my manager in Lake Havasu used to say, not a cloud in it. Looking up from the Volks, I remember the white edifice looking like a giant snowdrift, and I hadn't consumed my first Natty Ice of the day—although I can't say as much for while I'm writing this so, uh, never mind.

My newfound confidence was holding up, as I led the way towards Miriam's office, to see the obese, husky-voiced administrator, who had fed me stories and kept me updated in those bygone days when I ran the *Review*. We wanted to see Police Chief Bowden to discuss the investigation, and I alerted Miss Iceland I was not going to take "no" for an answer.

"No," said Miriam.

"Um. What?" I replied.

Miss Iceland feigned pressing her watch like she had been timing me. "Good comeback," she said. So much for my confidence.

"Why?" I pleaded, in a voice that was only digging the hole deeper.

"Because he's working from home today," she informed me, between forkfuls of cottage cheese. "He and Wes (Mayor Willard) are having their offices painted."

That seemed convenient, then again, maybe it wasn't. Neither knew we were coming. My mojo, such as it was, seemingly had worn off. I thought about going next door to the police, but between my reputation with the Chief, the Mayor, and my brother-in-law, that seemed a dead end. My best shot at getting info was with Miriam.

"On a diet?" I began, pointing at the cottage cheese. Miriam was always on a diet, so it was safe ground. "I thought you looked slimmer, uh, in the face." I quickly added the last part, since her body was draped in a floral-print housecoat that looked like it had previously been on an actual house. Either that, or a couple of bedspreads were missing from a rent-by-the-hour motel up on Route 7.

"You know, always trying. I just started this one, but I've lost two pounds already."

"Yeah, and I threw a deck chair off the Queen Mary," is what I thought. "It's paying dividends," is what I said. "Like that Enron stock I still own," is what I thought next.

Or maybe I said it out loud, because her mood changed. "I know what you're thinking," she stated, disapprovingly. "You're thinking, 'Two pounds, that's throwing a barstool over the rail of the Titanic.'"
I sheepishly replied, "Uh, deck chair, Queen Mary, ah, but you know, not here to quibble. Can we just see the investigation files on the double murder/suicide? No one will be the wiser."
"Around here that last part is axiomatic, but I can't give you access to the investigation files for Sheehan/Carson even if I wanted to," she continued. "They're locked in the Chief's cabinets, and I don't have the key. Listen, hon, you know I support you. I came to your breakfast, and I'll back you in whatever you do next. But this is over. It's a tragedy, but it's over. Time to move on."

I looked to Miss Iceland for help, but she had nothing. We had several disjointed clues, but nothing to tie them together. Nothing tangible to take to the State Police. So, Gladys and I would clean out the office next week. And from there Miss Iceland and I—if she would have me—would live on love and dried farts, as my grandmother used to say, till we both found new jobs.

As we stepped out of Miriam's office Miss Iceland, surprisingly, didn't seem as apprehensive about this possibility as me. A sure sign she was through with me, I thought, until she turned to me with a smile and asked, "Do you know where the Chief's office is at?"

"You shouldn't end a sentence with a preposition," I replied, smarmily.

"Sorry. Do you know where the Chief's office is at, asshole?"

"Why? You heard, Bowden's not in."

Just tell me where it is and try to keep up."

Fortunately for her, I'd follow that ass off a cliff, so I gave her directions and re-enacted the final scene of *Thelma & Louise*.

"Ah, you see there is a method to my madness," she exclaimed, pointing at the open door to Bowden's office.

"I'd say it's about 70-30 in favor of madness," I cracked. A couple of paint cans held the door open, and a drop cloth peeked out into the hall. "His office is open, but he's still not here."

"Shh!" She began sneaking up to the door on tiptoes, back to the wall. It was so cartoonish; I felt any second pizzicato violin strings were going to accompany each step.

"What are you doing?" I said in a whisper, though I wasn't sure why.

She stuck her head around the door frame and said in her normal voice, which now seemed exceptionally loud, "OK, it's all clear."

Chief Bowden's office was impressive, in an Old-World kind of way. It had high, vaulted ceilings, cathedral windows, and a pedestal cornice three-quarters of the way up the walls. I was not sure why Mayor Wes Willard agreed to move out and take a smaller, less ostentatious office, when he hired Bowden, but maybe the old bastard had a senior moment, and the Chief pounced.

Meanwhile Miss Iceland was moving around the office looking under tarps for something. Finally, she deemed me integral enough to clue me in on what she was doing. "You've been in this office before, I assume, help me find the filing cabinet with the investigation in it."

"To what end? You heard Miriam, it's under lock and key."

"So, you were a boy once, didn't you learn how to pick simple locks," she uttered over her shoulder, still maniacally searching.

"Was *Angels with Dirty Faces* on AMC last night?" I questioned. "I'm not from Hell's Kitchen. I'm from Vermont, literally, Heaven's Rec Room."

"Come on, it's a filing cabinet. Not like I'm asking you to break into Al Capone's Vault."

"Really, that's the comparison you're going with. You expect me to risk a felony charge for that kinda risk-reward ratio?"

"I found it," she said, throwing back a drop cloth. She hadn't. I knew it was behind Bowden's desk. I was just about to let her know when loud, unfamiliar voices came from the hall.

Seconds later, in walked the painters, splattered overalls and all. Only I immediately noted these were not just any painters, but the two guys from Pete's Pub that tried to run Miss Iceland and me off the road. Fortunately, they hadn't recognized us. I pivoted to get behind Miss Iceland, which is in the Top 3 of least chivalrous acts I've committed (yes, there are two that might beat it, but don't ask). From there I took out the flip phone and texted Bean and Tombs our location, just in case.

Miss Iceland and the painters stared at each other, uncomprehending for a few seconds. Unfortunately (Why does there always have to be an "unfortunately" coupled to every "fortunately" in my life?), her comely visage is considerably more memorable than my ordinary mug and, soon they made us.

"Hey, you're the girl we saw in that bar last week," one of them stated.

Meanwhile, behind Miss Iceland, my text of "BOWDENS OFFICE," kept coming up "BOWLING ALLEY," as apparently, I'd picked the wrong week to switch to T9 texting. Finally, I hit SEND and jumped in front of Miss Iceland, which only made her chuckle.

"Oh, and it's you too," said the tougher looking of the two, though they were pretty much neck, and tattooed neck, in that department.

I thought about saying, "Yes, it's me!", but Miss Iceland would probably bust a gut at that, and I needed her to get help when they were kicking my sorry ass.

The one who spoke reached into the front of his coveralls for something. Chances were good it wasn't a gun—he wasn't going to shoot us in the actual police department—but I was thinking more with my sphincter, and less with my head at that point. In fact, it felt like I just had a bag of those Olestra chips from the 90s, anal leakage was a very real problem. Miss Iceland's olfactory senses probably told her I was better off still behind her at this point, but there was no time to get into my, literal, intestinal fortitude now.

He pulled out two pieces of paper, to my underwear's relief, and slapped them on my chest with authority. One was a copy of some form. The other was a pink carbon copy.

"That's the estimate for the damage your piece of shit car caused to my truck," he said, as he and Mr. Silent brushed past us. "I'll collect it next time I see you. Now get the Hell out of here. We're working."

Thinking near-defecation was the better part of valor, we took his advice and high-tailed it out of there. Well, Miss Iceland's tail high, mine more between my legs. Last stop, the coffee shop.

AT THE COFFEE SHOP: As we headed towards Johnny Java's, I fielded two messages that apparently came in during our parley with the painters. Charlie Grissom found the State Police detective that signed off on the Artfield PD's version of the Carson/Sheehan double murder-suicide but was unable to make a connection to Chief Bowden. He said he would continue to search. We were officially pissing in the wind now.

The other call was Sandy Molesworth, reporting that she had nothing from her liaison in the state legislature, due to a falling out over sexual yearning. I listened through him wanting her to do something called "a Lake

Champlain Luge," but when she got to the drizzling of warm maple syrup, and where, I was, out.

"Nothing from the 'Dream Team'," I deadpanned.

"I thought you referred to them as the 'Mod Squad'?" Miss Iceland answered.

"I'm trying to update my references; I may be looking for work soon."

"Yeah, I'd shitcan all your jokes in that scenario. Plus, those aren't the kind of *references* you need to update. But, c'mon, we're here. Let's go in and have a coffee and try to make sense of what we have," she rubbed my head like she was taking her 8-year-old nephew for ice cream. "Ew, what's that in your hair?"

"Hair spray. Do you think this all just happens?" I replied, patting my 'do.

"You need a haircut. What is that style anyway?"

"My barber calls it 'Lesbian Cop', but I prefer 'Girl Band Bassist.'"

We went inside, and I ordered something that sounded like an Italian stripper ("Coming to the stage: Caramel Macchiato!"), from a girl that had earrings in every orifice on her head BUT her ears. There she had spacers, as I believe they are called. Now, I'm not a "get off my lawn" sort, but when did long, floppy earlobes become a fashion/sexual statement. What's next? Neck rings or foot bindings?

Rant concluded, we paid for our coffees, and took a seat in the nearly empty shop. Karina dropped her bag on the table and headed for the Ladies' Room, while I put my head in my hands, in what one might caption, ABJECT BLEAKNESS.

I knew Miss Iceland would be back soon wanting to talk about this, she was annoyingly optimistic. She would put what we uncovered into a neat theory and try to get the State Police to re-examine the whole thing. I thought it was a longshot, that even Derf wouldn't touch, but I didn't want to appear like a total sad sack to the only good thing to come out of these past two-plus weeks. So, I tried to organize the clues we'd uncovered in my head, but everything kept spinning in a vortex.

It was kind of like being in one of those glass booths on a game show, where air blows money around, and you have to grab as much as you can. But each bill I grabbed swirled away, just before I closed my hand.

Finally, I decided to lick my forearms, in a purely metaphorical sense, and see what stuck to me. I cleared my mind, threw back my head, and closed my eyes. Slumped in my chair, I must have looked like a mafioso who had just been whacked.

Suddenly, though, things started to stick. Not to my forearms, but to my brain. Frankly, at this point, I trusted my forearms more, so I quickly grabbed Miss Iceland's reporter notebook and her pen and began to write it down. Then, I tried to put it in some semblance of chronological order, and this what I came up with:

1. Jeremy, hipster reporter, is a phone whiz.
2. Police drinking lattes–Why?
3. Bowden gambling–owed Derf $100.
4. Sheehan/Monica close in high school–extracurricular.
5. Town Council members run the town *their* way–see burglaries.
6. R. James–planning board problems.

7. The bank cut off our loan.
8. Debra Townes—Sheehan apartment behind church.
9. Coffee shop—best commercial spot (R. James).
10. Episcopal Church is Anglican—Book of Common Prayers.
11. Chicken or Rooster on alley wall.
12. Dennis Trevino says Curly is not drinking—police theory.
13. Jeremy/Monica dated.
14. Historic site paperwork.
15. R. James beat up.
16. Willard hires union workers

    Miss Iceland finally returned from the bathroom and gave me a not-so-playful slap on the back of the head.

    "Hey, what was that for?" I started, though I realized there was a litany of possibilities. "Uh, I'm trying to concentrate."

    "You and your stupid bed, if it can be called that, gave me a yeast infection."

    "Good. I won't have to get an $8 muffin with my coffee now," I cracked without looking up.

    "Speaking of coffee, why didn't you pick ours up? They're sitting there on the counter," she said, annoyed.

    "Kinda in a zone here." I kept my head down, trying to put the clues I compiled into complementary pairs.

"Freakin' twilight zone," she muttered and went to the counter.

I continued my calculations, such as they were. 2-3 (Police connection to coffee shop), 8-10-14 (old building, historic?), 5-15 (town run like dictatorship of council), 1-13 (Jeremy has a connection), 6-9 (prime real estate, council too late), 4-12 (Curly knew Sheehan/Monica close), 7-16 (never before occurrences) and 11 (final link)

By the time she got back, I was ready to present my case. I pushed the list of clues in front of her, while keeping the page with matches in front of me.

"What am I looking at?" she asked, immediately.

"That's the clues as they came to me, out of the air," I began. She arched an eyebrow at "air," but I didn't have time to explain my "process," such as it was. That it would have hardly upped her confidence level, was also a factor in that decision.

"Bear with me," I explained, not for the first time to a woman I was dating. In fact, I used it as a pickup line for a bit. "I've paired the clues up, and I think I have a sense of what went down with Sheehan, Monica, and Curly."

She took the lid off her coffee, blew on it, and when a couple of seconds passed without a snide remark, I went on.

"OK, here it is, look at 2 and 3. These show the Artfield PD has some connection to this coffee shop. Why else switch from McCarthy's, where they got coffee for years, to a place that serves drinks with a 'spraw' in them."

"What's a 'spraw'?"

"Combination spoon/straw, like you get with a Slurpee. I'm hoping it catches on," I explained and continued. "Next, there is 6 and 9. Rick James said this is the prime commercial spot in town. Even I could see that. But it was already 'glommed up' before he got to it, so he settled for cutting deals with the owners of the rest of this strip."

"'Glommed up'?" Miss Iceland interrupted. "You know what? You're on a roll, just carry on, and we can go over these colloquialisms of yours later."

"That's probably for the best. OK, 1 and 13 tell that kid Jeremy has a connection to this. Then take 4 and 12. Curly had to know Sheehan and Monica were close; he had custody all through her high school years. But he's sober now, and if somebody showed him that cell phone, he might have thought he missed something during those years. Something unsavory," I said.

"And if Jeremy's a phone whiz, like Glenn Hubbard said. And Curly wouldn't know a flip phone from an iPhone from a hole in his ass," Miss Iceland interjected.

"Whoa, let's have a bit of decorum for the time being," I said. "But yes, I like where you're going with that. Next take 5 and 15. This town has been run by the same people since I was in high school. Mugabe in Zimbabwe had a lesser run as dictator. Then there are 8, 10 and 14."

"Wait, I thought you said you broke them up in pairs?" she questioned.

"If you're going to be pedantic about semantics, this will take all night."

"If you're going to rhyme things with Mugabe and pedantic, you're kinda tyin' my hands here," she retorted.

"Fair enough. But this, uh, trio could explain why Monica and Ted Sheehan were contacting the Historic Preservation Society. Throw in that 7 and 16 are things that never happened before, and I think I know who is behind this whole cavalcade of crap, to turn a phrase."

"Who?"

"Do you have the name of the LLC that owns this building?" I asked.

Miss Iceland grabbed her notebook from me and began searching through the pages. I noticed for the first time she didn't question me. She just did what I asked, which told me I was on to something, and felt a bit creepy. A take-charge guy, I was not.

"Here it is," she said, finally. "Yellow Rooster Investment. I told you it was some silly bird name."

"Come with me!" I grabbed her hand, left $25 worth of coffee and pastry behind and dragged her out of the shop.

I led us to the narrow alley between the church and coffee shop, where Rick James had caught me sticking my head between the buildings. I couldn't see much but a sense of color and an outline previously. Miss Iceland, however, with a smaller, less Charlie Brown-ish dome, for lack of a better or more dead-on term, could, most likely, see what the old-timey advertisement on the wall depicted.

"Stick your head in there," I said, pointing to the attenuated aperture.

"Why?"

"There may be a clue in there that could wrap up this whole case," I pleaded.

She looked me in the eye, then started to get in position. "Wait, are you going to do something to my ass, while I'm in there?" she queried.

The suspense of what was on that wall was killing me. I thought I had solved the mystery of what happened that tragic night at Ted Sheehan's house. So, I snapped at her, "I'm gonna kick your ass, if you don't get in there and tell me what is on the church wall."

When you live your life in a perpetual state of semi-inebriation, like I do, the few times you get assertive, really knocks them on their ass. She did as I asked. Stuck her head in the opening, turned to the right and blurted out, "Son of a mother—it's a giant yellow rooster!"

Epilogue

We took what we gathered to the Vermont State Police, and they half-heartedly agreed to look it over. Then our photographer, Charlie Grissom, discovered Chief Bowden, and the detective who signed off on Artfield PD's theory, went to the State Police Academy together (Bowden dropped out and took the Artfield job). But when Derf identified him from a picture as a fellow denizen of the dog track, who suddenly retired and claimed his pension, they cranked it up to three-fifths-heartedly (wait, that is more than half, right?).

They even took our advice to focus on the hipster reporter, Jeremy—Monica Carson's ex. On hearing the word "prison," he apparently folded like origami, and cut a deal faster than Monty Hall. Once he sang, the investigators were able to piece together this timeline:

Artfield Mayor Wes Willard and his council cohorts, upon hearing about Rick James' plans to build an upscale development, sought to cash in, much in keeping with their dictatorship of the town, which Gladys had pointed out. They then purchased the hottest commercial property in town, according to James, and turned it into the only thing they equated with Gen X/Millennials, a pretentious overpriced coffee shop. Hence, the Artfield PD switched from McCarthy's to Johnny's Java, and Chief Bowden took that hundred from the till to pay off Derf. With money being laundered through Johnny Java's, Willard & Co. could dip into the police petty cash allowance without being traced.

Unfortunately for Curly, Monica, and Sheehan, this was not the extent of gentrification as Rick James envisioned it. When James started buying up property on the main drag, Willard knew he'd missed the boat. No one was going to profit off the town, except him and his cronies. So, they threw up a roadblock via the zoning board, and put James off temporarily, but they knew once he brought lawyers in, they would point to the coffee shop, and its eyesore of a sign, and their cover would be blown.

That left only one property unaccounted–the Episcopal Church. James, not knowing the fading faith of the community, assumed it was not for sale. The council members were under no such illusions. They realized Reverend Brooks' rantings had forced the faithful folks to neighboring towns to worship, and that the episcopate was itching to downsize. When they made an offer, the powers that be in the Episcopal Church couldn't refuse, it set into motion Brooks' retirement, and his focus on the neighboring coffee shop and the changing face of the town, for all the woes that befell him.

Enter Ted Sheehan and Monica Carson. Sheehan had once lived behind the church per Debra Townes. He knew the historical significance of the building, as part of the Anglican Church brought over by the original settlers of this area. Hence, the Book of Common Prayer I saw piled in the church hallway. It's amazing how much one can get done if one is not half in the bag, playing softball, and reading out-of-print British novels all the time. I took the aforementioned approach and did nothing but lament the changing landscape of the town. Sheehan, however, had a more spirited style. Thus, he contacted Monica, back in town after college, and the dynamic duo of do-gooders set out to foil Willard's plan, by getting the church listed as a Historical Site.

That's when hipster reporter, and Monica's ex, Jeremy shows up. As I thought, Monica dumped Jeremy, and he was looking for some way to get back in. Well, I predicted the latter. In town to interview Mayor Willard on something for *The Burlington Bee*, he mentioned he dated an Artfield girl, Monica Carson, in college. From the stack of Artfield High yearbooks in his office, spanning the years Monica attended, Willard probably came to the same conclusion as Gladys and I that Monica and Sheehan looked a little too chummy.

Willard kept tabs on Jeremy over the course of a month. Satisfied he was trustworthy (in an Honor Among Thieves way) and a sneaky, little shit who wanted to get back with Monica, Mayor Wes sprung the lie on him that Ted Sheehan and Monica Carson were in an on-again, off-again relationship since high school, and it hit all the right buttons.

Willard had no proof, but Jeremy wanted it to be true, so somewhere between greed and lust, they found their happy place (mine is between drunk and misanthropy). They couldn't put it in the *Bee*, obviously. So, the jilted Jeremy, a phone whiz, as Glenn Hubbard informed us, concocted a plan that took advantage of Curly Carson's technological obliviousness (which apparently everyone knew but me, though I assume folks put me in the same category), to get him to confront Ted Sheehan and, hopefully, run him out of town.

He bought a burner phone, loaded it up with text messages from the phone itself, and took it to Curly, claiming it was Monica's. That a 24-year-old would own such a device or let her phone out of her sight for more than 10 seconds, never occurred to Curly. Instead, he was focused on messages that would make Ron Jeremy blush. According to his statement to investigators, Curly became so enraged that Jeremy, not the most resolute of men, hightailed it out of there, without bothering to get the phone back.

One might think in his recently sober state, Curly would be capable of more clear-headed, deliberate decisions. In Curly's case, however, alcoholic abstinence had set every nerve on edge. Remembering all the times she had mentioned Sheehan back in high school, really set him off—as supposed pedophilia will. So, gun in waistband, Curly set out for Sheehan's and the rest is tragic history.

Wes Willard was arrested. He was charged with criminally negligent involuntary manslaughter—or some such thing. Miss Iceland wore a denim jacket with a short denim skirt that day—which I believe is called a Canadian pantsuit in these parts—and I was distracted by her legs. She was back with the *Burlington Bee* covering the trial.

Willard fought the charge. He faced only between 18 months and 3 years if convicted, but he saw this as a death sentence. This was partly because he was older than a Soviet Georgian in a yogurt commercial (I may have over-referenced, but YouTube it if curious), and partly because he could never rule Artfield like a pale, Yankee, Idi Amin, ever again if he confessed—and after all, that's what he lived for.

At the trial, Old Wes showed up complete with a rolling walker from the Harvey Weinstein Signature Series and doing his best Vincent "The Chin" Gigante impression. But Jeremy turned state's evidence, and the State Police produced an overwhelming amount of the circumstantial kind, because Willard never thought to cover his tracks, thinking he was bulletproof within the confines of Artfield. He got the maximum. Good riddance!

Jeremy received immunity for testifying. Willard's cronies on the council quit and retired to their lake houses to live out their not-so-golden years. Hank Chase took over from The Crypt Keeper at Green Mountain Savings and Loan, and our line of credit was restored. That just left Chief Bowden and his coverup of the double-murder/suicide. But despite a trail of shady financial transactions between him and Willard, a litany of debt (some above, some below board), and due to a lackadaisical investigation by any standard, he walked. The mayor, to his credit, wouldn't give up his Chief of Police, and the county DA surmised Bowden looked just stupid enough, that a "dimwit defense" might be enough to sway a jury. Apparently, ignorance really is bliss (though it never seems to work for me).

The line of credit covered our considerable debts, but it wasn't enough to get the paper up and running again. Fortunately, Max Lipper came through with his promised fundraiser at Pete's Pub. He called everyone on his extensive "Contacts" list, which meant that a ton of softballers showed, and a substantial number of strippers from area clubs didn't.

There was a large water jug at one end of the bar for donations. It was three-quarters filled with change, bills, checks, and two scratch-offs Derf found in his otherwise empty wallet—the latter coming with the qualification that if we hit, we'd split the proceeds with him 50-50. It was more than enough, from my cursory estimates, to get the paper up and running again, and I contemplated pocketing the excess to pay my personal debts. This was a proposition that did not sit well with the younger, more idealistic, Miss Iceland. Just one more way she was like no woman I had ever dated before.

Besides, skimming off the top wouldn't be that difficult, now that I was considered Savior of the Town, which seemed to be a rather grandiose term, akin to calling that little bubble at the end of the condom a "reservoir tip." That was because I was not only credited with putting Wes Willard behind bars (though it was more of a team effort), but also putting the brakes on Rick James' gentrification of downtown (that was me with an assist to Miss Iceland in a tank top). He agreed to keep the properties he bought on the main drag in his portfolio. Though he was going to give them faux colonial makeovers, to get a quaint, village-y feel (Miss Iceland's cleavage could only sway him so much).

But all anyone wanted to talk about was how I landed Miss Iceland. They had seen me with attractive women, and they had seen me with intelligent women, but not at the same time. Several regulars suggested she must be a heavy drinker, but Max Lipper assured them he'd seen her sober, and she hadn't been repulsed by me. I thanked him for the ringing endorsement when my sister came up to introduce herself.

"Karina, this is my sister, Amy O'Sullivan. Amy this is Karina," I stated simply, making sure not to put the words "girl" and "friend" in close proximity to each other.

"Yeah, you're the girlfriend. Nice to meet you," Amy said, smiling at me.

"Yes, nice to meet you too," Miss Iceland answered.

Amy gave her the once-over, after three kids, I assume discreteness falls by the wayside. "She's nice, Luke."

"Thanks, I raised her from a pup," I replied, because I had no clue how to respond to that.

My brother-in-law Andrew came up just then and threw a beefy, freckled arm around my sister. "So, you gonna introduce me, Fuckface?" he demanded. Miss Iceland's eyes looked to me a little too quickly at the utterance of this term of disparagement. Ah, family.

"Karina, this is Amy's husband Andrew, aka, The Mad Shitter," I sallied back.

"Yeah, that was me," he admitted.

"So, you came over in the middle of the night, stood on my car and shat a geometric design on my hood?"

"Of course, not, Chief Bowden had us surveilling you when you questioned his theory of the crime. I had the overnight shift; I was bored, plus I never did like that crack about me and Will Rogers—and, by the way, I was going for a bow."

"Lovely."

"What's that about Will Rogers?" Miss Iceland interjected.

"I once said Andrew is the man Will Rogers never met," I replied.

"No, I mean who is Will Rogers?"

"Not important."

"How did you know it was me?" Andrew asked.

"I didn't at first, but the second time I figured it out."

"Second time?" He seemed sincerely befuddled, but that was his usual demeanor, so hard to tell.

"The second time, you know, when you left me the envelope. You glued it to my window with, uh, shall we say, excrement," I answered.

Andrew began laughing, "That wasn't shit. I'd get hungry on those surveillance runs, so I took along one of the kids' snack packs. That was Nutella."

"Well, you had me seeing shit everywhere. One thing, though, if you hated me so much you crapped on my car, why give me the clue that took down Willard and Bowden?"

"OK, I'll make it up to you," he announced.

I was skeptical.

"Here's a scoop for the first edition of your new paper. The new Police Chief of Artfield is yours truly!"

Well, sonuvabitch!

Made in United States
Orlando, FL
08 July 2024